GHOST OF THE STREAM

ISLE OF INTRIGUE

BILL PEARCE

authorHOUSE

1663 Liberty Drive, Suite 200
Bloomington, Indiana 47403
(800) 839-8640
www.authorhouse.com

© 2004 BILL PEARCE.
All Rights Reserved.

No part of this book may be reproduced, stored in a retrieval system, or transmitted by any means without the written permission of the author.

First published by AuthorHouse 10/21/04

ISBN: 1-4184-5897-X (e)
ISBN: 1-4184-4040-X (sc)
ISBN: 1-4184-4041-8 (dj)

Library of Congress Control Number: 2003098535

Printed in the United States of America
Bloomington, Indiana

This book is printed on acid-free paper.

TO

A number of people had a hand in the production of this book. Among those were author **Sara Rath**, for her hands-on-help, leadership, ideas, editing, guidance and encouragement. **Peter Ward**, the computer mastermind, who accepted - with dedication and good spirit - every challenge, chore and task necessary to convert these scribblings into a book. **Leann Moore,** for her detailed proofreading, language and grammar skills and for patiently "being there" to solve problems, answer repetitive and mundane questions. Wife **Ann,** for years of typing - even before the computer - and proofreading and years of love. Daughter **Pam** my apologies for all the years of lost time together because of my work. And for **every author** who has written *anything* about this interesting, unique and exciting place called Florida.

Jerry & Karen

Great Friends

Grand Neighbors

Bill

This is a work of fiction, meant for entertainment only. With the exception of the names of a few actual persons, places and things identified as such, the characters and incidents in this volume are entirely the products of the author's imagination. They have no relations to any person or event in real life. Even when persons and places are referred to by their real names, the reader should understand the events set there did not occur nor did the persons participate. Their names are mentioned solely for the purpose of saying "thanks" for being a part of my growing up in south Florida. Additionally, I'm indebted to many more folks - not mentioned - who played a role in my incredible and near idyllic youth.

Prologue

I first met Tuck covering most, if not all, of his many press conferences following his return from "missing at sea without a trace". Even the finality of those words did not rob him of his good humor. I found him to be personable, intelligent, and a decent, unassuming young gentleman. (Good copy my editor would say.) A good Scout is more accurate. He is quick-witted, clever and can think on his feet. Innovative with a zest for living - not just life - and there is a difference, Tuck is alive! Alive with enthusiasm, excitement, challenge and a youngster's appetite for "what's next".

As to be expected, initially he waved me away, unwilling and actually recoiling at the idea of me telling his story. I persisted, believing and arguing that he had a responsibility to answer all the questions arising from his lengthy survival at sea without, what many thought to be a likely explanation. As a rare survivor of the Devil's Triangle he could shine a light, first hand, on that mysterious region of the Atlantic Ocean. He could explain what actually happened to the five Avenger torpedo bombers, that left on a routine training flight, only to never return and became known worldwide as *The Lost Patrol.*

After many sessions together, a smidgen of research - only to clarify certain details - we finalized Tuck's story. And it is *his* story: told here - by a fourteen-year-old - as *he* told it. Keeping the facts as he remembered them was as easy as recalling a good storyteller's tale. I can assure you his story is not an invention of the mind, as many of the media suggested and did not come from some standardize cookie cutter. It's an adventure story of excitement, mystery, intrigue and a little danger. He - or they - did not use sky-hooks, special effects or bodacious embellishments to "accomplish the mission". Instead they used what was at hand: their wits, common sense and...a little baling wire or chewing gum now and then.

Utilizing his language as he spoke was no chore. He talked matter-of-factly, refusing to dwell in gutter slang, while maintaining a sense of decency, loyalty and humor through out. He even captured Billy Jim's tone of "butchering the King's English" without belittling or poking fun at his friend. (A Tuckism: Friendships need full time skippers.)

As I said, Tuck is a fine, young gentleman of notable character and I believe his tale. Characteristically he refers to it as a "romp" - a challenging adventure - that any other Kendall kid could have taken in the mid 1940s. Perhaps. But I think he's an unusual lad. And because of his keen enjoyment - his gusto - for a full life, we'll be hearing from him again in the not too distant future.

The Author

I
Shipwreck

JUNE 1946 -- It was unreal that a 40-foot boat could leave behind such a small amount of debris. Nevertheless, except for a few pieces of splintered wood, a scattering of floatation and one gray hatch cover with a young boy clinging to it, there appeared no other tangible evidence the *Nomad* ever existed.

On instinct, using his hands and arms, he frantically paddled the hatch cover about. Raising his torso, holding his head as high as possible for a better view, while careful to maintain his balance, he called out for his shipmates. "Buddy! George! Herb! Captain Bannerman! Anybody? Anyone out there?"

He was shouting, but couldn't hear himself. Touching his throat and finding no wound, he screamed again. With his fingertips, he felt the vibrations on his neck, but still, he heard nothing. He existed in a vacuum, hearing nothing and seeing only a bright noontime sun, blue sky, puffy white clouds, boiling about like sea foam, and a horizon-to-horizon aquamarine carpet; the Atlantic Ocean.

Struggling to hear himself, he was reminded of a recurring dream in which he needed to run, only to find his feet were tangled in fishing tackle, lines and nets. It took awhile, but eventually he understood. Apparently he had not only lost all of his shipmates, but his hearing as well. Blood seeped from a small cut above his right eye and he frequently splashed it with seawater.

Initially, he wasn't certain what had happened. He was numb. Groggy, like first awakening after an extended sleep. He appeared completely detached from everything.

The universe stood still. He shook his head to clear his mind. Lacking full comprehension and overcome with grief, he lowered himself, from his upright position, to lie stomach down on the hatch cover. He folded his arms, resting his chin on them. At the moment, he was in limbo: no light, no darkness, no questions, and no answers. He simply stared ahead in wide-eyed wonderment.

In time, blessed time, however, he began sorting through the facts, as he could recall them. He was a child playing pick-up sticks. Eventually his mind cleared and he was able to focus on the present.

"Was it only this morning?" he questioned aloud, squinting at the sun. He felt he was spinning, being sucked into a whirlpool of blackness. Spinning, tumbling out of control. Was the hatch cover truly bouncing about, or was it only in his mind? Darkness seemed to close in on him. Is this shock? he thought. Tuck's hallucinations are so very real he doesn't realize they are a common occurrence in situations such as his. He slapped his face and wrists and splashed water in his face in an effort to clear his mind. Regardless how hard he tried; he continues to fail and eventually is satisfied to drift in mind as well as body. Where was he? Where had this journey begun, he wondered?

Tuck was 14 the winter of '45 when he signed aboard the *Nomad* as first mate-cook-and-gofer. First mate was his title. Cook and gofer were the job descriptions. His duties, as explained by the Captain: "Whatever I tell you they are. And another thing, I can't very well be hollering a mouthful of titles when I need you, now can I? If I want you to handle lines or pull up the anchor, or make a sandwich, it'll probably be 'matey' or most likely just 'boy'. Might even call you Tuck now and then." The Captain's sea blue eyes crinkled when he was "pulling a funny".

Tuck plunged in love with her the first time he saw the *Nomad*. So blinded by that affection, he saw the 40-foot charter boat as a gleaming white motor yacht with few, if any, equals. Be that as it may, the boat could be more accurately described as a clean, mechanically sound, ancient barge. If one forgot the sleek lines of more modern vessels, ignored a loose plank here and there, a few rusty nuts and bolts and a contrary electrical system, the *Nomad* wore about her a mantle of dignity, warmth and experience. Much like the honored, white-haired judge or successful businessman of a small community.

The boat appeared to have an aura about it. For example, it seemed to attract people. Upon entering a marina, whether its own in Miami or a strange port-of-call, folks were drawn to it...pulled as if by some magical force. If it wasn't to inquire about the day's catch, it was to discuss the boat, its age, history or just to listen to Captain Bannerman spinning tales of yesteryear.

"Hey, skipper, what'cha git today?" someone would holler from the dock as the boat pulled in.

"A *Coke* bottle full and then some small ones," he'd answer, with the wry smile the regulars had come to expect.

Or when he was asked the age of the vessel, he might reply it had been the dingy Noah towed behind his ark.

The original "hail fellow well met", Captain Bannerman was a fine tuned "fishing machine". He enjoyed the reputation of thinking like the fish he was seeking, be it the elusive bone fish or the giant marlin. Always eager to try something new, he refined kite and balloon fishing. He was even apt to lay down a trail of newspaper sheets to attract dolphin that liked the shade it provided. Those assets, plus an engaging personality, ready wit and contagious laugh, made his charter business the envy of Florida's Gold Coast.

Tuck had no idea how long he'd drifted in what he would later determine to be a hypnotic state. The placement of the sun indicated several hours. He was thirsty and in spite of splashing himself with water, he felt like a sun-dried hank of seaweed. Gradually he began to get in touch with his senses and surroundings. The hatch cover rocked slightly in the light chop, washing it with salt water and an occasional piece of sea grass. Yielding to the soothing rhythm of the sea, he relaxed somewhat. In time he lay his face down on the hatch cover savoring the coolness of its surface against his cheek. Just before dozing off, he realized his arms were dangling in the water. Quickly he jerked them upward, turned over and sat upright.

The sea was cobalt blue, indicating great depths and big fish, including sharks. He gulped in great mouthfuls of air to help calm and steady his emotions. Cupping handfuls of water he splashed his face and body. The water tasted and smelled clean, with a whisper of crisp, sea mist. The sun was scorching and he knew he would probably blister, nevertheless he tried to keep his clothing moist in order to delay the inevitable. He had a ruddy complexion, thanks to a Cherokee grandfather named Mantooth several generations past and was usually bronze in color by early summer.

Tuck could not admit to being comfortable with the situation, however, he felt he was as calm and in control as circumstances allowed. Spending most of his life in Florida, a peninsular surrounded by the Gulf of Mexico and Atlantic Ocean, plus a major portion of the past ten months on or near the water, had heightened his affinity with it. Like some men take to the air, Tuck enjoyed the water. Ocean, sea, lagoon, pond or puddle, it didn't matter, so long as it was wet. He hoped this fondness would serve him well because he envisioned a very, very damp future. He was also glad that he was an excellent swimmer.

Letting his mind wander, he found himself at the claypit, a local swimming hole left behind after the builders of the Tropical Park Race Track extracted the necessary clay for its running field. For the moment

Tuck imagined himself with a gang of regular playmates, including a handful of Seminole youths from a nearby camp, jumping and diving from the dock Billy Mac constructed one day while skipping school. The grunts of the gators or a snake nearby didn't deter any of them from their "jaybird" revelry. Nor did the colored women fishing for supper or the visiting wife of the dragline operator as he harvested the remaining white sand for W.T. Price and Company's road building. Tuck found himself smiling and longing to be home.

The winds picked up slightly and together with the natural flow of the Gulf Stream, he figured he was moving northward at about six knots. Shielding his eyes, he scanned the horizon for signs of rescue. Even though he was usually optimistic, little spears of doubt stabbed at his brain. Often he could drive away unpleasant thoughts with a quick "get out doubts", but today he wasn't so successful. He wondered if the distress signal had been heard? If so, why hadn't someone picked him up? He didn't think he was more than 25 miles from Miami. Why hadn't he seen any planes or boats? Had the Coast Guard launched a search? What were the chances for survival? He was aware that to dwell on such questions was dangerous...well harmful, in any event.

Aloud he joked. "Well, Captain Bannerman, this is another find mess you've gotten me into." He knew unless a plane or one of the many ships plying the sea-lanes to and from South America spotted him, or he made a landfall, there was little hope for survival. And regardless how hard he tried, he could recall no land in the ocean pathway northward: nothing but wide-open sea and weather of all descriptions.

To take advantage of the easterly breezes, when possible, he formed a sail using his tee shirt. By lying on his back, putting his arms inside the shirt, and extended them into air; he presented a flat surface to the winds. Twisting his arms allowed a steerageway of sort as he sang for the whole world to hear: "I am Tuckster the sailor man. I live in the garbage can. I take care of the chickens; they stink like the dickens. I am Tuckster the sailor man."

His "make shift sailing", while hardly discernible, fulfilled his need to be doing something. And any activity that took him closer to the Florida coast was uplifting. Often he was entertained by flying fish and made a game of it. He challenged himself to see if he could hold his arms skyward for the flight time of five fish? Who would give up first? He won as many as he lost. Later a brief shower, common in the Caribbean basin, offered him some much-needed moisture. Quickly removing his shirt again, he held it out flat to the rain until it was soaked. Squeezing it over his mouth, he swallowed a small glassful. As the rain began to subside, he once more allowed the shirt to collect as much water as it would hold. He then twisted a small portion of the shirt into a cone shape and sucked the wet cloth. And so went another couple of hours in the afternoon.

He caught a piece of seaweed and shook it over the raft. As he suspected what would happen, tiny, flipping, shrimp dropped out: a food source if necessary. Heading towards the lowering sun a school of nosy, but friendly, porpoises surfaced from the depths of the Stream joining him long enough for a bump, chatter, click, squeak and squeal. Quickly casting him aside as too slow, they moved on for swifter company, but not before a jump, a roll and a splash that left him soaked. "That's right, go on and leave me out here all by myself," he hollered, shaking his fist. "I thought you were suppose to help by bumping me ashore someplace. I hope you have to eat dead pinfish tonight."

While shifting himself on the cover to relieve his aching bones and muscles, he lost his balance and tumbled into the sea. Very quickly - without even getting his head wet - he was back on board, feeling the wind against his wet tee shirt and jeans causing him to shiver. Like a lightning bolt, the tumble rekindled his irrational anxiety over what might be lurking below, reawakening his lifelong fear of sharks. He reminded himself to be more cautious. A shark handled or viewed from the safety of a 40-foot boat is one thing, he thought, being on a little slab of teak in deep water, with arms and legs dangling like live bait, was something else.

An unsettling picture came to his mind and regardless how hard he tried he couldn't get past it. Just last year the cruiser *USS Indianapolis* was sunk by a Japanese sub after delivering vital components of the atomic bomb dropped on Hiroshima. Because of a naval snafu and radio silence, no one knew they were missing. So for five nights and four days no one searched for the survivors and very quickly they became victims of the sun, saltwater and sharks. When the few hundred, from a crew of over a thousand, were finally picked up, there were more body parts floating about than survivors. One of the rescued confirmed there are no atheists in foxholes - or on tiny rafts in the middle of the vast Pacific Ocean. Many of those saved, believed he was delivered by a Higher Power. One survivor added, "It's probably a good thin' we didn't know nobody was lookin' fer us. Been fewer of us, I'll tell you."

Tuck tried, with little success, to erase from his mind the picture of sharks circling and swimming through the groups of men. He imagined the men kicking, striking out, but to no avail. Then suddenly the shark strikes, grabbing one of them in its teeth, twisting and turning it finally dives with the victim still screaming, flailing his arms and legs.

Eventually, perhaps his life vest, if he had one on, popped to the surface for the use of someone else.

Soon fatigue helped him back away from the mental picture he had painted. He rested his arms along side his body with his sneakered feet dragging in the water like a useless rudder. Believing he might look like a corpse from the air; he rolled over on his side drawing his knees to his chest. I might be a smaller target, he thought, but was convinced a person – dead or alive - was unable to float in this position. If they see me, they'll have to investigate, he reasoned.

For short periods of time, he turned over and lay on his back with knees drawn up, but being unable to watch the horizon, he favored the flat-on-the-stomach position. Looking towards the west, he judged it would be dark in another couple of hours. He knew if he hadn't been picked up by then, rescue would be unlikely before morning. To pass the time, he busied himself with a trick he used as a child while waiting for his parents; talking to himself, often aloud. "Rehearsing his defense", his Mother called it.

Actually, Tuck did more than "talk to himself". He was a cogitative or thoughtful thinker. As a natural part of his mental process, he looked at each aspect, pro and con, weighing its value against the whole. For example, he might role-play each person's part as if in a play. While sometimes cumbersome, Tuck was, for his age, an exceptional problem solver.

He recited Sunday School verses: "Yea, though I walk through the valley of *doubt* - changing the word from *death*..." He tried to recall the families that had been a part in his life while living in South Florida. Names began popping about like kernels of corn in a hot skillet: Denmother Dot, Aunty and Uncle Jack Rogers, the McSwains, Mom and Pop Thomas, Parkers, Williams, Pearsons, Ozannes, Moyers, Richards, Kendalls, Durnells, Currys, Hances, Pattons, Forsyths, Lewises, Hills, Dices, Grahams, Sheppards, Matthews, Bjorks, Speeds, Killerlanes, Moores, Claypools, Ouseys, Tuttles, Suggs, Whites, Powells, Saposes, Kirklands, Wipprechts, Uncle Bill and Aunt Tine Carter.

Now on a roll, he rehearsed the ritual of getting the *Nomad* underway: "Open all the hatches, start the blowers, check the oil and gas levels, bilge pump, batteries, radio, fresh water supply, food, etc., etc."

Still plaguing Tuck was the demise of the *Nomad*. The weather hadn't caused its sinking, that was for certain. It had been a perfect day to cover the fifty miles between Bimini and Miami. It might have been a gas leak or a mine, he thought. Gas leaks are always a threat around boats and that's why all safety precautions are observed, before starting engines. But then, also, World War II had ended less than a year ago and he questioned that every mine in the South Atlantic had been recovered.

Regardless of the theories, he couldn't make all the parts of the puzzle fit together. A mine made the most sense, but he couldn't remember an explosion. He suspected the media would add the disappearance of the *Nomad* as another chapter to the growing legend of the Devil's Triangle. He thought of the *Island Princess* that had disappeared in 1945 without a trace - never to be heard from again. Mulling over the conclusion those words implied, he wondered what the bottom of the oceans looked like and if man would ever have the capabilities of fully exploring them. "Wow!" He uttered. "What a sight to behold."

He had now drifted at least eight hours and the sun was sinking rapidly. It had been a ritual aboard the *Nomad* for all hands to gather on the bow and watch the sun set and guess how long before it was completely out of sight. (A few minor bets were not unheard of.) It always seemed the sun moved more quickly at the close of the day and today was no exception. Cupping his eyes, he continued staring to the west in hopes of catching the small green flash in the sky that so often follows the setting of the sun at sea.

With darkness came the worst feeling of abandonment - total aloneness - he had ever experienced. He had been alone before, but nothing like this. It was as though he had been plucked from planet Earth and placed in a black, watery, hole on some alien soil. The blackness was so complete he couldn't see his hand in front of his face. He spread his finger and waved his hand before his eyes as proof. His mind plunged into despair.

Tuck thought of his Aunt Grace, with whom he lived, and what she might be doing. "Cooking dinner, I'll bet." he spoke to the envelope of darkness. A lump welled up in his throat as he remembered her softly calling each evening, "Tuck, it's suppertime." She was a beautiful young woman, full of joy and charm with a happy heart, mind and soul. Always at ease, usually singing aloud as she went about her chores, she radiated a warmth and love to everyone about her. Even her name seemed to fit, but "comfortable to be with" best described her. Tuck loved her as he loved no one else. And he knew beyond a doubt he was loved and reveled in that knowledge.

All of a sudden, his reverie was interrupted, big time! Periodically, Tuck periodically scooched around on the cover, in order to scan the 360 degrees of his world of water. This time, however, he saw two running lights bearing down on him! Coming fast, not 25 yards away! With little time for anything, he let out a "Yeowee" and pitched off the raft. Kicking hard, he dove deep and swam away. The sound of the throbbing props and turbulence of the water made his skin prickle. Understanding how close he was to becoming chum, he continued to swim downward. After what seemed an eternity, the lift of the water, as the boat passed by, pushed him upward. He surfaced, gulping in great mouthfuls of air. Shaking the water from his eyes, he saw the stern light rapidly disappearing. Luckily the bow wake and hull shoved the cover towards him. With the help of the swirl of phosphorescence and a few minutes of swimming and splashing about, they were reunited. The entire episode happened so quickly, he didn't have time to be disappointed or despondent. Perhaps that's good, he thought.

Once back aboard the cover and calmed a bit, he had time for a replay. The event itself aside, several things plagued his thinking. It was a strange vessel. The running lights were close together for a boat that size and they were located near the waterline. That's unusual as the lights are usually elevated for visibility purposes. Another thing; the hull seemed much too narrow and longer than would be expected for the small cabin area he had seen. He resisted jumping to a conclusion that it was a submarine, but that's what his brain told him. Nevertheless, he was certain the boat wasn't looking for him. It was going much too fast for any lookout to adequately survey the area and there had been no searchlight beams raking the surface. Most likely it was a charter boat, maybe a "head boat", on its way back after a day of fishing. In any event, it was making over 10 knots and in no time its light was barely visible. If that was a dress rehearsal for finding him, he thought, it would be like trying to locate the "crab" in crabgrass. He watched in silence until the stern light had fallen from sight. Then, he became discouraged…briefly.

What's the old saw about silver linings, he thought? Four things became apparent to Tuck: he was lucky to be alive. Could have gone the other way quite easily. Apparently the water pressure of diving deep had restored his hearing and he now knew there was traffic about. And then there was tomorrow. Ah yes, tomorrow. "Tomorrow will be my day," he shouted for the entire world to hear.

The night cooled and he longed for a blanket, but had to be satisfied with hugging himself. He tried resting on his stomach, with his face turned to the side, but the sloppy waves kept washing over the raft and he spent most of the time sputtering and spitting salt water. At last he decided to lay on his back and breathe through his mouth.

He was emotionally and physically exhausted. It had been an exceptional day on anyone's calendar. He calculated aloud how far he had traveled since the sinking; "Let's see, eight hours at five or six knots; that's about the distance from Miami to West Palm Beach." He strained to picture the charts of the area, but the only islands he could recall were the northern reaches of the Grand Bahamas.

He recognized he was weary. Like after a long day on one end of a two-man crosscut saw; he was totally weary. His arms felt like he'd followed a mule plowing all day. He was too tired to eat, even if he had something to eat. Earlier, when a hunk of seaweed or grass washed upon the cover or brushed his arm, he jumped. Now, as fatigue took over, when that happened, he simply pushed it away wanting only to survive the night.

Finally settling down, he gazed into the heavens and saw the coal colored sky had given away to a canvas of blues, purples and indigo, splashed with the Milky Way and a sprinkling of closer stars. Visibility had improved greatly and eventually he slept soundly, if not for very long. On one occasion he awakened to learn he had turned on his side, knees drawn up, with his hands between his thighs without toppling off the raft. He was adapting to his circumstances, he thought.

He had just eased his way back into a tranquil state of sort, when he was startled with a milk-souring scream. "TUCKKKKKK"! Suddenly he was engulfed in flailing, swimming arms connected to a soft, pudgy "body" climbing atop him and the raft. His first sleep-laden thoughts were that an octopus or giant squid was attacking. Fearing he was about to be dragged from the raft into a lair hundreds of fathoms below, he screamed like a banshee and rolled from beneath the monster. Propelled by fear and adrenaline, Tuck pushed hard against the cover, swimming many strong strokes before stopping and looking back.

"Tuckster, it's me, Buddy!" the pain racked, panting voice called out. "You gotta hep me. Hurry! I been chasing after you ever since the 'splosion, hollering my lungs out trying to git your attention. Why you didn't stop to hep me?"

Tuck wiped the water from his face and turned his ear towards the sound. Initially, he could neither trust his ears nor fathom their meaning. How could he have missed anything as big as Buddy all day? Treading water, he was afraid his mind was playing tricks of sort. Finally, challenging, he stuttered, "Who-who-who ever you are; how, how did you get the name Buddy - if you really are?"

"Why, Tuckster, you give it to me. A nickname for Melvin, which I didn't like. Did you already ferget? Tuck, I'm hurt and you gotta hep me. Come on back!"

Relieved, Tuck swam toward his friend, "No, I didn't forget, but I had to be certain. Lordy, Buddy, you surely scared the begeebers out of me. I suspect I'm down about three lives from just this alone."

"Never you mind all thet. Right now, you gotta hep." Holding his ankle tightly for Tuck to see, he said, "Thet boat's prop nicked me when it came by and I'm bleeding like a stuck porker at butcherin' time. We gotta fix me a tournekey or I ain't gonna see 'nother sunrise".

Not being able to see well Tuck, treading water, felt for Buddy's foot and what he called a "nick". His stomach churned as he felt the cut. He swallowed hard. What he touched was a leg with a huge gash at the ankle. He held it briefly and felt the warmth of the escaping blood. Although he couldn't tell for certain, he knew the water around them was already crimson with Buddy's blood. Without proper care - now - he could not survive much longer. Additionally, he knew at that very moment, every shark within a few miles were honing in - with that mysterious capability of theirs - on the blood and were steering their deadly course towards them. Quickly tearing away a strip of pant leg he tied off the wound, slowing the flow of blood, and plopped the torn foot on top of the other leg. Buddy moaned weakly. His foot hung like a hank of rope.

Between clicking teeth, Buddy questioned, "How come you didn't answer me when I called out? I could see you at times; when you was on a crest. But you never did even turn around."

Tuck explained the loss - and the regaining - of his hearing. "But, I certainly never saw you and I scanned the area constantly. You know I'd never leave you intentionally. Don't you?"

"Course I do," he said through chattering teeth. "But right now I'm too cold to think or care about it."

Tuck rolled Buddy's long sleeves down and fastened the buttons at the wrist. He felt his pulse, rubbed his arms and chest vigorously and put his decision into action. After centering Buddy on the hatch cover, he struggled into Buddy's life jacket and began propelling the raft parallel to the running sea in an effort to thin the trail of blood. He knew he couldn't outrun the sharks, but was hopeful he might outsmart them for a bit, giving Buddy as much time as possible. Between his grunts and deep breathing, he asked Buddy about what happened to the *Nomad*.

Putting his arm over his forehead Buddy mumbled quietly. "'Splosion of some sort. Devil's Triangle I 'spose. You know all them stories. Mysteries. Ghosts. Mines left over from the war. Them darn

Krauts. The deck jest sort fell away from under me. It was like one of them carnival sink tanks, where you hit a target with a baseball and the clown gits dunked." He continued with pauses, chattering teeth and moans. "Tuck, I'm so cold. But, you can chalk the *Nomad* up to another of 'em 'vanished without no trace'." Rolling on his side, he put his hands between his knees and curled into the position of a baby. He fell silent. Tuck steadied the raft against the shifting weight, but kept pumping his legs in the unforgiving race with the sharks.

Buddy was not one of Tuck's favorite shipmates. Much of it was due to Buddy's relaxed attitude about everything. Rarely serious; he was lazy, overweight and seem to care little if school kept or not. Just getting by, appeared to be his code. Tuck thought his head looked like a fat sausage with a rubber band around the area of his eyes. He was reminded of the character, "Fat Stuff", in the popular comic strip *Smilin' Jack*. Due to his ample belly, "Fat Stuff" was continuously popping off a shirt button that was always caught in mid-air by a naked chicken. Tuck chuckled to himself being able to conjure up the image at such a serious time. Shaking his head, he said, "You're over the edge, Tuckster,"

In less than an hour, Tuck felt the sandpapery skin of the circling marauders brushing against his body. He cringed. His lifelong fear of sharks was managed only by an almost super human control and the realization there was little, if nothing, he could do. He again envisioned the survivors of the *Indianapolis* and wondered how it would feel to be ravaged by a school of sharks. Probably painless after a few well placed bites, he thought. He recalled how a shark's teeth seemed to come forward, almost out of its head, when taking a large bite. He believed he would live but a few seconds after the initial attack. Screaming underwater a time or two scattered the sharks if only for a brief period. A swat on the nose or a punch in the gills repelled the beasts for a moment. In the end, however, he had little choice but to remain calm, control his anxieties and imagination and await the inevitable.

Be calm, Tuck, he cautioned himself. Be calm. Lose your cool. Lose your life. He squinted, ground and clenched his teeth, hard. He prayed. Oh, how he prayed. He knew it was just a matter of seconds before the sharks attacked his pumping legs. And he could imagine what his bloody, little butt would look like hanging out of his ragged jeans. As a temporary solution to his thrashing legs, he hooked his toes on the leading edge snuggling his body up underneath the raft as close as he could. He was thankful for Buddy's life jacket, as he was able to remain motionless for long periods of time. But, his brain would not let him forget it was just a matter of time and believed the sharks had not yet attacked because of the thin trail of blood. He wished with all his might the porpoises had stayed around, as they were a superior foe of the sharks.

Buddy was no longer responding to Tuck's questions. His body was cold and stiff to the touch. Gritting his teeth, summoning all the strength, nerve and courage he could ever hope for, Tuck performed a task he would forever remember and re-think the rest of his life. One more time he touched Buddy's neck, satisfying himself he was dead. He then, in one fluid motion grasped Buddy's collar, rolling him into the churning sea, quickly taking his place on the raft. Pulling his feet into a sitting position, hugging his legs with both arms, he rested his head on his knees saying a silent prayer for the soul of his friend, asking at the same time forgiveness for his own action. By the time he looked up, the sea about him had become a pool of thrashing dorsal fins, flashing white teeth and churning water as every shark imaginable competed in the feeding frenzy over the body of his shipmate.

Tuck remained in his sitting position, hugging his knees as his small chip of wood continued its northward journey, gradually leaving behind the rampaging predators. He knew he could never, ever reveal what just took place. For the sake of all, Buddy died with his shipmates. "How could I ever explain to his Mama what happened?" He mumbled. "How could I convince her or anyone else Buddy was really dead before I pushed him off the raft?" He wouldn't even consider the implication of his having Buddy's life jacket. Tuck was now weeping for himself as much as for his friend.

Sometime during the early morning hours, Tuck became aware of the sound of breakers. It was still too dark to see well, but he heard the unmistakable sounds of surf. Not caring if it was a sand bar, a reef or an island; it was land! And he wasted no time sliding from the hatch cover in order to begin propelling it towards the sound. Holding on with both hands he stretched out behind, kicking in powerful, even strokes. "Sharks be gone! I'm heading home!" he cried.

It was difficult for him to accept the sound as being real because he believed the closest land - after passing Grand Bahamas - were the Bermuda Islands. He knew he had not drifted long enough to travel that far. Fifteen, sixteen hours at six miles per hour, a hundred miles, probably close to Ft. Pierce. "I'll worry about that when I get there." Right now it was one kick after another. Kerthunk! Kerthunk! Kerthunk!

As dawn gradually arrived, he made out a dark, thin profile on the horizon. An island as best he could tell, looking like a rolling porpoise, with its highest point in the center tapering to nothing at both ends.

Although worn out, he continued kicking and steering the hatch cover toward his target, knowing if he let up even momentarily, the Gulf Stream would whisk him right on by. Again and again: Kerthunk! Kerthunk! Kerthunk!

With full sunrise, he could better tell he was making headway as the landmass was growing and he was still on course. As his strength ebbed, he challenged himself with another hundred strokes, counting aloud: "1-2-3..." After that hundred, another and another. It was a system he'd developed while picking oranges, planting tomatoes and cabbage. It eased the boring tedium if not the mind and muscles.

After he could no longer see clearly, think or understand, and was functioning only from habit and will power, he felt the pallet grind onto the pebbled beach. After a final dozen or so "kerthunks", he stopped his scissoring legs, pulled himself upon the hatch cover and collapsed into that great chasm of relief - exhausted sleep. Deep, deep, sleep.

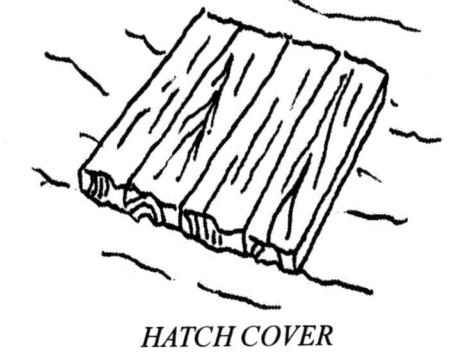

HATCH COVER

II
Land Found

Tuck wasn't alarmed at awakening in unfamiliar surroundings. As a child, he had lived the nomad's existence of migrant workers. "Many times, in the darkness, we would pack up and move just a step ahead of the sheriff with a warrant in hand or a company store employee with an outrageous bill 'fer them dang, deadbeat Fryers." He explained to the one person he cared about most; his Aunt Grace. "After awhile it seemed 'them dang *SABAL PALM* Fryers' was used as a way of explaining everything that was wrong with humanity: theft, sickness, fire, bad weather, you name it. For a time I avoided using my last name whenever possible."

On several occasions he had been sent back home by a family member to whom he had been "hired out", 'cause we jest can't keep care of 'im no more'. Once, when about ten, he was sent home on a *Trailways* bus from someplace in north Florida. The bus was crowded; standing room only. After leaning against a hang pole, then shifting from one foot to the other he was pretty miserable. He could've sat down on his suitcase, but it was made out of cardboard so he knew it would just collapse. Finally, a colored lady on the back seat slid over a bit and motioned to him. Not caring a whit that a few people called him 'white trash' and 'nigra-lover', he gratefully scooted in next to her. And slept the remainder of the night, with her arm around his shoulder and him leaning up against her enormous, soft, bosom. So, over time, Tuck had grown accustomed to being bumped and thumped and bounced about, with little or no warning, regardless of the time, day or night.

Cautiously he cracked his eyelids and without moving his head, surveyed the dim room. The semi-darkness and his slitted-eyes made it difficult to see well. But what he saw was a mixture of brush, limbs and a few planks propped against the trunk of a tree forming a natural teepee. Sunlight wiggled into the cavity through the many holes in the makeshift structure. He could tell it had not been in place very long, as the greenery was still green and only a tiny portion wilted. There were no holes for windows and the door was simply an opening in the brush, so small one would have to duck, in order to use it. The floor was raw earth covered with a thick layer of fresh Australian pine needles. Their pungent, spicy aroma filled the air and suddenly he was overflowing with thoughts of

GHOST OF THE STREAM

The Home. He rolled over ever so slowly, as if in sleep. The deception, however, was short lived. Opening his eyes, he was snapped wide awake and into a sitting position, trying to crab backwards looking for a limb or rock to use as a weapon.

Finding himself in unknown places might not have disarmed him, but peering into the wrinkled, coarse, old face of the huge woman at his bedside certainly did. He involuntarily winced and was immediately ashamed for his action. The gentle giant placed a hand on his shoulder and Tuck felt a touch of warmth as his fear evaporated like a wisp of smoke. In the future, Tuck would experience, on many occasions, the peace and security she projected. "Isn't nothin' to be afraid of youngan," she said calmly. "Take this here." Raising a metal cup, she spooned mild soup to his lips. "It's conch broth. Be good for you."

"Ma makes the best conch chowder in the Keys," testified a tall, thin boy standing at Tuck's feet.

"Hush!" demanded the woman. "What's your name, boy?"

"Tuck. Ma'am. Tuck Fryer. My real name's Thom - spelled T-h-o-m, but I'm mostly called Tuck."

"What kind of name is Tuck?" questioned the boy now collapsed in a heap, leaning against one of the many curving tree roots. "That's the craziest name I ever heard." Pointing a finger at Tuck, he added, "And ya didn't fool me fer a minute playin' you was 'sleep. Seen light bounce offen your eyeballs the split second ya opened 'em."

"Make your manners, Billy Jim. You knows it ain't polite to fun a body's name. Anyway, Mr. Tuck, this here is my boy, Billy Jim and I'm Hannah Hamilton. You can call me Ma or Hannah, but ain't gonna have none of this Miz Hamilton stuff." Offering the spoon again, she ordered, "Here, eat."

Sitting up, resting against the tree trunk, Tuck chewed the tiny bits of tough conch with his front teeth. Between ladles of soup, he asked the usual polite questions of strangers. The answers came freely until he asked, "Where are we anyway? I'm afraid I lost track along the way, but figure somewhere near Daytona Beach." Hannah kept a spoon of broth at his lips constantly until he felt like a baby bird, sitting opened mouth in a nest, being fed by its mother. He gently pushed her hand to a stop.

Billy Jim stole a quick glance at his mother and squinted at him. "We're on an island in the Atlantic Ocean, but don't know exactly..."

"Billy Jim, if you ain't a jabber-jaw," interrupted Hannah. "It don't matter where we are just now. Plenty of time for that later. Right now, this youngan needs to rest. Why don't me and you go get us something for supper."

ALOE

Lying back, wallowing out a place in the needles for his shoulders, Tuck recognized the tree as a Serpentine Banyan so named for it's many twisting, curling roots. Touching the crude bandage encircling his forehead, he felt no pain and smelled aloe, a member of the lily family known for its healing juices. Shortly he was again asleep; soothed by the lullaby of the wind humming through the branches and trying to figure out what Billy Jim meant when he said they didn't know where they were.

Sometime later, he awoke feeling rested and refreshed, if not totally ready to tackle the immediate future. Looking down at him was Billy Jim Hamilton. Tuck stirred uncomfortably, but would eventually learn Billy Jim was an untidy, uneducated, clever, tough-minded rascal with a natural ability of survival. A character right out of Mark Twain, Tuck decided: Tom Sawyer, perhaps. A year older than Tuck he walked as though all of his joints were doubled hinged. Loose, like a puppet, he stood and sat ill at ease.

Only when he flopped down, like he had no bones, did he actually look comfortable. His lanky frame was only a few inches more than five feet, but his dangling arms, the too short pants and a thin, elongated neck made him appear taller. Long, protruding front teeth, a large Adam's apple, sad droopy eyes and a button nose that lifted his upper lip, gave him an appearance of weariness. If he were an animal, Tuck thought he would be a Basset Hound and every person in close proximity would pat his head, scratch his ears or talk kindly to him.

"We gonna have lobster tonight," Billy Jim announced, crumbling into a space between two roots. "You like lobsters, Tuck?"

He nodded his fondness of crawfish, or more commonly known as Florida Spiny Lobster. Raising himself in order to lean against the trunk, he again approached the subject of their location. "Billy Jim, where are we really?" Briefly outlining his journey as best he could, he did admit that he didn't believe they were in the Keys.

"Naw, we ain't in the Keys. Never said we was." Billy Jim laughed. "I said Ma made the best chowder in the Keys. We lived there a while back. Still operate out of Marathon when we fish the Gulf. Moser Channel through the Seven-Mile Bridge allows us to fish both sides. You know the Atlantic and the Gulf." For a long moment, Billy Jim just stared at Tuck. He gave the impression of debating whether or not to trust telling him a secret. Eventually, again squinting, looking about as he scratched his neck, he whispered. "Tuck, we's in the Devil's Triangle. That's where we're at. Ma don't like me saying it, but old Satan hisself done up and snatched your boat out from under you. Same as us. And that's why we're here, on this island, just Ma and me and now you. Ma thinks we're on some part of Atlantis, seeing how that diver-fella found them underwater walls or roads near Bimini. But, I calls it Mystery Island 'cause it is."

Tuck was aware of the legends of the Devil's Triangle having read everything he could find on the subject. Although he didn't believe there was anything mysterious or supernatural about the area, he knew there were many reports of unusual happenings. By nature he was curious and interested. "Billy Jim, I just can't believe all the hocus-pocus blamed on this area. Bad weather, human error or faulty equipment can explain almost every event. You know yourself how quickly the weather can change in the Caribbean."

For a brief period, Billy Jim said nothing. He simply stared with squinty eyes that bored so deep, Tuck became uncomfortable and actually began to squirm and look about. Billy Jim's cheeks flushed and his jaw muscles twitched as he clenched his teeth. "You calling me a liar?" He got to his feet.

Tuck forced a smile. Stiffly he raised up, extending his hand as a gesture for him to remain. "No, Billy Jim. Please stay. I'm sorry. I didn't mean to sound so flip. Of course, you have every right to your belief. I just don't happen to believe there's anything different about this body of water over any other. Did you know there's suppose to be a similar area in the South China Sea?"

"Don't doubt it for a minute. Makes sense to me. Ain't that what they say about digging a hole straight down here and you wind up in China?" Billy Jim angrily punched a finger at him. "When you get better, I'll show you some things I ain't even told Ma about. Then we'll see what you say!" He headed for the opening.

"Wait, Billy Jim," Tuck said, getting up carefully, playing favorite to his cramping, aching, shouting for attention, muscles. Touching his arm, he admitted, "I forgot my manners. I'd like you to show me any secret you want to. Sometimes I can sound like a know-it-all and for that, I'm sorry."

Billy Jim stopped and turned. "Well, that's better. I ain't got no time for people what's agin me." Tuck sat back down in his nest and leaned back against the tree trunk, glad he had not alienated his new found friend. Billy Jim flopped on the ground. Stretching out, he leaned his head against a root and stared at Tuck. "What'cha thinking about?"

"Billy Jim, I'm trying to figure out what happened to us - my boat, it's crew - and me. We left Bimini for Miami on a clear, sunny day without the hint of a thunderhead. In fact, a welcomed breeze provided the only movement, other than our boat and an occasional flying fish or water bird.

"We were only a couple of hours out when we began taking on a little water; which wasn't unusual for the *Nomad*. I mean the boat was old, but we had good bilge pumps and they were working fine. The skipper, Captain Bannerman, decided to let someone know just in case we might need assistance later. He was cautious that way."

Billy Jim was listening like he might have been on board. "So, did he raise the Coast Guard?"

"That's just it. We had trouble with the radio right before we left *The Complete Angler*, but the technician didn't have the proper part. He did a temporarily fix, soldering in a piece of nik-chrome wire in place of a transistor, and thought we'd be okay for the crossing. We all agreed to try it. The short story is that we don't know if we ever got through or not. We couldn't receive and never heard from anyone. Anyway, the Captain thought it best if we prepared for the worse. I was already aft getting the inflatable raft ready when I heard a rumble, or perhaps it was a growl, from the engine compartment. We had already slowed to a crawl, so I'm guessing we were taking on more water than we thought."

"Why didn't nobody check? Could have been the pumps was plugged or shorted out."

"There wasn't time, Billy Jim. By now everyone was rushing around trying to find his life jacket. The skipper was hollering into the microphone and slapping the radio, trying to make it come to life. There was more than a little excitement. Lots of noise, raised voices, shouting and panic. Pandemonium! You know it's not every day you find yourself preparing for a disaster at sea regardless of how much you think about it or trained for it in advance. The strangest part was that it all seemed, to me, to be happening in slow motion. I remembered falling off a bicycle once, and while sliding across the street into traffic, I had time to think how long it was taking me to stop sliding. I know it was all in my mind, but that's the way I saw it.

"The next thing I know the boat starts shaking like a wet dog and everyone's losing his balance. Then - and I'm not absolutely certain about this - I seem to recall a muffled explosion and then the boat kind of collapsing within itself. Billy Jim, did you ever see a man crush a beer can with his hands? How it sort of gave in at the sides first, then the center wrinkled and crumbled inwards and finally the ends crunched downward. That's just the way the *Nomad* died and everyone on it, except me." After answering Billy Jim's questions about the sinking, Tuck realized he was perspiring heavily. Pausing for a moment, wiping his forehead with the waist of his tee shirt, he continued.

"Somehow I wound up on the hatch cover paddling around screaming for everybody. The only thing I saw was the boat stick its bow up in the air, like a rapidly surfacing submarine, then slide backwards into the Gulf Stream leaving a string of bubbles racing to the surface." At this point Tuck was emotionally drained having finally said aloud what he had before just committed to the mind.

He was met with silence. Billy Jim sat and again stared at him. After awhile, he asked, "Tuck, that 'zample of the beer can gittin' squashed. You can't see no likeness to that and a hand reaching up from the bottom of the sea and yankin' your boat under? Maybe King Neptune. He carries that three-prong spear, just for that reason, you know. So he ain't no Santa Claus."

"No, Billy Jim, I really don't. Besides King Neptune is made up, a myth. I see the *Nomad* as a victim of faulty equipment, gasoline explosion or a mine left over from World War II. No flimflam, hocus-pocus, smoke and mirrors or...Devil's Triangle."

"Well, you tell your story with a lot of ands, ifs and buts, and yet you ain't seeing no mystery in it. I think you ever write it all out, you'll see it. You oughta make a diary or something."

"All I'm really trying to do, Billy Jim, is to make some sense out of it all. Trying to determine what happened and where we are. The nautical charts we used in and around the Bahamas continued to float through my mind." He fluttered his hand, imitating a falling feather. "I'm amazed I can recall depths at certain spots and pinpoint spoil banks and reefs. I can mentally track my entire journey on the hatch cover - up to a point."

Early June

Finding a stubby pencil and a few scraps of paper washed up on shore, while walking to the point, I really didn't have an excuse not to keep a journal as Billy Jim suggested. To be honest I wanted to try. Thought if I wrote down some of those things nagging at me, they'd lose some of their sting. I still don't know exactly what happened to the Nomad. *The last thing I remember was Captain Bannerman shouting, "Mayday! Mayday!" into the microphone. "This is the* Nomad. Nomad. *We are sinking and need assistance. Can you read me? Over."*

He was met with silence. Again and again he flipped switches, twisted dials and even resorted, a couple of times, to slapping the ancient transmitter with an open palm. *His efforts went unrewarded. The signs were there of the turmoil the Captain was facing as he concentrated on the problem. His usual expressive – almost elastic face was flat. The normally laughing eyes were dulled with a far away, glassy look. There were no witty comments.*

Not even the crackle of static, so familiar with the aged boat's radio, could be heard. "Mayday! Mayday! This is the Nomad. Nomad. *En route to Miami from Bimini. We are taking on water and need help. Mayday! Mayday!" He looked at each of us, apologizing. Making surrendering motions with his hands and dropping his shoulders slightly, he signaled he had done his best and it wasn't enough.*

Hands behind his head he now spoke more comfortably. "If I were a seagull looking down, I'd see myself on a small block of wood. Then at the whims and dictates of the winds and water, I quietly began drifting north from the mid-point between Miami and Bimini. Swirling, spinning, circling, I pass Great Isaac, Northwest Providence Channel and Freeport. Finally, I slip between the northern tip of Grand Bahamas and West Palm Beach. From that point I can count off the places along Florida's east coast as I skitter by: Riveria Beach, Jupiter, Port Salerno, Hutchinson Island."

Billy Jim tossed back his head and laughed. "Good golly Molly, you sounds like one of them dispatchers at the *Greyhound* bus station."

Tuck was frustrated and a little irritated that Billy Jim did not appear the least bit concerned that he didn't know where they were. Had he known Billy Jim better he would have guessed him to be like a hermit crab - always at home wherever he was. And when he outgrew one shell, he comfortably moved to another without upset or fanfare. The possibility that he did know crossed Tuck's mind, but he could come up with no motive for him - and his mother - to withhold that information. "Well, we can't be on Bermuda. I wasn't adrift that long. If the Stream is moving at five knots this time of the year, I couldn't have traveled more than 75 miles. A hundred at best."

"Me and Ma figured you weren't out there more'n two days. You wasn't too dried out. Little sunburn and cracked lips. Weren't no barnacles starting to grow on the cover yet. So 200 miles at most."

"That puts us where? Daytona Beach? St. Augustine?"

Billy Jim paused long enough to taste the bittersweet juice from a pine needle causing him to spit. "Based on our mishap we know it's more like New Smyrna or Cape Canaveral."

Tuck jumped as if struck from behind. From a kneeling position, he almost screamed. "Cape Canaveral! Billy Jim, that's where a rescue plane, a flying boat, took off from to look for the *Lost Patrol* - Flight 19 it was called. Five Avengers, torpedo bombers, out of Ft Lauderdale, disappeared while on a routine training mission. That was just in December of last year! Six or seven months ago! Gone! Heard from, but never seen again! And then a search plane, a Martin Mariner with 13 men on board, didn't return either." Realizing the pitch of his voice, Tuck silenced his rapid-fire speech and took a big breath of air. He could feel the tempo of his entire body responding to the excitement he felt. Feeling sheepish, he squatted back on his heels.

Billy Jim continued to chew on the pine needle thoroughly enjoying Tuck's anxiety. "Tuck, me lad, you need to calm down. You gonna bust a gullet. You don't believe them stories about the Triangle. You told me so yourself. Remember?"

"Oh, I believe most of the reported events happened. I just don't believe there's anything unusual or mysterious causing them. You know, UFO's, magnetism, ghosts and that sort of thing. At least I don't think I believe them." Now it was Tuck's turn to pace.

"You believe you can be on an island that don't 'zist...at least not on any chart?" Billy Jim asked in a monotone whine accompanied by his twisted little grin. "And an island like you ain't never seen before."

"What does that mean?" Before Billy Jim could answer, Tuck continued thoughtfully. "I must admit it's baffling. Of course, it may just be a coincidence, too. By that I mean New Smyrna or the Cape. We might be on an island too small for the charts and we just never heard about it"

"You really believe that?"

"I don't know Billy Jim." Tuck answered absently. "How large did you say this place is?"

"Based on the land we once farmed near Everglades City, we figure about twenty acres. Irregardless, it's too big to miss for long and we ain't seen no boats, ships or airplanes. Leastwise, Ma ain't."

"What do you mean? Billy Jim, why all these riddles?" He was annoyed.

"In time. In time. You'll soon see for yourself. Maybe tomorrow, if you're up to it."

Tuck sat back down asking about the island and how long they had been here.

"Going on a week. But not long enough to learn all about it. It's got a good supply of drinking water. A fresh water spring in a saltwater ocean I suspect, like the pirates knew about. And plenty of tropical fruit and seafood."

"What happened to you folks?"

"About the same as you. Old Satan pulled the plug on Pa's trawler and down to the bottom it went." Using his hand, Billy Jim indicated a direct plunge straight down. "Like an anchor."

"And your Pa? Your father?"

"Oh, he wasn't on it. He's been dead fer years. Buried back at Lostman River in the Glades. Got hisself killed while "borrowing" phantom orchids from Fakahatchee Strand in Big Cypress Swamp."

Tuck looked incredulously. "What's a phantom orchid? Never heard of such."

"Phantom or ghost." Billy Jim stirred the earth with his knife. "I don't know if they're called that 'cause they's very, very rare and orchid folks want 'em or 'cause so few people ever seen one."

"What do they look like?"

"Never seen one, but Pa said they ain't got no leaves. Just one satin white flower of five thin, ribbon-like pedals in the shape of a starfish. Out of the center is a squid looking shape with only two, long, thin tentacles. Pa said the tentacles reminded him of an ole Chinaman's mustache. You know Charlie Chan or Foo Man Choo. Around the whole thing is a bunch of thin green roots that looks like somebody's fishing reel backlashed on him somethin' terrible.

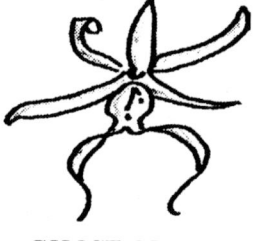

GHOST ORCHID

"I don't bleve Pa cared nothin' about the flower business," Billy Jim added with a grin. "He just like the challenge of gettin' more than anybody else and 'course the money's good. They's found mostly in swampy areas, in Alligator Apple trees. Hard, nasty, work to get at 'em. Mud so bad it can suck your shoes off, accordin' to Pa.

"We think he probably got caught raidin' somebody's 'private nursery'." Billy Jim rolled his eyes. "Anyway, some snake hunters for *Ross Allen Reptiles* found him spiked on a Judas Thorn tree. He was a goner from the git-go. If the spines didn't kill him the poison sap would." Tuck winced.

"I 'spect he was left there as a warnin' to others. Now me and Ma runs the boat. Snapper fishing mostly, off the Banks." Pausing, Billy Jim added, "Pa said the unusual thing about the ghost was that the roots blend in with the tree bark and it appears to grow in mid-air. Maybe that's why they's called ghost. I don't know."

"I'm sorry about your father," Tuck said, extending a hand towards Billy Jim.

"Don't matter none. Pa died long time 'fore he got killed. The day he got the telegram about my brother Henry Lee gettin' killed in a little, old German town that don't amount to spit, he started dying from the inside out. Took to shinin', drinkin', poachin', and plain ole meanness...like he was always hankerin' for a fight. Mad at the world it seemed. Just went through the motions of living after that." He paused as if he didn't believe what he was about to say or didn't want to say it. "You know the only thing I can remember Pa ever saying about Henry Lee, was that his boy didn't count for nothin'. That ain't much to say about eighteen years of livin', is it? Reflectively, he added, "I guess it hurts most to lose your first born."

Tuck explained that he thought his Pop meant that Henry Lee's death didn't accomplish anything. Billy Jim paused and looked at him. Tuck digested what little he knew about his new friend. Finally Billy Jim broke the silence. "Whatever. We did lose our nigra, though."

Tuck tried to conceal his surprise at hearing Billy Jim's obvious disregard for human life. "That's no way to talk about a person," he finally managed to say.

Billy Jim did not move a muscle or show a twinge of emotion. "Waden't no person, just Russell. Russell Fussell. Ain't that a handle? Can't you just hear his Mama yellin' for him when he was a youngan? 'Russell Fussell, hustle yo bustle.'"

Billy Jim's rhyme helped remove the pebble from the shoe. Tuck managed a smile because that's exactly the way Candy or Mamie, two colored women at The Home, would summon their broods: "Goot, yo best scoot. Zeke, we gotta meet. Buddle, Buddle, git out dat puddle." But, Billy Jim, he thought, if I could have introduced you to Sam, you'd never, ever feel the same about colored folks.

Billy Jim took from his pocket a smooth piece of shell and began rubbing it between his thumb and forefinger. "What's that?" asked Tuck.

Looking at it, holding it between a finger and thumb for Tuck to see, Billy Jim said, with a grin, "That's my future and fortune." Pronouncing a long E, he added, "It's called the E-zec-a-tive pacifier. Seen one in a novelty shop in Miami. I figure me to start collectin' 'em, polishin' 'em up and sellin' 'em wholesale."

"How does it work?"

"When big shots get to feelin' antsy, they just rubs the smoothness and their troubles melt away. 'Calms the body and soothes the soul' is my sales pitch. Gonna drill a hole, add a chain so they can be hung on their key rings. I 'spect to be living on Biscayne Boulevard in downtown Miami, afore I'm old enough to vote."

Tuck pinched his lips together to cover a smile. "How much do you know about marketing?" Before Billy Jim could tell him "nothing", they were interrupted.

"What'cha youngans up to in there?" Hannah called from the outside before stooping to enter the room. Her enormous size still amazed Tuck. She was six feet tall, wearing men's clothing: long sleeve shirt, army surplus pants and high top tennis shoes. The graying hair was cut short, obviously with a knife or dull scissors. Years of hard toil in the sun had wrinkled and browned her face. High cheekbones, pencil line lips, slits for eyes and prominent chin gave her face a "pushed in" appearance. She was quick of hands, but they were creased and puffy like those Tuck had seen on people he had worked alongside. (Aunt Grace explained it as the results of years of manual labor and poor diet.)

As she stood with hands on hips, Tuck again experienced an overwhelming comfort in her presence. It was a feeling of security and safety he had felt only rarely. "How you feel Tuck?"

"Feel just fine Ma'am." And he really did.

"It ain't Ma'am," she said, ruffling up his hair. "Ma or Hannah, remember?"

"I remember and I think I'd like to call you Hannah, if Billy Jim doesn't mind. I've seldom called an adult by their first name."

Billy Jim shrugged his shoulders. "Don't make me no never mind. She ain't your Ma, no how."

"Hannah it is then," said his mother, slapping her palms together.

After a filling meal of guavas, bananas and papayas, Hannah cleared the table, fashioned from several planks. "Suppose you'll want to be seein' your new home, Tuck?" Before he could answer, she added, "Billy Jim, why don't you give Tuck a quick visit. But, you listen to me; he ain't a hundred percent yet, so go easy. Besides, lookin' at the weather we may have us a cloud directly." Hannah pointed to skyscraper thunderheads building in the east

Walking from the shaded area, Tuck had begun thinking of as "base camp", he had to shield his eyes from the bright sunlight. Looking north, he could trace the eastern boundary that rested on the sheer, western side of the Gulf Stream. By the dark blue color of the water he estimated its depth to be several hundred feet at the edge of the island.

"This here is what we call the 'dome' because the way it's shaped. That there's the 'point'. The north end," offered Billy Jim, waving his arm. "It's about a quarter of a mile from the southern tip. Huge rocks there and gets deep in a hurry. Good fishin' I'll bet."

Peering to the west, their vision was limited by the elevation of a ridge and lush, green vegetation. Regardless of what the Hamiltons told him, Tuck continued to believe the island to be part of the Bahamas. He recognized he wanted it to be...very badly. If it wasn't Grand Bahamas, then perhaps it was one of the smaller islands that appear as stepping stones around it. Like a mountain goat, Tuck scampered up the knoll for a better view.

"Hey man, take it easy," cautioned Billy Jim, following. "It'll all be here for a good long piece. You don't have to take it all in with one look-see."

The scene from atop the ridge was breathtaking. On the western side was a natural lagoon. The water was so clear the various depths could be seen from this vantage point. The light blues, deep purples and mint greens blended to form an electric abstract. A logical place for red snapper, yellow tails, and nameless reef fish, swimming in unison, to race about. "Billy Jim," Tuck said pointing to an outcropping of rocks, "Can't you just picture fat groupers, with their perpetual frowns, backed into the earth's recesses? Or Queen conchs lying over there in the turtle grass? Florida lobsters and plump shrimp resting under the ledges and in the surface holes?"

Billy Jim shook his head. "Fish is fish," he said. "I want poetry I'll go to the *Buzz Inn* for some Country and Western, guitars and fiddles."

In spite of Billy Jim's lack of interest, Tuck's excitement was well in place. He could now see the entire southern tip of the island, proving if there was a town, it had to be on the northern end.

As they began walking the ridge to the north, Tuck became aware the island was like nothing he had ever seen. The landscape was filled with palms, the deepest, dark-green imaginable and loaded with coconuts. Avocado, guava, banana, wild orange and papaya trees strained under an abundance of fruit. A scattering of long-leaf pines and giant water oaks reached widths and heights he never thought possible. The undergrowth looked like a botanical garden of blooming hibiscus, juniper, cedar, philodendron and colorful crotons. "Plants that grow in the Caribbean basin, but only with constant care, seem to flourish here," Tuck noted.

"Apparently unaided except by nature." Billy Jim was not into botany either.

Stopping to look about, they could now see both sides of the island. Together, they estimated it to be no more than 200 yards wide and maybe six or seven times that number in length. "I think a pilot would see this as a long thin emerald on a piece of rich, blue velvet," Tuck said to Billy Jim. "You and Hannah have been joking with me, haven't you?" he challenged. "This must be a part of the Bahamas. No island this size and beautiful can go undetected in today's world."

"Whatever. Believe what you want to." Billy Jim shrugged. Waving toward the natural run of the ridge, "The growth ahead, gets thicker from here on in. It'll be easier goin' along the ocean side." Without waiting for Tuck's confirmation, he turned and began threading his way down the knoll, over the gigantic dome of rock towards the shoreline. Pastel butterflies jumped into flight as he bulldozed his way through the thick underbrush.

Tuck followed, pushing the low branches out of the way as they swished back into his face. "Are there any animals on the island?" He hollered.

"Strange as it seems, I ain't seen none. Just the usual insects, mice and a few birds". Reaching the shore, they walked in silence towards the north end of the island. Occasionally, Billy Jim would stop, skip a flat stone into the midnight blue Atlantic and make a pronouncement of sort. "I 'spect it's near a thousand feet deep out there." Or, "Bet the Stream is movin' six knots 'bout now." At last, rounding the point, Tuck's worst fears were confirmed. There was no settlement. No people. No colorful, native boats bobbing at anchor. Just the large, protruding rocks like Billy Jim had described and the large expanse of water.

Tuck was devastated, because he had been so certain there was a small village or town at the point. He was sure his disillusionment and dashed hopes showed and he was glad Billy Jim, who was already busy jumping from boulder to boulder, did not see his disappointment. Finding a comfortable place beneath a palm, he sat down to sulk, think and pick away at his frustration.

With ease he allowed his memory to drift back to The Home, and what Sam had said about times like these. "Sometimes, son, when you got nothing but failure or disappointment staring you in the face, you gotta reach down deep inside yourself to see if you really gonna come up with a 'handful of empty'. Weighing everything, most likely you won't." Sam displayed his hand with the missing thumb, loss to his ax having been bitten by a deadly coral snake.

"You all right?" asked Billy Jim, coming up from the boulders below. "You look like you been rode hard and put away wet. I 'spect you're tiring. Why don't we head for home? You get sick and Ma'll tan my hide saying I let you over do it."

"I'm okay. To prove it I'll open us a coconut. Then we can go." Picking up a dark brown nut about the size of a soccer ball he shook it next to his ear to ensure it contained milk. Dropping to his knees, he began pounding the pointed end on a stone. After a few whacks small splits began creeping up the three flat sides. Even after the husk appeared to be well loosened, he continued pounding. Experience had taught him to quit too soon, regardless of appearance, would make removing the inner nut very difficult. A few more whops and the husk pulled away with ease.

Using his knife, he punctured the soft eyes and drank some of the cool, sweet milk, before passing it to Billy Jim. After smashing the nut, he dug the rich, white meat from the shell and together they enjoyed the semi-sweet taste.

Opening the coconut somewhat settled Tuck's mind. Suddenly, he felt a turnabout, a companionship - a calmness - as they began the trek southward by way of the lagoon. It was a restful walk. Billy Jim pointed up to several outcroppings along the way. "I think them holes are really caves. Ain't had no chance to 'splore them yet."

Tuck suggested they take a look. "Might be pirate caves. Hidey-holes. You know filled with treasure. Black Caesar roamed these waters. *Caesar Creek*, south of Elliott Key, is named for him."

Billy Jim nodded his knowledge of Black Caesar. "Even got a fancy restaurant named after him down there in the Old Cutler area: *Black Caesar's Forge*. To rich fer my pockets, howsomever."

As they walked Tuck told of his reading about the pirate. "You know, one story I read tells of him and another pirate, Captain Flood, actually fighting at the mouth of a cave they had hidden their loot in." Tuck pointed upwards. "Those could be the very ones. They seem to fit the picture in my mind's eye. The book called it a precipice, a steep cliff." Quickly he added, "I had to look up its meaning. Nevertheless, supposedly old Flood pushed Caesar over a cliff and believing he had killed him went about his business. Unknown to Flood, Caesar grabbed some bushes, limbs and roots on the way down and survived. Eventually he made his way back to Port Royal, got well, came back and waited for old Flood's return. When he did, Caesar killed him, took all the spoils, his booty, ship and crew."

"You believe all that stuff and won't have nothing to do with the Devil's Triangle." Billy Jim shook his head. He was bewildered. "I guess we best take a look, but right now we better head for home."

That evening, poking at the coals of the perpetual fire, Tuck thought he had a good layout of the physical island. What he couldn't fathom was the many unusual aspects about it. This island seemed too large to remain unnoticed by air and sea traffic and chart makers from all over the world. The rules of nature apparently didn't apply to this enchanted land. Outside forces or elements did not seemingly influence it in any significant manner. It was as if there was an invisible dome covering this spot of the world and within its boundaries, there existed a Garden of Eden - a paradise. He couldn't begin to explain it, but there nagged at his brain the constant thought he was on to something not easily explained.

Before he went to sleep, he drew in the sand, with Hannah's and Billy Jim's help, what he thought the island might look like from the air and where they might be in relations to Florida. Unable to sleep Tuck wrote again in his journal.

June ? 1946

I still think about Buddy every day and don't know if I did right by pulling him from the hatch cover and taking his place. He was dead, of that I'm certain. I also know together, we could not have survived on the raft. It was just too small. One of us would not have survived dangling from the raft. The sharks would have made quick work of those pumping legs and perhaps spilled the other to a certain death.

So why do I get this hollow feeling in my gut when I think of him? I really didn't care for Buddy. I mean he wasn't a best friend, but hey, I didn't want him dead. Having seen what sharks did to a live whale, I've just had to close my mind to what I imagine his body went through. Ugh...

I've thumbed through my underdeveloped list of emotions and you know what I feel mostly about Buddy? Sadness. Sadness and loneliness. I can't get it out of my mind that forever Buddy will be out there all alone. His mama won't have a marker to put flowers on. He won't ever have a family and kids. Even though I was with him when he died it isn't the same as having a member of your family present. I guess dying without a loved one present is really dying alone.

Kinda reminds me of a tombstone in the corner of the cemetery at The Home. Off by itself. No writing to identify the person buried there and I never saw a single flower placed there during my stay. Just like Buddy; dead, all alone and not one person to cry or mourn.

BILL PEARCE

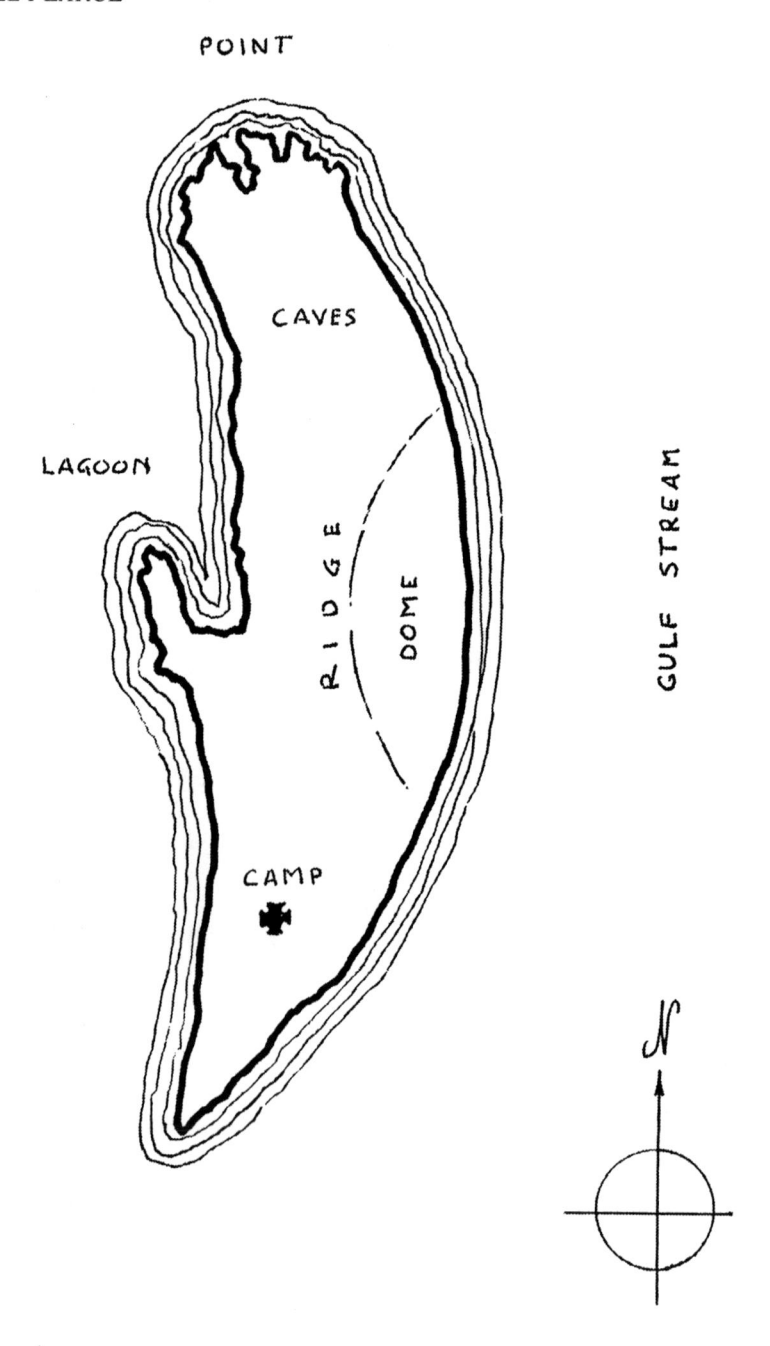

POINT

CAVES

LAGOON

RIDGE

DOME

CAMP

GULF STREAM

N

III
Mystery Island

SQUID

"If you's up to it, we can take a gander at our new home," Billy Jim invited. "Got somethin' to show you." Providing themselves with two straight limbs to serve as staffs, they began their journey up the center of the ridge towards the north. "Travel's gonna be slow till we get outta this mess, but the trip's gonna be worth it, I promise." Billy Jim spoke as they broke their way through the entanglement of vines, weeds and brush. Within a few minutes, the underbrush gave way to small, lush groves of guava, mulberry and papaya trees: all heavily laden with fruit.

The landscape again changed and very soon they were in a forest of mahogany, oak and pine with vines dangling about. The coolness of shade was a welcomed relief from the oppressive heat. "Did'ja notice how the sun can't reach down here so there ain't much undergrowth, just leaves and needles?" Billy Jim asked. Tuck could feel the padding beneath his feet and acknowledged the thick foliage of the trees and weedless ground. For the next hundred feet or so they were in a canopied forest except for the few places where a tree had fallen and small plants had quickly sprung to life filling the void in the island's tapestry. "Just nature's way," observed Billy Jim over his shoulder. "Pretty soon a tree will sprout and claw its way towards the sun until its shade kills the stuff at its feet. In time, the dead weeds will feed the very thin' that killed it. Ain't that a hoot?"

"Seems like nothing is wasted," Tuck said, recognizing the cycle of nature. "Each action has a reaction." He told Billy Jim that mankind should pay detailed attention to nature and incorporate more of its components into its daily lives. He knew the Everglades were suffering because of the Corp. of Engineers meddling in nature's business and the Florida Keys had changed dramatically in his short life.

Exiting the forest they entered into a thick jungle of head-high scrub oaks, bamboo and ligustrum, some of it growing almost parallel with the terrain, battered victims of the ocean winds at this elevation. "Almost there," Billy Jim promised. At their feet were the coontie plant, saw palmetto, snake cactus, lantana and periwinkles. Tuck remembered from his scouting days the starchy coontie plant was poisonous, but could be made edible.

"Billy Jim, do you know how to eat the coontie plant?"

Barely slowing down, he turned and glared at Tuck. "Naw. I ain't no squaw. But, Ma probably does. The Seminoles make a flour out of it called sofkee. I know it has to be washed a time or two during the cookin'. Did'ja know they also use cattail roots to make flour?"

Again and again they stumbled, tripped and pushed their way through underbrush so thick, at times visibility was but a few yards. Limbs, branches and vines reached out to snag their clothing and tangle their feet. Adding to their misery was the hot, muggy weather making Billy Jim ask, "Is this here trip really necessary?" Exasperated, he talked ugly on several occasions, but Tuck kept his sense of humor.

"I feel like a fly caught in the web of a daddy-long-legs."

Billy Jim didn't respond. He was too busy stumbling, turning, twisting and falling as they continued their erratic journey. At last, quite abruptly, they emerged from the entangled jungle and stood in a grassy opening at the very top of the ridge. In the center of the cleared space squatted the remains of an airplane. Billy Jim spoke as if he might be ordering a *NuGrape*. Pointing his staff in its direction. he asked, "You 'bleve that's one of them Avengers you was talkin' 'bout?"

"It *is* an Avenger!" Tuck cried, throwing down his staff and racing past Billy Jim. "I can tell by the lines and cockpit canopy." Hopping up on the wrinkled wing, then using the toe hole, he pulled himself up the fuselage until he was able to look into the cockpit. "Yeowee, Billy Jim, there's a skeleton in here." From the center seat of the plane, staring up at him from a pile of bones and tattered, khaki uniform, was a toothy skull. All at once, he felt a wave of excitement as he experienced another direct contact with death. He wasn't shocked or afraid, but felt instead privileged, to have been allowed a certain closeness with one of life's mysteries.

Peering aft through the Plexiglas into the gun turret, he saw nothing. Wasting no time, he hand walked himself to the forward cockpit where he leaned over inside in order to get a better look at the instrument panel. "It is an Avenger TBN-3! Here's the Grumman's ID plate. Manufactured in 1944." Feeling a compassion for the dead man aboard, he knew it would be difficult to explain his feelings to Billy Jim. Tuck had always experienced a fascination about the "mystery" of life and death. And not so much death, but the remains of death: the body, the human skeleton, epitaphs and graveyards. "Morbid", the kids at The Home called him. Nevertheless, that feeling, that fascination, that excitement, that wondering about the person's history was very, very real. As he hung to the side of the plane, he realized his nearness to something quite special. He savored the moment, enjoying the excitement and emotions that had taken over his mind and body. Looking back, he came to realize; because he was so caught up in the thrill and fascination, he missed a very important point that would cause him embarrassment in the future. He would have hung there indefinitely if Billy Jim had not broken the spell.

"You been there long enough. Come on down. Ma will worry if we ain't back directly. Besides, got a couple of more thin's I want to show you."

Tuck let go of the cockpit, dropping to the wing then jumping to the grassy earth below. The fall, however, was nothing like he had ever experienced. He felt as if he had fallen in slow motion landing into a soft pad. At first he attributed it to his mental state, but quickly aligned it to a similar occasion.

Once while running for home ahead of a thunderstorm, he had raced along the banks of Snapper Creek Canal at superhuman speeds. At least he thought that was the case. Even today, he can still recall the sensation of literally flying over the rough trail of ruts, roots and holes with his feet hardly touching the earth. Several times since, he has dreamed of running so fast, holding his arms out to the side like wings, he flew, floated or glided for short distances. The one thing that always snaps him back to reality, is that "Tank" Thomas, not known for his speed, was right along side him during that "beyond human" jaunt.

"Ain't that the dangest thing you's ever felt? The floating, I mean."

"You felt it too, Billy Jim?"

"Well, of all the...course I did. What'cha think I brought you up here for? This whole place is like that." He spread his arms indicating the cleared space. "Watch this." Without fanfare or further explanation, Billy Jim jumped into the air and rolled into a backward somersault. His feet barely touched the ground before he sprung forward into a flip, landing with a soft bounce.

Tuck stood awe-stricken. Outside the circus, he had never seen anything like it.

"Close your mouth, Tuck, before you catch a fly. And you better put your eyeballs back in your head before they springy-sprong themselves silly."

For the next few minutes they jumped, dived, ran, flew, hopped, skipped and floated through space. They satisfied, to a degree, mankind's universal desire to spread their arms and fly like a bird - limited as it was to one general area.

"Watch this!" they challenged each other as they jumped from the plane to projecting rocks only to float back to earth with the ease, if not the grace, of the Great Blue Heron. "My guess is that gravity is lessened by 30 to 40 percent. Maybe more," Tuck said. "Just enough to keep us grounded, but adequate to make our steps lighter. I believe astronomers think the moon has a gravity similar to this."

Billy Jim reached into a hole at the base of a tree nearby and produced the compass he had taken from the plane. "What'cha make of this here?" he asked, handing Tuck the instrument.

Tuck turned it over carefully in his hands; not knowing what Billy Jim was expecting him to say. "It's an ordinary compass isn't it? I've seen many quite like it, especially in the war surplus stores." Examining it more carefully, he saw nothing unusual about it.

"Stand right where you are and point it to the north."

He pivoted his body until the needle lined up with the large black "N". But, he couldn't hold it there. "The needle keeps moving." Creeping ever so slowly clockwise, he was soon facing to the northeast by the time he had the needle aligned once more. After a second or so, it started moving again. Regardless, how hard he tried; he couldn't hold the needle steady.

"Now turn to the south, fast."

He did as he was told and the compass began spinning so rapidly he could not read the numbers. It continued for sometime before it settled down to a slight crawl. He couldn't fathom what he was seeing. "I don't understand. Perhaps the compass was broken during the crash. Or maybe there is a large mineral deposit on the island."

"Maybe, but it don't act up that way nowhere but up here. Below the ridge it behaves mostly like a regular compass. What'cha make of it? Tuck."

"I don't know, Billy Jim. This is the highest place on the island. Maybe it's a focal point of sorts. It's pretty strange all right. What does Hannah think about it?"

"She don't know nothin' about it and I don't want you tellin' her. You hear? She worries about things like haints and ghosts and spooks. She don't even know about the airplane. It would just put another bother on her."

"There's probably a lot of things on that plane we can use. Maybe we can even construct a boat from the canopy. She'll need to know."

Billy Jim scanned the canopy. Hopping up on the fuselage, he slid the hood over the pilot's section forward, noting the seams were airtight. "Yeah, I can see how that might work. Turn it upside down, add an outrigger... I wouldn't want to trust it in rough weather, but paddling around the lagoon might be fun. We'd have a glass boat instead of one with only a glass bottom." He grinned at the prospect.

"You know Hannah is always telling us to find a boat and get us off this island. Sooner or later she has to know about the plane."

"I heard ya. We'll make it later. Let's put the compass away and go back to camp."

"In a minute," said Tuck. Backing away some distance, he began walking towards the plane with the compass stretched out at arm's length in front of him. After encircling the plane, he told Billy Jim how the compass had performed. "If I had relied on the compass, it would have actually steered me away from the plane. A ship or airplane within its range, would experience the same results," he reasoned, "thereby avoiding the island altogether. Hey, wait a minute, perhaps that's the answer; it's the island with the magic. Not the plane."

"If your idea is correct, that'd explain why we ain't seen none. How you suppose the plane got here?"

"One puzzle at a time, Billy Jim. I think there might be a large mineral deposit here, like the magnetic north. I guess the plane could have gotten hit by lightning and is now putting off some sort of power or energy. Like a magnet, but perhaps in reverse. Instead of attracting, it pushes it away."

"I seen that before in elementary school. Point two magnets towards one another and they push each other away. Opposin' magnetism, we always called it."

"I suppose negative or reverse magnetism or interrupted polarity could explain it. The scientists can figure it all out when we get home."

"If it messes up the gravity, why don't the plane float? It seems to me, it oughta."

"You'd think so, but maybe it's just the source of the energy and it's not actually affected by it. Of course, it might be too heavy. I suspect that plane weighs several tons."

"Another odd thing about all of this," Billy Jim added, again indicating the immediate area. "It ain't here all the time. The low gravity, I mean. I been up here when this area's natural. Normal. It's almost like somebody can flip a switch turning it off and on or it's on a timer. That's one reason I took it out of the plane. One day it's spinning out of control. The next time it's pointing north like it's suppose to."

"Perhaps, it has a cycle. Maybe the Earth's revolution has a bearing on it. I don't know." Tuck was baffled and simply looked quizzically at Billy Jim.

Walking home, Billy Jim asked Tuck what he really thought about what they'd found.

"I honestly don't know. It's beyond me," he admitted. "The compass. The low gravity. It's all so very different...so strange." The word 'strange' came out raspy as if it was difficult to say. "Nevertheless, I do believe the possibility of the Avenger being one of the *Lost Patrol* is very, very real. I can see how it could have caused them to appear to be lost. And according to what I've read, that's what the transmissions from the pilots seemed to indicate." They walked on in silence until Tuck stopped and took Billy Jim's arm. "Billy Jim, I don't know how to say this, except just come out with it. "I apologize for being a smart-mouth when we first met. This truly is Mystery Island."

Billy Jim's ears turned red as he kicked at a tuft of grass. "It's okay, Tuck. I don't 'spect friends gotta agree on everything." He gave Tuck a friendly punch to his arm. Yet his next question was baffling. "Tuck, did'ja notice anything else unusual at the plane?"

Tuck thought through what they had just experienced and couldn't come up with anything he felt out of the ordinary. "Not really, Billy Jim. What did I miss?"

"How many skeletons did you find?"

"One."

"Does that seem strange for a plane that usually carries three men?"

"Well, I-I guess so," he stammered. "Do you suppose the others bailed out? The plane can be flown from the center seat, even though it's where the bombardier sits." Then answering his own question, said, "No. That wouldn't work. The bombardier and gunner are usually enlisted men. Probably didn't know how to fly and surely the pilot wouldn't have left them if they were still alive. It doesn't appear the plane crashed as we think of a crash."

"So?"

Criminy, he can be frustrating, Tuck thought. "Billy Jim, I'm sure you know the answer, but my guess is we have at least one, maybe two, others on the island with us. If that's the case and they are from Flight 19, they can solve one of the most popular aviation mysteries of the 20th Century. What did happen to Flight 19 on that - ordinary turned unordinary - day in early December 1945? Sorry, I failed my first test. Anything else?"

"Yeah. And you didn't fail, just didn't get no 'A'. Your thinkin' is okay, your powers of observation need a little fine tunin'." He flashed that hint-of-grin smile of his, indicating that was as close to a compliment Tuck would get. "Let's go down to the lagoon. Another test. Stay on your toes."

As they walked towards the lagoon, Tuck ran over in his mind what he might be looking for. Why the lagoon? Why not base camp or the point or the Stream? What's unique about the lagoon? Immediately sand came to the forefront! It's the only beach on the island with sand. Even the area I landed on was pebble. Okay, Tuckster concentrate on the sand.

Arriving at the beach, Billy Jim asked him what he saw. Tuck walked the water's edge looking out over the lagoon and then towards the ridge. After his second trip from one end of the beach to the other, he saw what he thought Billy Jim might be referring to. "Footprints! One set barefoot the others with shoes. Not necessarily together, in fact I'd say not together."

"Give the man a cee-gar." He bowed from the waist and pretended to present Tuck with a stogie. "Very good Tuck. How you read it?"

"My guess is that 'barefoot' is the downed pilot. The 'shoes' are boaters that stumbled upon the island, much as we did. Except they got off. Probably fishermen. They didn't take the pilot with them or we'd heard about? Why not? What do you see?"

"Pretty much the same. The shoes have me stumped, howsomever."

"Meaning what?"

"Well they's all men. Women don't boat in this area? Ever? Women who have been separated from their menfolks for years are gonna let them go off fishin' by themselves? I don't think so. And the prints don't show a clear indent of a sole. More like a slipper, no heel. They ain't the usual types of boat shoe found in ship's stores or marina shops. And it's almost like the 'shoes' don't worry about leaving tracks, while 'barefoot' is very, very careful. Plus the barefoot prints are the only ones that changed since I've been checkin'."

"Meaning he's been out and about since our arrival: probably observing us."

"Lots of questions just climbin' all over each other. Howsomever, I ain't got enough answers to go around. Before you got here, I spent many hours lookin' fer him." Pointing upwards, he added, "I believe he's up yonder in the thickets on the ridge or in one of them caves. That's why I took you up to the plane the way I did. I wanted you to see how a body could be really close by and you'd never see him. He's either very good or he's gone underground. Either way, now that there's two of us lookin', we'll find him one of these days."

"A rabbit just ran over my grave, Billy Jim. Knowing someone else - perhaps a pilot from Flight 19 - is here with us, is even more tantalizing than finding the Avenger."

Mid June ?
I can't begin to explain what it felt like "flying" in the low gravity area. It was a universal dream come true! I've never been up in an airplane, but can imagine what it must be like having talked to folks who have flown.

First would be the feeling of unlimited power as the plane rolls down the runway faster and faster. Then at reaching flying speed, the ground gradually begins to fall away; trees and buildings become smaller and a thrill of being free overrides fear and sometimes common sense.

Suddenly, you are a master of the universe gliding over your kingdom that stretches as far as the eye can see. You dive, dip, turn somersaults and pull up to a stall before falling off into a recovery. Long before you're ready, it's time to quit and head for home. It is said the landing is the most dangerous part of flying, but I'm quite comfortable and confident as I point the nose homeward. Reducing power, holding the plane level and on target, I apply a little rudder for a minor correction, softly kissing the ground and taxiing to the hanger.

(After re-reading the above, I'm reminded Billy Jim said a journal must be honest. In view of that, I

admit to using a tad of active imagination.) I also made a promise to myself, once I get home, to go Brown's Airport for a free ride with Paul or Hunter, a couple of wartime pilots that still fly for fun.

With a plentiful supply of food readily available and the abundance of fresh water, Tuck had only his shelter to think about. He didn't think it would be fair to continue living with Hannah and Billy Jim in their crowded quarters. (While he wouldn't speak of it for fear of hurting their feelings, he also valued his privacy.) So, for the rest of the day, he spent his time constructing a house from fallen fronds, using the hatch cover as a threshold.

Even though finding the pilot was uppermost in their minds and they were constantly on the lookout for him, a typical day had lapsed into a routine of chores. Daily they gathered firewood and walked the shoreline looking for anything they might find useful. They collected coconuts and picked ripe mangos and other fruits or gathered up a conch or two. Using the canopy-boat, explained to Hannah as some plastic they'd found, it was easy to locate food under rocks, in caves and holes. Tuck even tried to catch the elusive lobster, but without success. He simply could not bring himself to plunge his hands into holes and crevices where he couldn't see. "I'm afraid of moray eels, sea urchins and crabs. I suppose, too, I wasn't hungry enough yet," he suggested, one night at supper.

Billy Jim had no such fear. He reached into holes with abandoned care. When necessary, he even swam into the small caves - sometimes upside down - in order to catch lobsters hanging from the ceiling. "Pluck 'em off, like pickin' oranges" he'd teased Tuck.

SPINY LOBSTER

Becoming more familiar and comfortable with the new boat, they eventually ventured out into the deeper waters at the north point in order to spear the octopus and squid found in the deep holes. On this day, for nearly an hour they had paddled about the large boulders without luck. Suddenly, Billy Jim stood, his spear readied over his head. "Easy, Tuck," he whispered slowly. "We're gonna have grouper tonight. Easy does it. Quiet now." Like a Zulu warrior, he stood motionless, his spear overhead, at the ready.

Focusing his sight *through* the water, to beneath the surface, it took Tuck a moment to see what Billy Jim was looking at. When finally he did see it, he recoiled in fear. "Good golly Molly, Billy Jim!" he shouted, waving his arms. "Don't spear that thing!" It was the biggest jewfish he had ever seen. While not necessarily a man-eater, both boys had heard tales of large jewfish attacking divers. "That thing will go six hundred pounds! Don't..."

Before he could finish, Billy Jim drove the spear downward and into the giant fish. For a second or two, as the shaft found its mark above the left eye, the monster fish appeared paralyzed. It simply drifted towards the bottom without moving a fin. It reminded Tuck of a fighter taking a stunning blow to the head. Before Billy Jim could ready another shaft, the Goliath fish quickly recovered, shaking loose the spear, and attacked the boat in full fury. Biting, snapping, pushing, bumping, it put its entire brute strength against the frail craft. Tuck and Billy Jim held on to the side with all their might as the glass boat spun, rocked and swirled in the churning, foaming water. Finally, having torn the outrigger loose, the beast lunged upward: turning the vessel over, spilling its contents into the sea.

"Head for shallow water," cried Billy Jim in mid-air.

Without difficulty, Tuck surfaced and swam with strong, fast, flailing strokes toward the closest boulder. Standing atop a crag, he searched the surface, finding only small ripples and tiny swirls. Spinning around and around, he expected to see Billy Jim's face pop up, teeth showing through its crooked little grin. But there was no Billy Jim, no boat and no denizen of the deep. "Billy Jim! Billy Jim! Where are you?" Tuck screamed over and over through cupped hands. The surface of the water was again glass smooth, broken only by the outrigger bobbing up and down; one end apparently hung up on something beneath the water. Tears streamed down his cheeks as the realization set in that his friend was gone. Billy Jim was dead!

Believing the jewfish had finally caught Billy Jim and drowned him, Tuck did nothing for a long time, but stand on the rock and rapidly scan the surface of the ocean. His body became cold and began to shake and quiver from the sudden expenditure of adrenaline. His thoughts tumbled over and over. He was drained of every ounce of strength and energy. His body actually sagged in dismay as though every cell, nerve, and muscle had become disassociated and detached. His arms dangled at his sides giving an appearance of being so alone. Forsaken.

Finally mustering courage enough, he swam to the outrigger. Wrenching it free, he was relieved to see it was not attached to the boat. Slowly he kicked back towards the island - his heart heavy. He cried in loud sobs.

Hannah screamed, wailed and fell into herself on the ground. Then picking herself up she ran, arms flailing, to the water's edge screaming,

GHOST OF THE STREAM

yelling and hollering for Billy Jim. For over an hour, she paced the shoreline shouting her son's name, futilely searching the sea.

Returning to camp, she did something Tuck would never forget. She took him in her arms, hugged him closely to her. With her chin resting on the top on his head, she spoke quietly. "Son, it ain't none your blame and you ain't never to fault yourself. Billy Jim could be reckless at times, but he was also brave and I gotta believe he died bravely."

"He did, Hannah. He really did," Tuck said with his arms wrapped around Hannah's waist.

Finally resolved to her loss, Hannah disappeared into her hut. Tuck had not seen her cry, but he could imagine the soft sobs tearing at her heart. Deciding she needed her privacy, he walked to the ridge and looked toward the Point scanning the miles and miles of ocean. He saw nothing of the boat, the fish or of Billy Jim.

Numbness was the best way to describe Tuck's feelings. Nothing in his life had prepared him for the devastating emptiness he felt. Sam's death, and even Buddy's, had been foreseen. Sam was an old, old man, and Buddy was seriously injured. But, Billy Jim... A youth, full of energy and excitement, cut down before he had a real chance at life. A future of perhaps sixty years reduced, in the blink of an eye, to zero. He pondered the "fairness" of life, with no conclusion.

That evening, Hannah sat staring at the food Tuck had prepared. "You gotta eat something, Hannah," not knowing what else to say. "Billy Jim would want you to". At the mention of her son's name, the wooden spoon dropped from her hand with a thud. "I'm sorry, Hannah." Tuck spoke quickly to fill the void. Walking behind her, he bent over putting his head next to hers and with his arms pulled her back into his chest.

After a moment, she patted his cheek. Then standing, excused herself. "It just hurts so bad, son," she turned to say. "Even worse than losin' his brother and sister or his Pa."

Tuck returned to his plate to stir and pick at the food. He was in no mood to eat either. He was about to toss it away when he heard from the edge of darkness. "Fine fishing buddy you turned out to be. Leavin' me out there all alone."

"Billy Jim!" exclaimed Tuck, jumping to his feet, rushing towards his friend. "Hannah!" he screamed. "It's Billy Jim! Come quickly!" With as few steps as possible, Hannah was out of the hut, hugging, kissing, crying and touching Billy Jim.

"My boy! My boy! You're home. You're safe." Then raising her arms to the skies, she shouted again and again. "Billy Jim's home. Billy

Jim's home. Glory, glory, bless the name of God. Precious Jesus, thank you, thank you, thank you."

Flustered by all the attention, Billy Jim did little more than stand silently first on one foot, then the other. "Hey," he finally spoke. "I'm hungry. Can't a feller git somethin' to eat? What'cha got, that's good?" Immediately, Tuck set about preparing another plate.

"Not that stuff," admonished Hannah, wiping away the plates with a swoop of her hand. "My boy's home. The 'prodigal' has returned! We needs a feast." Guiding Billy Jim by the shoulders, Hannah said, "Honey pot, you set yourself down and rest. Me and Tuck'll fix you a supper you ain't soon gonna forget. "Tuck, go git me a couple of them lobsters and a stone crab from the pens." Then adding, "And a hand of ripe bananas and a lime or two. Stoke up the fire. Set a new place."

During dinner, Billy Jim told them again - in detail - how he escaped. "When that monster turned us over... Tuck, you ever seen a bigger jewfish? Golly almighty it was big!" Holding his hands out about three feet, he added, "Eyes musta been this far apart! E-normous!" Hannah smiled knowing a fish story when she heard one. "Anyway. I went down deep then, turned 'round and swam right back into the upside down boat. It had a sizable air pocket in it, so I just laid up on the underneath side of the seats and waited it out."

"Billy Jim, I didn't see you or the boat after you overturned and I waited, looked and searched a long while."

"Don't surprise me none." Billy Jim tore into another lobster plucking out a hunk of the snow white meat. "The boat being made of glass and mostly submerged with my weight in it, don't expect there was much to see. And the current was moving pretty fast, by then. Wasn't no time till we was some distance from ya. Me and that dang jewfish!"

Hannah sat silently, listening, admiring her son. Occasionally she would reach over and touch him as if to reassure herself he was real.

"Did you actually see the fish underwater?" asked Tuck.

"Yep, sure did," answered Billy Jim, plopping another piece of lobster meat into his mouth. "That, devil..."

"Don't talk with your mouth full, son."

Wiping his mouth with the back of his hand, Billy Jim continued. "That devil wouldn't die - and it had a sizable cut just where I hit him - and he wouldn't go away. It kept followin' me, comin' at me, tryin' to take a bite, but couldn't figure why he couldn't sink 'em pearly whites into me. Lordy, I was scared. It would come at me full force, big old mouth wide open trying its best to take an arm or leg. Its eyes were blood red with rage. It'da smash into the boat, then shake like a pit bull tryin' to git to an alley cat. All the while I was laid out straight as a fence post on them seats, hanging on fer dear life. With my head up in the air pocket, I was a-grinning at that dumb old jewfish and praying away."

Tuck was surprised. "You prayed, Billy Jim?"

"Like a Sunday-go-to-meetin' Preacher, with the town drunk at the altar."

"Billy Jim Hamilton, how you carry on?" Hannah rinsed her hands. "You ain't never seen no such thing."

"No, but I can 'magine."

"How'd you get out?" asked Tuck.

"Wasn't long before the Stream pushed me onto the shelf into shallow water. And soon as I could reach down and touch bottom, I pushed and pulled myself along until the water wasn't deep enough for the fish. 'Spect I looked like a horseshoe crab pullin' myself along, lookin' fer a girlfriend. Finally, the fish lost interest and moved on. I figured it was safe. So I slithered out of my crystal cocoon and walked-crawled-swam home by way of the lagoon. Wish I could'a saved the boat, but it's gone."

"Doesn't matter. You're safe and that's all that's important," said Tuck.

"Amen," said Hannah. "Right now, I want you youngans to get to bed. We've all had a big day." As an afterthought: "And don't let's none of us fergit to say our prayers. We got lots to be thankful for. All of us."

One night, lying in his temporary shelter, a few days after building more fish pens so each species could have their own, Tuck reviewed his actions. He realized he had subconsciously been planning to remain on the island for some time. Again he recognized he had not seen or heard a plane or ship the entire day, but now attributed it to the low gravity area and its influence on a compass. Over and over he mentally reviewed Captain Bannerman's nautical charts. Still he could not remember one parcel of land between Grand Bahamas and Bermuda.

His thoughts danced between the pilot, the unusual island, and the low gravity area. Something is very strange about this land, more than just meets the eye or touches the senses. It's mysterious, foreboding, ominous, he reasoned. He believed he stood at the portal of one of life's mysteries and didn't know which way to turn. What piece of information held the secret? Something nagged and pulled at his brain. In addition to the pilot, he wondered what else he had missed? Something that could shed light on the island's makeup, it's character? He picked away at each day's events as though he were dissecting frogs in biology class. Cut away a layer of flesh, pull it and pick at it with tweezers. Look at it. Examine it. It was a baffling performance, but one that would continue, he was certain.

Mentally exhausted, he snuggled beneath a stiff piece of canvas he'd found, and looked forward with zest and excitement to the next chapter. While he was safe and relatively comfortable, he did wonder how Aunt Grace was handling his absence. But the last thing he remembered as he lay on the soft carpet of perfumed pine needles was the cool breeze encircling his shelter and the hypnotic rhythm of the teasing sea against the beach. Whatever is out there will keep till morning, he thought. "Right now, I'm like a *Carnation Milk* cow: contented. I'll let the subconscious do its work," he murmured sleepily.

They did find the pilot - or more accurately he found them - quite by accident. Nevertheless, it was by them doing something they thought the proper thing to do.

Mid June?
I just took a solitary walk around the island. This place is something else. There seems to be no limit to its characteristics. Take the weather for instance. At times clouds can build up all around us and while it might be storming 360 degrees, we get a fine mist of rain with gentle winds. And it appears to rain when it needs to. I've seen no evidence a hurricane has ever paid a visit. The only proof of strong winds are some of the trees nearest the Stream and on the ridge have been assaulted.

Haven't seen a bird of any kind, which defies explanation since I know the sooty tern has established a rookery at Dry Tortugas. I seem to recall that's sixty miles from Key West – a distance much greater – than we think we are from the coast of Florida. The agriculturists, botanists, engineers, architects, "the bug folks" and Grady Norton, our Miami weatherman, are going to have a field day when they get here.

IV
Old Resident

Usually the airplane was the boy's favorite playground. Nevertheless, the day they decided to do their Christian duty, brought a new dimension to Mystery Island. "Billy Jim, I think we should bury the bones in the plane. You know dig a proper grave, complete with a marker."

"Guess it won't hurt none. Besides that way we won't ever have to tell Ma about him."

The musty air trapped beneath the trees hung like stalactites. Billy Jim dug with his hands and a pointed stick while Tuck used a thin board like a shovel, as they scooped out an adequate hollow beneath a chinaberry tree. "I think he'd like it here, if he had a say," Billy Jim said, looking up at the umbrella shaped tree. Wiping his sweating forehead on his sleeve, he looked at the cross, fashioned with limbs tied with a piece of electrical wire from the plane. "Wish we had more than his dog tags to mark his grave, but guess they'll have to do." Moving to the plane, Tuck was about to lift out the bones of James McCoy to Billy Jim's waiting hands, when a gravelly voice stopped them cold.

"Get away from that plane! Don't touch a thing! What do you think you're doing anyway?"

"What the heck...?" Tuck cried, dropping the bones and jumping from the cockpit onto to the wing. Surprised and frightened, both of the boys turned towards the sound. On the edge of the clearing crouched a shaggy creature with long hair and beard, shaking a stick, raised over his head. Waving in the other hand, was what appeared to be a large caliber pistol. He looked formidable, but not aggressive. In his stooped stance, he gave the appearance of being unsure of himself and ready to run in any direction if necessary. He wore ragged pants that ended at mid thigh, a tattered shirt opened down the front and no shoes. Once more, he jabbed the air with his stick and stared at the boys. "Do as I say! Get away from there. Leave everything just as it is. Now move!"

"It's barefoot," Tuck exclaimed, under his breath, jumping down from the wing to where Billy Jim now stood.

Through clenched teeth, Billy Jim whispered, "Let's go after him from each side. That way he can't get us both. When I give you the signal, do that crazy chicken thing you do, making lots of noise." Before Tuck could protest, Billy Jim started crabbing toward the scarecrow, talking all the time. "What'cha doing here? We thought we was alone on this place. How'd you get here? What's yer name? Can you talk English?"

"You understood me when I yelled at you, didn't you? Now, both of you stop right where you are. I've got this stick and pistol and I can take off either your head or foot. You decide. What do you think you're doing? Be gone with you."

The boys slowed a few yards from him, but continued easing up on him while Billy Jim kept talking. "You ain't got no cause to be upset at us. We's shipwrecked, stranded, just like you...by your looks."

Billy Jim's aggressiveness surprised Tuck, but he could tell he was getting through. The man relaxed slightly, stuck the pistol into his waistband and began slapping his empty palm with the stick. "We're shipwrecked," Tuck offered. "How about you? How'd you get here? Fly in this thing?" He pointed a thumb over his shoulder at the downed aircraft. "My name's Tuck. This is Billy Jim. What's your name? We're Americans. We really are friends."

Still several yards apart, they were now only a few feet away from their target. The ragged man retrieving his pistol, standing with his feet apart, began waving his weapons again, pointing first towards Tuck then Billy Jim, letting them know he was still in control. For a second he paused as though thinking. Billy Jim cried, "Now!" With that, Tuck let out a war whoop that would have made any Seminole warrior proud: "Ya-ya-ya-ye-ye--yeeeee" And went into his imitation of a drunken ostrich strutting about on high-stepping, unsure legs, arms flapping and shaking like wings. The disheveled creature yanked his face towards Tuck and got to say no more than, "Wha..." before Billy Jim tackled him, pinning his back and both shoulders to the ground. Quickly Tuck stopped his charade and landed on the flailing feet and legs wrapping them tightly with vines.

Disarming the prisoner and quickly tying his hands behind his back, the boys dragged him to a sitting position and began asking him questions. Tuck thought he saw some teeth, although he couldn't be certain through his beard. He hoped it was a smile. "How do I know you're really who you say? How do I know you're not one of them?"

"We'll ask the questions," Billy Jim said, poking the man in his ribs. Looking to Tuck for his approval. "Who's 'them'?" he asked.

"The Germans. From the U-boat." He nodded his head in the direction of the Gulf Stream. .

"Don't play us for no dummies." Billy Jim was incredulous. "Germans! What Germans? The Germans surrendered over a year ago. The Japs quit this past August. Don't you know thet?"

"Of course I know that. I fought in the war. What I don't know is why there's still a U-boat operating out there. It might not look like a U-boat anymore, but it is."

Tuck was baffled and looked at Billy Jim. "Is it possible there's a U-boat that doesn't know the war is over?" He thought about the boat that nearly ran him down while on the hatch cover. "Remember the boat I told you about. It could have been a sub, Billy Jim. I thought so all along. Now, I'm almost certain."

"I just can't believe it, but that's a creek to forge later. Right now we needs to find out what this here bird knows. Perhaps a little torture will help us learn what we want to know. Let's stretch him backward across a wing."

"No. Wait. Let's try something else." Turning to the man, he said, "We've told you our names. What's your? Maybe we can convince you we're on the same side."

He relaxed a little, dropping his shoulders slightly. "Name's Jones. Navy pilot. Serial number 418-94-45. Last billet, Ft. Lauderdale. That's all you get under the Geneva Convention. Now, who are you and how do I know you're telling the truth?'

"Well, my name is Billy Jim Hamilton. I live or did live on a boat out of Green Turtle Cay. Bahamas. Commercial fishin'. Fished out of Marathon some. Tuck, here lives in Miami."

"Where in Miami?"

"Ever hear of Kendall? Dinner Key? Coral Gables?"

"I know of Dinner Key, old Pan Am base. Used it during the war when I was flying PBYs looking for U-boats in the South Atlantic. I've been to Key Largo, north of Marathon. What's the name of the famous Club there?"

Billy Jim laughed. "We ain't old enough to drink, but it's the *Caribbean Club*. Made famous by the movie *Key Largo*. You know, Bogie."

Tuck told him Dinner Key was where they tied up the *Nomad* and it was a base for Pan Am's first flying boats back in the thirties and forties. "Did you know it got its name because so many families ate their Sunday picnic dinners there while watching the airplanes take off and land? I was little, but I remember seeing men in one-piece bathing suits float the wheels out to the planes where they were attached. Then big heavy tractors pulled the planes ashore up a ramp."

"Didn't know that. I guess I'm safe since you appear to know more about the area than I do and you don't sound German. Okay, my name's Jonesy. Lt. Taylor Jones, USN, and yes, I flew in that thing." He indicated the Avenger with an uplifted chin. "I've been watching you for days, but it wasn't until you were fighting your way up the ridge that I got close enough to hear you speak." He motioned his head at Billy Jim and chuckled. "You could be a sailor the way you talk at times." He continued. "At one point, I wasn't twenty feet from you." Tuck could tell he was now smiling. "I was still afraid that you might be some of the Germans. Many speak English very well, but I couldn't take a chance showing myself or leaving tracks." Tuck's skin became gooseflesh at learning they had been so close to each other and he wasn't aware of it.

"How do you know they speak English? Just maybe you're one of them." Billy Jim said.

"Do I look like a Kraut? Do I sound like one?" Jonesy spread his arms looking down at himself.

"Wie heissen Sie?" Tuck said abruptly. Both Jonesy and Billy Jim looked quizzically at Tuck

"I know a few German words and just asked him his name. I believe he's who he says he is." Thinking Hannah should be brought into the picture Tuck added, "Since there appears lot to learn and share with each other, why don't we go the camp and get you something to eat? Maybe we can sort out all of this."

Jonesy readily agreed. "That sounds good to me. Why don't you untie me?"

"Just your feet," said Billy Jim. "Your arms stay tied 'til we know for sure what yer all about. After untying his feet, standing him up and giving him a push, he was directed to walk ahead. "Remember I can still bop you a good one." And periodically the 'thunk' of the stick against a tree trunk could be heard.

Nevertheless, after walking awhile, listening to the boys chatter, Jonesy seemed to relax somewhat. "I've been in hiding ever since you guys arrived and haven't been able to replenish my cupboard. I'm starved. Who's the tall woman with you? And what was she wailing about a few days ago? I heard her, but couldn't make out what it was all about. Was it some sort of ceremony or custom I'm not familiar with?"

"That's my Ma. Hannah Hamilton. She'll put some meat on your bones. And yeah, that was a war whoop you heard. She's part Injun, so don't cross her. She'll cut your heart out and put it in one of her stews." Billy Jim looked at Tuck and winked.

GHOST OF THE STREAM

"Come on. You can put that stick down. I believe we're on the same side." As they entered base camp, with caution Billy Jim did lower the stick, but did not discard it.

After introductions and several probing questions, all were eventually comfortably seated around the table located beneath a sapodilla tree. Hannah quickly put Jonesy at ease, as Billy Jim knew Mamas like his would. A few explanations and conch chowder followed by a plump lobster and fried bananas, Jonesy began the dialogue. Struggling, he began telling his story. "Perhaps it was the war...the fighting...the killing. I suppose I'm a little daffy, mad, crazy or all of the above. At least for a period, I was." Time and again he repeated how happy he was he had been found and took every opportunity to look at each of them with sincerity as if to prove himself.

"Maybe talking about it, will help," Hannah offered, pushing another serving of dessert towards Jonesy. Billy Jim and Tuck leaned forward, huddling over the table, not wanting to miss a single word. With the ease of an experienced storyteller, Jonesy told of Flight 19's practice mission and of his ultimate crashing on Mystery Island.

"Having gotten lost, nothing seemed to add up. But, from the beginning. After leaving Ft. Lauderdale we flew north of Bimini. There we were with the cockpit cover pushed back, skimming along a few feet above the occasional white cap, enjoying the day, making a practice torpedo run on the old cement ship as we had many times before. I'll bet all of you have seen it." The three looked at each other, nodding as having seen the old relic. "Did you know that during Prohibition the old ship was to be used by bootleggers as a liquor warehouse just off the three-mile limit? A storm, however, upset that plan by grounding the vessel where it broke up and subsequently became a practice target for planes during World War II."

Tuck said he had dived on the crumbling hulk many times and remembered the numerous bomb fins still visible along with some sizable fish. "Big groupers down in the dark holes, but difficult to get to and then back out. Lots of sharp metal, pipes and bulkheads." He shivered at the untenable situation. "During season, lots of scallops in the grass-beds."

Jonesy continued. "After our torpedo run, we *SCALLOP* were to fly 160 miles east, turn north for a brief period, then return to base. We did all that...except return to base. Somewhere along the last leg of our flight, we encountered a strangeness none of us could explain. It was like nothing any of us had experienced before." He

49

shook his head as if to clear his thoughts. "I just don't know. The planes developed an unfamiliar vibration and were electrified with low voltage or static electricity. My hands actually tingled at the touch of metal. Not one electrical instrument registered a correct reading. Fuel gauges flittered. Batteries seem to discharge rapidly for no reason. It was mass confusion. I was sweating even though the air was cool. I know my pulse rate was over a hundred. Bet the others were feeling the same."

Jonesy paused for a drink of water, tossed a stick of wood on the fire and wiped his brow. "Radios didn't work properly. Compasses spun until they became just a series of blurred numbers. Static. Humming. Loud, piercing squeals that penetrated the brain making you yank off your earpieces. The noise just added to the confusion and chaos." Almost pleading for understanding, he walked about muttering to himself, but he continued. "We had been trained to handle emergencies - of all kinds. My, God, I survived first as a fighter pilot then as a bomber pilot. Wasn't an Ace, but had dogfights with several Germans fighter planes including the ME109. I mean, I was acquainted with accidents, mishaps and misadventures, but I wasn't up to what was thrust upon us. None of us were." He fell silent.

Hannah and Billy Jim looked over at Tuck. He showed them his empty palms, shrugged his shoulders and touched his finger to his lips. Jonesy reminded them of a roller coaster. The pitch of his voice rose and fell dramatically. As he spoke he swung between being wild-eyed mad and a compassion-filled Dr. Albert Schweitzer. It became his pattern to walk about, wave his hands, gesturing excitedly, exhibiting the body language of a great orator. Then without notice he would fall silent for a few moments. Once again regaining his composure, he would continue more calmly.

"Now that I've had over six months to think about it, I don't believe all of the transmissions, the voices, were those of ours alone. Between planes, I mean. I believe they included some of an unknown source. They were like a foreigner who had learned to speak fluent English by rote or formula, without the benefit of the idioms and colloquialisms."

"Say what?" asked Billy Jim, seated on the table with his knees pulled up to his chin.

"The voices didn't know our slang and they seemed to speak with a formula, Billy Jim," explained Jonesy uneasily, as his eyes began to blink sporadically. "For example they might say 'how are you called?' We would say 'what is your name or number?' If I said, 'I'm going to hit the hay', would you know what I meant?"

"Sure, you was going to bed."

"And if someone kicked the bucket?"

"They died."

"Full plate?"

"More to do than ya got time to do it."

"Right. That's slang known to all Americans, but not to them. The voices. They were, how do I explain it? They were too precise. Too perfect. Like our own air traffic controllers - no time for nonsense." Jonesy's shoulders slumped as he twisted his hands inwardly. He was looking for solutions he didn't have.

"Why did you listen to the voices?"

"In all the confusion, Tuck, we were ready to listen to anyone that made just a little sense. Don't forget, we were up against the wall. We had just so much gas, so much time and had to get back to Ft. Lauderdale or ditch in the Atlantic Ocean. And the voices did seem to clarify the muddled mix-up. They had the power to command. 'Fly one seven eight degrees north. Come right to one niner three, altitude six thousand.' I'd boost the power, kick the rudder pedal and push the stick to the right." Beads of sweat again formed on Jonesy's forehead as he moved his hands through the air indicating the movements of the aircraft. "'Come left twenty degrees to one seven three.' Again, I'd punch the rudder and move the stick left. I came to believe the voices were playing with us as the maneuvers they were putting us through, were doing little more than wasting time and burning fuel.

"Regardless how hard I tried it was too late to get the Squadron together again. The voices had us under their control. They were that good! In our attempts to discover where we were and return to base, we listened to anyone and everyone with a reasonable idea. It was mass confusion. We were beginning to panic." Jonesy tugged at his beard. "It was getting dark. We were about out of fuel and knew we would most likely have to ditch in the water. Not a pretty picture, especially at night, with no hope of rescue. In the end, we did exactly as the voices commanded and ended up at the slaughter house like so many sheep."

Anxiety was building and Jonesy began pulling at the flesh of his palms. Sensing his uneasiness, Hannah suggested they call it quits for the night. But he waved his hand and continued. He wanted to talk. He needed to, it seemed.

"I know it's pretty hard for you to understand how a group of grown men, with years of flying experience, could become disoriented, confused and lost on a routine practice run most of us had made numerous times before. But we did. We reached the point we didn't even know which side of the Florida peninsular we were on. The little bit of land

I could see didn't look like any part of the Florida I knew. We did not know north from south. Our instruments would tell us one thing and our instincts another. On one occasion, I looked straight up and saw the ocean. Yet my instruments indicated I was flying right side up without the first hint anything was amiss. Finally, after we were totally exhausted, mentally and physically drained, the spirits..."

"The what?" exclaimed Hannah, leaning away from Jonesy.

"Spirits, forces, powers. Hannah, I don't know what else to call them."

Billy Jim was about to tell Jonesy about the compass, but Hannah nudged him to be quiet. "Let him talk. I want to learn about them haints."

"There's not much more to tell. I now believe they purposely were directing us away from this island. One by one we began falling from the sky. One was out of fuel. His wingman began circling. I suppose to try and help. Another just seemed to give up and ditched in order, I assume, to be near someone. We were like a bunch of lighting bugs in a jar with the lid on. We couldn't get out and sooner or later we all had to die. It was like a puppet show. Five planes flying all over the place, but only as far as the puppeteer's strings would allow. It was total, final hysteria! Mayhem! We couldn't comprehend anything." Agitated once more, Jonesy wiped his face with his shirttail.

Tuck wanted to hear more about the U-boat, as he was sure Billy Jim did, but decided to stay with the subject at hand. "How come you survived?"

"It was a desperate, last-ditch effort, Tuck. I turned my plane away from the group and began flying by what the seat of my pants told me was west. I don't know why, I just did it. Instinct perhaps, but it saved my life." He looked down at his body and offered, "Whatever that is."

"Why didn't you fly towards the sun?" Tuck questioned.

"There was no sun. Had been, but now there was an overcast and it was getting dark." Jonesy was in agony and his audience should have given him a reprieve, but he appeared to want to continue and they wanted to learn as much as they could.

"It was then that I saw the cone of light," he said. "Or at least think I did. It might have been a hallucination. But there, as plain as day, were the faint glittering rays much like a searchlight only wider and not nearly so bright. Imagine the shape of an inverted pyramid or a squat triangle."

"Probably sun rays." Hannah said. "You can get 'em in the evenings. It's bits of dirt and dust I been told."

"Perhaps Hannah. I know what you're speaking of, but these were different. Astronomers call them aberrations. They were emanating from a single source below me that I couldn't see. I don't believe there was enough sunlight to illuminate them. Remember that I'd see the sun for a longer period of time up in the air than someone on the ground.

"Anyway, I flew into it, this cone of light. My plane faltered and began losing air speed and altitude. I pumped the throttle, pulled back hard on the stick. Even lowered my flaps for more lift. But without airspeed they were of no help. More like brakes. I tried circling to keep from stalling. Instead of crashing, however, I began floating...downward. That's when I saw this island. 'Thank God,' I said aloud and told McCoy to prepare for the crash. But, no crash ever came. At the time, I supposed I had slipped into an air stream that gave me an unnatural lift. Whatever it was, I gently floated - almost like a pie tin pancaking through a light breeze - to where you found the plane." He floated his hand about to indicate how he gyrated to earth. "You can tell it's not too banged up. Anyway, I grabbed my side arm, crawled out on the wing and headed for the woods at the run. Thought James would follow me."

At hearing the word "plane", Hannah stood up, put her hands on her hips, looked at the boys and asked, "What plane, Billy Jim? Tuck? What's he talking about? You ain't said nothin' 'bout finding no aryplane. I want some answers and I want 'em now. You hear me."

With his hound dog eyes, Billy Jim pleaded with Tuck to take the floor. He did. "Hannah, we did find a plane up on the ridge. We didn't tell you the whole story about the plane and canopy-boat because we didn't want to worry you. Beside, it's a tough place to get to. Almost impossible. In fact Jonesy told us he was within a few feet of us and we didn't know it. So you see, we were really thinking of you first. And except for the low gravity area there isn't much to tell."

"And the spinning compass, Tuck. Don't forget the compass."

Tuck rolled his eyes. "Thanks. Billy Jim."

"Yes Tuck, I'd be most interested in a spinning compass." Jonesy was standing over him, hands on the table. His look was more indignation than anger. Like he was hurt they had withheld something from him.

"Jonesy, we weren't trying to keep anything from you. We simply had been so interested in hearing of your accounts, we just didn't want to interrupt you."

"You must be Irish, me lad," he said. His eyes and the movement of his head giving Tuck the go ahead. "Tell us about the low gravity area and whirling compass, for surely you have the blessing of the Blarney stone."

"Ma and Tuck don't want to believe there's anything strange going on out there." Billy Jim pointed towards the darkness. "But we's in the Devil's Triangle." Hannah flushed.

Jonesy was quizzical, but eased the tension. "I don't want to believe it either, but the facts remain. There is something strange happening out here. At least there appears to be. That in itself is strange. Having been here awhile, with time to observe and think, I know things are different."

"What'cha mean, Jonesy?"

"Well, Hannah, how do you explain the absence of traffic? The unusual landing I made? This island paradise? Now the low gravity area and the whirling compass? Do you think we're imagining all of this?"

Tuck spoke up. "Jonesy, are you familiar with the Devil's Triangle? I mean did you ever hear the term while you were flying in the Miami area?"

"Oh, sure. There was small talk, but we tried never to pay any attention to it. After each mysterious happening it was referred to as Hoo Doo Sea, Rum Punch Alley or the Witch's Basin. Wish we hadn't been so flip about it now. That kind of chatter does not fit well with responsible flying. Why do you ask?"

Tuck tried to be brief, telling Jonesy of the theories and interest in the area known as the Devil's Triangle. "It seems that no matter what happens within this area of the Atlantic Ocean, it's blamed on the Devil's Triangle. It can be a ship, boat, barge, or airplane of any size. It goes down, fails to show up on time or sinks in a hurricane, it's the fault of the Devil's Triangle. In fact, Jonesy, the most recent interest was spurred by the disappearance of your patrol - Flight 19 - and the seaplane, a Martin Mariner as I recall, from the Banana River Naval Station sent to look for you. Your flight became known as the *Lost Patrol*".

"Well, I was part of Flight 19, but outside an occasional remark about the unusual number of accidents, little was said and less believed. There certainly wasn't any paramount interest shown. Naturally, I wouldn't have known about any rescue plane. I do know the Mariner was joked about being a flying gasoline can."

"The Devil's Triangle is for real," said Billy Jim. "Even if Tuck makes a funny outta it." Jonesy, recognized the differences of the boys and continued his story.

"Tuck, I never heard the depth of the accounts of the Devil's Triangle as you tell it until this moment. I only know what I felt and saw. However, based on what you say and what I experienced during those terrifying moments up there, yes, I do believe there is something unusual going on. But, now I see it as more than the flat surface between Miami, Puerto Rico and Bermuda. There is another dimension, a cone shape energy that emits and delivers a force capable of bringing down an airplane to a landing softer than a mother's kiss. Perhaps instead of a triangle, it should a Devil's Pyramid"

Tuck smiled at Jonesy. "You're going to be famous when we get home. You're the only person alive, as far as we know, that can tell us exactly what happened to Flight 19. You can't imagine how many records you can set straight by just telling what happened to you."

"Or how many more I can confuse."

"Jonesy, why didn't you git yer crewman out?" Billy Jim wanted to know. "You know we found his remains. And wasn't there three of you on board?"

Before Hannah could react to more surprising news, Jonesy spoke up. "That's another strange thing. We talked to each other periodically all the way down. But, when I jumped out of the plane and hustled for the woods, I thought James would follow." Almost as an afterthought, he added, "It's funny, but we always called him James. Never referred to him as Jim, Mac or Kid, you know the boxer, Kid McCoy. It wasn't until much later, when I went to check on him that I discovered he was dead. There were no marks on him or signs of blood. He had no health problems. I thought he was literally scared to death. Now I wonder if a death ray of some sort possibly killed him? In any event, I thought it best to leave him there until I got a lay of the land. You know he could have been the pilot and I was hoping anyone checking the plane out would assume he was. And yes, there are usually three to a crew, but one - the gunner - canceled out just before takeoff. Probably saved his life."

"So you just left him? McCoy, I mean." Tuck asked.

"I left him as though he were alone in the plane. I didn't like it - knowing he would soon begin decomposing - but in my mind it was the best thing to do under the unknown circumstances. After all, if the plane was found and one day there was a body in it and the next it was gone, the Germans - of course I didn't know they were Germans then - would know there was someone else present. It was a matter of self preservation."

"Jonesy, if I could prove you were on the Atlantic side of Florida, would you know about where you'd be in relations to the coast?"

Jonesy scratched the side of his head. "Well, Tuck, I don't know for certain, but based on what we did before crashing, my guess would be no further north than West Palm Beach."

Being impatient, Billy Jim was ready to move ahead. "Well, it's more like Cape Canaveral. Now, what about them Krauts - the Germans and the U-boat?"

"Yeah, Jonesy tell us about the U-boat," Tuck encouraged. "I might have seen it while I was adrift."

He cast Tuck a questioning glance, but dismissed his news with a shrug. "Fellas, I'll tell you all about it real soon. How about tomorrow? But right now it'll to have to wait. As my Aunt Mary would say, 'I'm plumb tuckered out'. I'll say my goodnight and take my leave." Exaggerating a bow, he kissed Hannah's hand saying, "Thank you my dear lady for the finest meal in a long, long time. Till tomorrow."

Still Mid June?

Wow, we just spent several hours listening to Jonesy. He's a wreck! A mass of contradiction. At this time it's difficult to separate fact from fiction. I want to believe everything he said as gospel, but I have my doubts. Serious doubts. The Miami Herald *did report the base had received radio transmissions indicating the squadron thought they might be over the Gulf of Mexico. That meant they would have had to cross the peninsula of Florida – a distance of over a hundred miles - without knowing it. I just can't understand how experienced pilots could have become so disoriented in a space they knew like the palm of their hand, doing a task they knew so well. Unless there's more to this Devil's Triangle than I want to admit...*

V
Island Lore

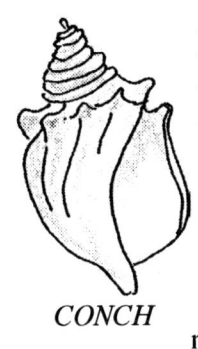

CONCH

Awakening earlier than usual, Tuck lay in his bed doubting that any of them had slept well last night. Each had much to digest, ponder and weigh. If the others were like him, he thought, it was mainly questions without answers and lots of tossing and turning. By the time he left his hut, Jonesy was already stirring up the fire waiting for everyone to assemble at breakfast. He greeted Tuck with "Morning, Sunshine." Tuck blanched slightly at the unusual, but for him, a familiar greeting. "Isn't this the kind of day that makes you feel fortunate to just be alive!" Jonesy's hair and beard had had some attention since last night. He looked less like a vagrant.

Tuck was not a morning person, usually, but the sun was blinking the Morse code, in golden pips, on the rippled surface of the ocean and the island bathed itself in a crisp, cool breeze. It was a brief, but welcomed reprieve from the customary blistering days so hot the weight of the heat could actually be felt on one's shoulders. A peach colored sky was accented with a kaleidoscope of rays: purples, blues and greens emanating from the horizon of a turquoise sea.

During breakfast, Jonesy told them about the U-boat that he'd been watching while he was stranded. "I think it would be valuable and necessary for you to see for yourselves where it ties up."

Together they walked towards the eastern boundary of the island. Along the way Jonesy pointed out certain details he had discovered while being marooned. His most shocking observation - discrepancy really - startled everyone. "You must understand this island is man-made."

Hannah stopped dead in her tracks, placed her hands on her hips and leaned towards Jonesy. "Say that again!" she demanded.

"Oh, it's designed as nature might make it, but the foundation of the entire island and the main stays of the ridge are constructed of concrete. Much of it covered by deep layers of different types of soil, conducive to the healthy growth of certain plants, trees and shrubs. That's one of the reasons for the lush sub-tropical vegetation. The sub pens, constructed of coquina and concrete, are beneath us, where we now stand." For emphasis, he stomped the surface of what Tuck, Billy Jim and Hannah referred to as the "dome".

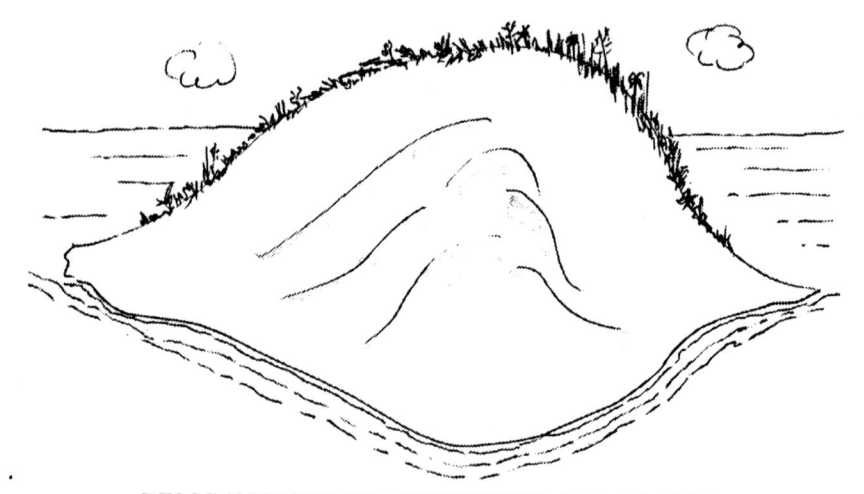

PELICAN VIEW OF MYSTERY ISLAND / DOME

    Having toured the Spanish fort, Castillo de San Marcos, at St. Augustine, Tuck knew coquina to be an unusual rock made up of seashells and corals and of its abundance in that area of northeast Florida. Looking at Billy Jim, he turned his thumb downward and laughed. "Well, so much for the caves and Black Caesar's gold. It's back to the sweat shop for both of us." They had to explain to Hannah and Jonesy about their hopes of finding pirate treasure in the caves on the ridge.

    Waving his arms indicating the island, Billy Jim noted, "Jonesy, it musta taken years to do all of this here."

    "I can tell you one thing," Hannah said, "I know most of the plants, trees and shrubs growin' here, grow in the islands and Florida. But it usually takes lots of care and water. Here they's growin' without nobody tendin' to em."

    "I'm not certain how they did it, but I think the Germans set this up as a combination greenhouse, laboratory and submarine base, probably back in the late thirties." Jonesy hesitated for a moment, looking out over the Gulf Stream, as though he were weighing something. "It's difficult to believe they could have been so advanced in their planning for the future. But, I'll bet you a pretty, history will prove this island came in very handy when the U-boats began attacking our convoys as they sailed to Europe with critical war supplies."

    With Jonesy's explanations digested, Tuck stood mesmerized, simply scanning the ocean north to south. For some reason the words from Longfellow's poem *Hiawatha's Departure* came to mind: "By the shore of Gitche Gumee... Shining Big-Sea-Water...." Let's hope it doesn't end for us as it did for Hiawatha, he concluded to himself.

Jonesy, watching the faces of his audience, understood their lack of knowledge and continued. "Don't you see after we entered the war, this island would have been a vital link as the Nazis turned their attention to the shipping in the South Atlantic, especially oil tankers. Did you know there were over 400 ships sunk off the coast of the United States? Forty of them right off Florida!

"Additionally, what they learned here would give them a hands-up when they occupied the Caribbean basin and Florida. And it also became a convenient stepping off place for Nazis to escape to South America during the final years of the war. Some of its uses were planned, some just happened, I suspect."

"How you know all of this?" asked Hannah. "Most of us know about the oil slicks and saw the glow from several tankers burning off Miami. Boys, you remember the little cans of kerosene at the beaches used to clean the oil off our feet?" Billy Jim and Tuck nodded. The three had become so mesmerized with Jonesy's tale; they had stopped on the dome, over top the sub pens, but gradually edged towards some shade under a huge sea grape.

"Well, Hannah, I don't know for certain, but I'm a history buff and everything I've learned during and since World War II, points to what I've just told you. At the beginning of the war, the U-boats operated alone most of the times. Because of little success, they finally formed 'wolfpacks' or groups to attack single ships and later convoys. For a time, that strategy was the very edge they needed and the U-boats made Europe and especially England pay dearly for each shipment of supplies they received from Canada and the US. Hannah, you probably remember we sent supplies and armaments on the lend-lease plan before we entered the war. Don't expect the lads would know of that." He tossed a small pebble in their direction. "And don't forget England was starving by this time. We had to help.

"Nevertheless all of us paid a price." By this time, Jonesy had stretched out on the ground, encouraging the others to do the same, and was speaking with ease. "Do you know some convoys lost over half their ships crossing the Atlantic. I'm talking about 40 million tons of supplies and 1000 ships went to the bottom in just the first half of 1942. Even with those terrible losses, and this is interesting, the majority of the convoys survived.

The Atlantic became a major battleground. We were trying to supply our Allies in Europe and the Germans were doing their best to prevent it. I can see this island playing a major role in that campaign as a repair, replenishing and supply depot. Actually, it wasn't until we invented sonar and broke the German's code - the Enigma - that we got the upper hand. After that the U-boats were at a disadvantage and lost as many as one of three. We began referring to them as 'iron coffins'. Their final cost was 30,000 men and boys. Three fourths of all the German submariners, never returned home."

Jonesy stopped for a moment lost in thought. Softly he said, "Can you imagine what it must have been like for those poor devils to be under attack by depth charges, bombs and hedgehogs up to twelve hours at a time? They were made of better stuff than I." Regaining his composure, Jonesy continued, obviously remorseful.

The sun had now traveled overhead indicating noontime. The group, still fascinated by Jonesy's account, moved to shadier spots. "There were instances of 40 subs in one wolfpack being lost! With 50-60 in each, that's over 2,000 men! Compare that to the total of only 52 subs, out of 288, that we lost during the entire four years of the war." We believe they had nearly 800 subs total." The high pitch of his voice added the only emphasis necessary. He began again. "Finally by early 1943, even though Germany was turning out 17 new subs each month, they were still losing the battle of submarine warfare. We had declared an all out attack on the U-boats because it was imperative we get supplies to Europe. By May we had the upper hand and that's when the U-boats directed their attention to the South Atlantic. There, they began attacking the oil tankers and shipments of rubber to the United States. And, in my opinion, at that juncture of the war, this place would have been operating at its peak.

"After the surrender, it was discovered that during the final years of the war, when the generals, admirals and other higher-ups knew the war was lost, they began shipping their loot - gold, jewelry, art works, money - you name it, to South America." Jonesy's eyes twinkled. "Of course you can understand, many high ranking officials decided this would also be an excellent time to accompany their goodies south. This island would have been an ideal stopover for them."

"How'd they do it Jonesy? Make the island, I mean. Wouldn't someone have caught on?"

"Tuck, my guess is this was done well before the war." Jonesy picked leaves from a twig while Billy Jim whittled. "It was probably an established base by the time the world learned of Hitler's plans of world domination. And if they had developed some sort of electronics that could gradually turn a compass away from here, as you and Billy Jim have discovered, no one would be the wiser."

"And before the transmitter, wouldn't someone have become suspicious of the construction? You know stopped by and asked what was going on?"

"Perhaps, but under the guise of marine research, botany, archaeology or one of the many sciences, almost anything could have been explained away. Don't forget that most of the world was quite peaceful in the early-thirties. This is in international waters well beyond any nation's control. Of course, these are just my thoughts. Guess work. That may or may not be factual. But having lots of time to think about it and trying to make the pieces dovetail with each other, this is what I've come up with." Jonesy shrugged his shoulders. Don't forget there weren't the number of boats and planes then that there are now or will be in the future. What is the population today compared to 1930? An additional fifteen million, even with the millions lost to the war? So in the '30's this place may not have ever been challenged."

"What about the subs?" Billy Jim asked, flipping his knife into the earth between his feet. "Where are they? I don't see no place for 'em to tie up."

"And you won't, even from the air." Jonesy continued. "This eastern boundary, the dome as you call it, is actually cantilevered over the Gulf Stream some thirty feet or so. The pens are inside the top half of a giant size clam shell if you will." He used his hands to illustrate a large clam opening and closing. Pointing to where they had been standing. "The pens begin about there." Then swinging his arm westward, added, "And stretch to the ridge which offers room for the conning tower and extended periscope. The subs enter underwater and don't surface until they are within the shelter of the island. Never to be seen from the land, sea or air. Very, very ingenious."

"How do you know that, if you can't see them?" Tuck asked

"Quite by accident, I assure you." Jonesy smiled, placing his hands behind his head, crossing his legs and looking comfortable – at peace. He continued. "I was on the ridge with my binoculars one day when I spotted the sub. Naturally, I was surprised to see a submarine out here, but I could just taste 'rescue' and began running down the ridge, jumping, waving my arms and hollering loud enough to start an avalanche. Probably looked like a mountain goat gone crazy. I could tell by the sound and the belching smoke, it was having mechanical problems and when it turned, I assume it was putting into the island for me. Anyway, by the time I arrived at the water's edge, it had completed its turn and coming directly towards me. I tell you I was ecstatic! My prayers were answered. I just knew they had seen me waving." Jonesy, unable to control his emotions, stood up and demonstrated by jumping about thrashing his arms. "I was overcome with joy. I knew for certain that they were going to get me off this place. Oh how I thanked God!"

A little embarrassed, he sat back down and eventually continued. "But rescue was not to be. No. Five hundred yards out the sub switched over to batteries and began submerging. I put my glasses on it and – immediately dropped to my belly! It was a German sub – a flaming U-boat! Afraid to move, I watched the trail of bubbles disappear under this island – right where I lay. From there on it was a matter of conjecture and at that moment, I began playing a very successful game of cat and mouse. The sub's presence challenged the endurance of my mind, body and spirit. It was like a spook, seemingly disappearing and reappearing in disordered irregularity. Trying to establish a pattern or schedule was as easy as grasping a wisp of smoke. In time it became my 'ghost of the stream.'

"You know over time, the sub has become more brazen, I suppose because the war is over. Complacency. When I first observed them, they departed and entered mostly at night. However, they now come and go pretty much as they please. It travels on the surface as much as possible, probably because it's saving its batteries and generator for the future. I don't imagine there are too many places a U-boat can pull in and ask for replacement batteries." Jonesy actually smiled at his humor. "In any event, once in close proximity to the island, it submerges and surfaces inside."

"Wow!" Billy Jim said. "How'd you know that? I mean about the surfacing underneath us?"

By nature, Jonesy appeared self conscious, but he spoke of his time on the island with ease and candor. "It was logical, but I had to prove it to myself. The first time, after the sub was gone for a few days, I swam in. I had estimated the distance, then stepped it off figuring I had to swim a little more than thirty feet underwater before I could come up for a breath. After practicing for some time in the lagoon, I was ready and made it on the first try. In retrospect, I could have come up within a few feet. The dome rim out there is only a yard thick. Later, I found an easier way in - through the caves and down several sets of stairs. I should have tried that first." He grinned.

"What's it like inside?" Hannah wanted to know.

"Come on and I'll show you. It'll probably be easier to understand if you see it."

They followed Jonesy over top of the dome, up the ridge towards an opening Billy Jim and Tuck had thought to be a cave.

He continued talking as they walked. "There are nine pens down below, but only two subs. I believe the spare is being cannibalized to keep

GHOST OF THE STREAM

the other one going. Incidentally, the sub no longer looks like a U-boat. The deck gun has been removed. I suppose it's on the bottom or in a storeroom. The conning tower has been cut down. Periscope shortened. Hand railings were scrapped and the sharp, metal, net cutter removed from the prow. Even has a small hand operated crane mounted where the deck gun was. Its profile has been altered considerably. If you saw a silhouette of it, you would not recognize it as a U-boat. Oh yes, it's now bright yellow with the name *Nautilus Scan* painted on both sides in bold, black lettering."

As they approached the opening, Jonesy explained. "If you look directly into the recess, that's all you see, an indentation. Through artistic shading, painting and using natural light, the cave entrance is masked. It's a deception you'll find used extensively in making movies. You must actually step into the recess to recognize it is the opening to something else...a stairway. All of the entrances are handled in the same manner regardless where you are on the island. Quite clever, I think. Most are simple openings, some are fakes, but many of the doorways are blocked with heavy metal or wooden doors. I suspect they are labs or rooms for special projects. It will be interesting to see what we find, once we get into them.

"A few of the entrances are sealed with balanced stone doors that can be accessed by touching a certain point. It then moves with the delicacy of a Swiss watch and usually leads to one of the more important chambers. There's apt to be a treasury of information behind such doors." Jonesy, with his index finger, barely touched the wall and it revolved 90 degrees to allow passage. "I'm not so cunning," Jonesy admitted. "I stumbled onto this by accident. Bumped my elbow and 'Shazam'. Watch your step and hold the handrail." Natural light, through mirrored skylights, and prisms comes in automatically as they descend the stairs.

"There are many things I don't know about the caverns and companionways. I haven't been able to explore all of them. But now that I have some help..." He turned and looked at them, sheepishly. "I was never able to know just how long the sub would be gone. If it surfaced and sailed away I could time my visits with some accuracy. But without that knowledge, it was hit and run as best I could."

After a series of passageways and stairs, the foursome emerged on the ground level into the cavernous opening containing the submarine slips. The pens can best be described by imagining two hands placed side by side, the fingers and thumbs being the docks and the spaces between, the water. In spite of the shameful reason the pens were constructed, they were beautiful to the eye. There was hardly a sound except a slapping wave

63

here and there. The air was cool and weighed only slightly with the odor of the sea and diesel fumes. Not altogether unpleasant, but a reminder this was not a leisurely walk in the country. The water, indirectly lighted by the sunshine outside, was a lime green with reflected rays splaying across the ceiling. It is best described as a green grotto.

FISH EYE VIEW OF SUB PENS / DOME

They were standing on the main floor at the forward end of the pens. Jonesy pointed in the direction of a workstation at the "bow" of pen number seven. "Once I was caught unaware over there. I had watched the sub surface out in the Stream and sail away to the south. Watched it until it was out of sight. I climbed to the ridge and entered through one of the passageways. It must have taken longer than I thought because when I entered the pens, I couldn't believe my eyes. The sub was surfacing! I could only imagine why they returned, but assumed they used the swiftness of the current to get back so quickly. In any event, I dived under that row of workbenches over there, thinking I could move from one to another if necessary.

"My heart was pounding so loudly I actually held my hand over it to muffle its sound. I finally released my breath that I didn't realize I had been holding and became light headed. I waited and waited fearing they might have canceled the trip. It was a pickle I was in if that were the case.

The funny thing though, and this is something we should remember, as the sub was surfacing it raised its scope and looked around 360 degrees. Only then were hatches opened allowing a group of sailors to emerge. There must have been a dozen of them. Certainly more than was needed to tie up the boat, connect electric and water and put the gangway in place. Lots of activity, confusion and milling about. Immediately, I suspected I had left behind a clue from an earlier visit and they were searching for me." He face twisted slightly. "My imagination takes on the role of Superman at times like those. You know, leaps and bounds. However, in the final analysis they didn't hook up the electric and water, I later assumed it was a ploy."

Tuck was paying special attention to Jonesy and what he was saying. He couldn't help noticing how he had changed since last night. He was calm, deliberate and thoughtful; even humorous at times. He thought it might be having the chance to talk, or perhaps the military bearing in him was being demonstrated. Regardless, Tuck found it enjoyable and comforting to have him in their midst.

Apparently, Hannah also recognized the change and decided to see if they could learn a little more about the pilot. "Where you from Jonesy? Your family and all?"

"Jonesy from New Jersey. Newark. Small family: parents and one sister."

"You married?" Hannah continued.

"No, Hannah." Then with a sparkle, imitating Groucho Marx raising his eyebrows and wiggling an imaginary cigar, asked, "Are you interested?"

Hannah threw her arms up in the air and laughed. "Hah! Glory be, heavens to Betsy, I'm old enough to be yer Ma."

Jonesy put on his very best pouty face: his puckered lower lip, downcast eyes and bowed head indicating his disappointment at his refused proposal. Looking up, smiling, said, "No, Hannah, war and a wife and perhaps a family is just not a good mix. Perhaps someday."

He continued. "Once more Lady Luck smiled. Three or four seamen made a dash for one of the rooms," Jonesy related. "I couldn't tell which one from where I lay hidden."

"Probably forgot to set the timer on the low gravity machine." Billy Jim offered with a chuckle.

"Could have been. I just wanted all of them back on the sub and it gone. It was then I realized I was shivering. I wasn't cold, but I shook like I had the fever. Adrenaline rush I suppose. I was so scared, I curled up as best I could and resisted any movement possible. It wasn't long before a couple of the kids returned from over there. He pointed in the opposite direction. Walked right by me. I didn't hear them coming because they were wearing rubber slippers or booties. They were so close to me, I could actually smell them. Looked like they each had an armful of charts and manuals. Anyway, my prayer was answered...again. With little noise, the sub settled where she lay. A sizable boil, a small wash, a hum and the *Nautilus Scan* was gone. I began calming a bit, but continued to reside under the benches. The only reason I could come up with for the return was the sub decided, by chance or by orders, to proceed to some place for which they didn't have charts or codes aboard. Thus the mad dash by the kids. I tell you, I was one scared little hoppy toad.

"I'm embarrassed to mention this, but one thing still bothers me - and this is very important: I swear three or four kids took off on the run, but I only saw two of them return and then from a different direction. I hope I just miscounted, but the thought has not left me that there is still a Nazi or two on this island with us. If they did see me running down the hillside, it would be logical to have someone spy on me. On the other hand, I haven't seen hide nor hair of another soul. And I've looked."

Tuck, Hannah and Billy Jim stared at each other incredulously, not knowing what to think except to be anxious and concerned. "Why the heck didn't you tell us this before?" Billy Jim demanded. "Don't ya bleve that's pretty important stuff?"

Tuck could see Billy Jim's anger and quickly interceded. "Why would they leave someone here except by accident?" asked Tuck. "What could a sub full of seasoned sailors possibly fear from one man?" Then answering his own question; "Of course, they may have thought you were one of many trying to spring a trap. After all, they're still hiding from something."

"I don't know, Tuck? I've come up with only a couple of thoughts. I suppose with that many men one or two could be left behind on chance. But I don't believe anyone would purposely jump ship at this lonely outpost. I can vouch it's not pleasant being here alone. The other reason I came up with - and this is the most plausible - they suspect they have a visitor. As you can imagine, before I knew they were here, I didn't conceal my presence. Had no reason to. It's quite possible they saw smoke, footprints, or other evidence of my carelessness. Who knows."

"And you've seen no indications of any kind, a footprint, an ash, a sound that he or they might be here?" asked Tuck.

"No, except the same old footprints you saw at the lagoon." Seeing their surprise, he added, "Yes, I observed you there also. But listen, I've concentrated on trying to determine one way or the other, but still I'm

GHOST OF THE STREAM

no closer to an answer. I apologize for the mystery. It's like a pesky toothache that comes and goes."

"What makes ya think ya miscounted?" It was Billy Jim, the most concerned of the four, rubbing his E-zectative pacifier.

"Have you ever looked at something directly," answered Jonesy, "but your mind was concentrating on what was around it? That's the way this thing is. Nothing positive. I compare it to a photograph that has been cropped or trimmed. The finished picture shows one thing, the negative something else. It may be nothing more than an uncomfortable feeling, you know a nagging of the subconscious that something doesn't square with the brain."

"I don't know nothin' about the sub-brain or whatever, but I know what you're saying about lookin' at one thing, but seein' something else," said Billy Jim. "Especially at night. You want to really see what's out there, don't look directly at your target; but aside it. I guess it's looking out the side of your eyes for a hint of something. A movement maybe." Both Hannah and Tuck nodded their understanding.

"He may know of our presence and playing a good game of hide and seek. I think we should be on our toes to the possibility we're not alone on Mystery Island."

"Thank you Jonesy. If you're trying to scare us, you're doing a fine job of it," Hannah said.

"By the bye, in time I snailed out, massaged my stiff muscles and began a circuit around the underground cavern. I took a cursory search of each pen, the available nooks and crannies, unlocked toolboxes and compartments. I was still pretty well shaken, but I was looking for anything that might shed light on this strange, bewitching land. I found what was expected, and more. In addition to the normal maintenance equipment, needed for up to nine subs at once - fuel, rations, ammo and such - there's an array of electronics beyond my comprehension, powerful electrical turbines and machinery beyond the imagination. I think the continuous current of the Stream has even been harnessed for electric power." Jonesy indicated the Gulf Stream. "I imagine they've positioned giant turbines out there and the water, traveling five or six knots 24/7 year in and year out, flowing against the vanes would be more efficient that windmills.

The electronics may be the source of the low gravity phenomenon, the cone, the magnetic mystery and who knows what else. And if I'm right, there's also a treasure-trove hereabout. Probably well hidden and or well guarded." He looked directly at Tuck, recalling his interest in pirate treasure.

"How you figure that?" Tuck wanted to know; his attention perked and interest tweaked.

By this time Tuck and Hannah had found a comfortable place to sit down or something to lean against. Jonesy selected an iron bollard; a mushroom shaped post used to tie up the U-boats. He continued his uncanny tale, Billy Jim being the only diversion, occasionally tossing a pebble, rusty bolt or washer into the pens, watching it sink from sight, many fathoms below. "Based on facts we learned after the armistice, I'm assuming the sub never surrendered, but continues to travel back and forth to the Caribbean and South America - countries friendly with the Nazis - particularly Uruguay, Paraguay, Brazil and Argentina. To do so they need money. They probably have many contacts from years past, but they'd still need money. Any covert operation takes money - lots of it.

"Don't forget the Nazis lost the war. They weren't going down there as conquering heroes. They were criminals going into hiding - at any cost - to avoid the hangman's noose. So it's logical to me, they must have hidden wealth to pay their way. I imagine fuel would be one of the most expensive items seeing that the 'milk cows' aren't delivering these days."

The term attracted Billy Jim's attention. He turned from the pens and giggled. "Milk cows, they got cows down here?"

Jonesy also laughed. "No, Billy Jim. The 'milk cows' were the huge subs that delivered fuel and supplies to subs at sea. Ammo, new orders, food, spare parts, equipment and so forth. However, rough weather was a constant enemy of the subs. Quite often bad weather would prohibit refueling and replenishing at sea. The subs would then have to return to Spain or France, the closest bases, for fuel and supplies. That took time away from attacking the convoys and the costs were exorbitant.

"It stands to reason, this spot would be an ideal depot. Regardless of the weather outside, in here, subs needing major repairs, could be worked on 24 hours a day." Jonesy flailed his arms about, as he had a habit of doing when explaining large subjects such as the pens and work areas between. "Those on patrol needing just diesel, food, supplies and routine maintenance, could zip in here, be serviced and turned around quickly. Having a spot this close to the supply lines would be a plus. Of course, once our planes started patrolling out three and four hundred miles, all subs were pretty well contained. As I mentioned earlier, mid-May '43 was the turning point for us. It was a time for us to celebrate. Submarine warfare in the Atlantic, as we had known it, was a thing of the past. Did I mention that in spite of the tactics of the wolfpacks, over ninety per cent of the convoys survived to deliver their shipments?" Jonesy seemed to relax, almost as if he had run out of steam or relieved to have passed along a heavy burden to someone else. In Tuck's mind, he associated Jonesy's turnabout to his getting well.

"Jonesy, do you think the sub is transporting Nazis from here? And if that's not their mission, why are they running south? Why not just stay put?"

"Good point, Tuck. I think they need more than this small island can offer. No girls, for example. No social life to speak of. After all they're cooped up in the sub for weeks at a time. Without the pressures of war - a common goal - I imagine all that togetherness could create an epidemic of cabin fever. Also, they might be transporting war criminals, wanting to avoid prosecution, between different countries down there. How better to get from Brazil to Chile than by submarine? Do you remember from your geography all the large rivers in South America capable of handling huge vessels, including subs? And if they wanted to run to any island in the Caribbean basin, who would question a bright yellow 'research submarine', especially if it had the money to pay for the very expensive fuel and supplies?

"But to finally answer your question, no. No, I don't think there are any more Nazis using this as a stepping stone to escape. Those that could get out, did. The sub might still have a meager business shuttling them to where they want to go...and can pay for it. But, I don't think there's a lot of movement about. To stay here would prove nothing and produce nothing. I imagine this is just a depot for them to do their repairs, maintenance and pick up some of their booty for the next business venture."

"I think we oughta sink it," Billy Jim said matter-of-factly. "It's time they paid for killin' my brother." He was looking as grim as Tuck had ever seen him.

Jonesy jumped from the bollard, offered his sympathy about Henry Lee, but put forth a strong argument against attacking the sub. "Why would you want us to take on a battle we can't possibly win, Billy Jim? They have everything going for them and we have what?" Jones held up his hands twisting them back and forth. "Laddie, they have experience, weapons and manpower. I suspect, with little difficulty, they could wipe us all out and not even miss breakfast. No. I think we should maintain a watch and a low profile. We will not show ourselves and survive with an appeasement not seen since Europe watched Hitler overrun Poland and drive France to its knees. I forbid any further consideration of taking on the Nazi submarine. With time and a proper amount of luck, we will get off this island, report to the authorities and permit them to do what's necessary."

Billy Jim jumped to his feet exploding! "Ferbid? You ferbid? You ferbid nothin'! You don't order me 'round, mister! How the devil you coulda stayed on this here island fer this long and not sunk them Huns is more than I can handle. And, don't you never talk to me like that again! I ain't in your flamin' army!" Billy Jim turned and walked away. He threw a washer, sidearm into the wall ahead of him. It bounced, spun a few times before rolling over the edge into the water.

"Jonesy, I'm sorry. He's still upset over losin' his brother." Hannah was trying to make amends, but looking at Jonesy, she knew she was failing. Her eyes watered and finally, she put her hands over her mouth. Turning, she drifted after her son.

Jonesy stood like a sentinel, arms at his side, with a very flush, crimson face, sputtering about not understanding.

To break the atmosphere, Tuck reminded everyone it was time to vacate the bunker since they didn't know when the sub would return.

"Tuck, you gonna hep me sink that there sub, ain't ya?" They had returned to the area of the plane, stretched out in the sanctuary of a stand of Australian pines. Both had camped many times in such places. The trees formed a natural encampment, with a thick canopy that filtered rain into a mist, and a floor of soft, brown needles. It was cool on the warmest of days. Deer loved such hideaways. Winds singing through the trees and branches provided a sympathy that soothed and quieted the most restless of campers.

"Hilfe? Ja, Nein. Ich weiss nicht. Ich glaube nicht. Billy Jim, I just told you in German, I'm not certain I can help. My Daddy is of German blood and he lost an American cousin in the war. I didn't know him, but I know how it hurt my Daddy." Looking away reflective, he added, "He has no idea how many German relatives he lost.

"During '44 and '45 I worked alongside the German POWs picking citrus for Herb Glassman, owner of Blue Goose Brand groves and packing house. I got to know many of them and to think I could now kill them or possibly some of their family is just beyond me."

For some time Billy Jim sat and stared as only Billy Jim could. When he was like this, Tuck compared him to an alligator. The small brain, adapted well to its surroundings, taking in what he saw, assimilating the information and deciding how and when to use it. Patience. Rarely did he betray his emotions. He was not distracted or made uncomfortable by his geography or environments. Patience. A scorpion could land on his nose, crawl down his lips and chin and he would not move an eyelash.

Patience. Seldom did Tuck know what he was thinking until he spoke. Sometimes, even then...

"What'cha mean? You ain't never told me you was German or you ever worked with 'em."

"It never came up, but yes, I worked with them. And, Billy Jim, many of them are kids just like you and me. One youth I met was twelve years old and was captured in his very first battle. Shot in the leg. You remember the old C.C.C. Camp in Kendall?" Billy Jim gave Tuck a questioned nod. "Well, it was turned into a German POW camp during the last years of the war. There were no serious criminals there, just low ranking foot soldiers that were no threat to anyone. Many told me they were better off here in the States than they would be in Germany. The conditions over there were deplorable. No food. No fuel. No family. No economy. They were, in fact, happy to be here and thankful to have something to do."

"How come they was workin', if they was prisoners?"

"To help the war effort. Most of our young men were in uniform. We kids couldn't pick all the fruit before it began to spoil. There weren't enough of us. So Uncle Sam asked for volunteers. Had more volunteers than we had guards for them. Finally, many of them were sent to the groves with no more than the truck drivers."

"Bet'cha had lot of 'scapes."

"No. Very few even tried. Why would they leave? They were well fed. Housed in clean camps and in addition, were paid for their work. Where would they go? What would they do? They didn't speak the language well enough to get along without raising suspicions. They were safer in camp than they would have been on the street. I don't think we spent any real efforts seriously looking for the few that did make it out. Anyway, I got to know many of them and learned a little German. And their English improved over time." He smiled at Billy Jim. "I suspect some of the local girls were talking to them through the wire fences."

"You knowin' German might be hepful to us when we go after the sub. It would only be the right thing to tell 'em to surrender first. That's probably more than they offered Henry Lee. Got any ideas how to go about it? Sinkin' it, I mean."

"I'm not certain we should go after it. Jonesy makes a lot of sense. After all they're seasoned submariners, accustomed to sinking ships killing dozens, scores. Billy Jim, I've never killed anyone and don't really get a thrill from hunting. I did hunt at one time, but only because it was a way to put meat on the table."

"You tellin' me you're soft? Can't kill if you have to?"

"That, I don't know. Never been tested. I suppose, if I were in the war, had been trained, I could. But I can't answer with certainty. I saw a man killed when I was younger. A colored man shot by a cop simply because he didn't stop when told to do so. It was scary. I still think about it at times. Have you ever killed? A person, I mean."

"Questions unanswered don't pick up no lies. What you don't know can't be used against me." He smiled that little ghost-of-a-grin that suggested mischief, but left Tuck wondering. It said more than any words might and again it said nothing. Did it hide his true feelings? His bravado? Macho? Fears? It gave Tuck a feeling he knew much more than what he was telling... Was he capable of murder? No, Tuck didn't think so. Killing? Self-defense or what he might assumed to be. Yes, I suspect he could, Tuck thought. In the end, Tuck had to admit he'd rather have Billy Jim with him than against him. Street fight, fox hole or even sinking a sub.

Right about then, Tuck wished he had some answers to the many questions he was always asking himself. He wanted to talk to Jonesy and Hannah, but he also needed to respond to Billy Jim. Saying a silent little prayer, he began: "Okay, for the sake of argument, let's say all efforts - whatever they might be - to get them to surrender, failed. How do we go about destroying a U-boat and a crew of say fifty who have years of fighting experience? Hand-to-hand combat is out. We have no weapons to speak of. So it's much like David and Goliath. You remember he swacked a giant with a stone?"

"Tuck, I went to Sunday School when I was little." He was sprawled out, head resting in his left palm, eyes twinkling, thoroughly enjoying Tuck's awkwardness. "Sounds to me like you stallin'. You stallin', Tuck?"

"Well, I guess I am. However, just as a game, let's see what we can come up with. I'm not saying I'll help. This is just thinking aloud."

"No. It's stallin'. But, go ahead." He smiled. Now sitting up, he played a game of solitary mumblety-peg with his own hand.

Tuck couldn't help being impressed at the skill Billy Jim exhibited throwing the knife deftly between his outstretched fingers. "All right, here goes. We can't ask them to surrender, because they will just laugh at us. Then they will shoot us and turn us into shark bait. So we must rely on surprise, total surprise. They can't even know we're on the island. That is if they don't already know. They must not suspect anything is different than when they left. I think we should learn all that we can from Jonesy. Seeing the entire inside of the bunker might give us another perspective. More ideas."

Billy Jim put away his knife and applauded. "We gonna have to knock 'em out and do it without 'em knowin' we're here. What do you suggest? Dynamite? Bombs? Lock 'em inside, then gas 'em? Smoke? Hey, how about flooding it and drownin' the devils? Let the sub sink right in its pen. It will tumble to the bottom of the Stream and no one will ever know what happened to it. That's pretty good, Tuck."

Tuck stood up to stretch and exercise his stiff joints, recognizing Billy Jim had embellished what he had proposed. "You know there's another matter we haven't taken into consideration. The war is over. We wouldn't be killing in defense of our country or ourselves. We would be killing out of revenge. And I believe we could be found guilty of murder, regardless, if we did it in justification of Henry Lee's death. And another thing, we haven't even talked about our casualties. Forget you and me. How would you feel if your Mama or Jonesy got killed? No. We've got lots to discuss before we decide to take on this project. Only then can we put a plan into action." Tuck was adamant.

"I don't mind exposin' Jonesy, if he's willin', but I don't want Ma involved. I was wondering if there's anything on the plane that we can use? Machine guns, live ammo, bombs, torpedo? Let's go find Jonesy."

Still June

Billy Jim remains an enigma to me. At times he's as bright as a hunk of coal. Other times he's a piece of that stone, cut, faceted and polished into something of substance. I like him and value his friendship, but don't know what to make of him much of the time. He can be as complex as the schematic of a long range radio transmitter, then as clumsy as a schoolboy trying to talk to his first love in the third grade. He can speak like a poet when describing their small piece of land in the Everglades; recalling trees and animals or giving a detail account of every bird, it's plumage and call.

Then he'll spit through his two front teeth and throw his knife, with deadly accuracy, into a tree trunk thirty feet away. I swear he'd be comfortable at the Waldorf in a tee shirt and sneakers. At the moment, however, he's in a rut about taking out the U-boat and it consumes his every thought, every waken hour. It's like everything else around him has closed down. Lost it's meaning.

> *Nothing I have said to him has deterred him one iota from his determination to take revenge on those he holds responsible for the death of his brother, Henry Lee. In spite of everything, it will be interesting to see where Billy Jim will be in ten years. I hope all of us are around to see it.*

After laying out their ideas, both Jonesy and Hannah said "no". "We ain't at war no longer and I don't want to lose my last youngan. That jewfish thing was as close as I want to git. So, jest put them ideas out of your head and spend that energy at gettin' us off this here island." Characteristically, she slapped her palms together, indicating the judge had ruled; court adjourned!

Jonesy reacted pretty much in the same manner. "Fellas, I've just about reached my end of the line. Feel like I've probably got more days behind me than in front. I've been through all I want during the last few years, especially this last six months. I've thought about destroying the submarine. Really discussed it with myself. My military duty says 'do it'. Make 'em pay to the last scintilla.

"The other side cautions me to 'let it be'. There's been pain on both sides. All of us have lost something." Arms out to the side, he twisted his body indicating a vastness. "But the Germans have lost it all. We still have our country intact. Most of our families are complete. So to continue the war to satisfy something personal, just doesn't seem right. Doesn't make any sense. Hannah, Billy Jim, you lost a son and a brother. Tuck, you lost a great uncle. I lost many, many friends, a cousin and as you know, my bombardier, McCoy. But I'm still optimistic. And I believe somehow the four of us will go home to our communities and neighbors and family members who will welcome us with open arms and shower us with love.

"But what about those poor boys on that sub? There is no home to return to. It's been bombed to smithereens. They aren't conquering heroes returning from battle. There will be no parades or shouting audiences as in the past. There's no community or family to hug and kiss them upon their return." He paused, sticking his hands in his pockets. "I'm not telling you this just to sway your thoughts about the sub. I'm also reminding myself, that for all we've lost, they've lost more, much more. Probably everything they - or their families - ever owned. We're far better off than most. Now, having said all that, I'll do what *all* of us, together, agree to. If we are to kill the sub, I'll give it my all." Unable to hide his satisfaction at Jonesy's decision, Billy Jim knew he now had to convince Tuck.

Hannah surprised everyone with her announcement. "I 'spect Jonesy has a better handle on these here matters than I do. After listenin' to him, he makes sense. I'll follow his directions."

"Ma, I wasn't plannin' on you gettin' involved. I think us men can handle it."

"I'm in, Billy Jim." Hannah spoke with finality. Further discussion was no longer an option.

Billy Jim, didn't like what he heard, but said, "Okay, Tuck, that leaves you. We got ourselves one positive and two maybes. All's you got to do is say 'yes' and we kill us a German U-boat." He gave Tuck a "thumbs ups".

Tuck was not swayed. "Billy Jim, I can't say just yet. There's too much to discuss. The two things we have on our side - I hope - are time and surprise. If the Germans don't know we're here and if we play it smart, we can learn more about this place and make better choices. I think the first thing to do is to find out all we can about their operation. Let's start by exploring this island until we know it as well as they do. That way we won't be open to surprises. Perhaps we won't have to, as you say, 'kill us a U-boat'. Maybe there are other options. Jonesy can we start by you showing us what you know about the 'inside' and any other ways to get into the pens? Are there any other secret passages?"

Jonesy perked up and smiled. "That I can do. We can start right away." Tuck looked at Hannah and saw that she was pleased with the outcome - so far. Billy Jim said nothing, but Tuck could tell he would have been happier preparing an explosion of some sort. Since there was no majority, they headed for the caves on the ridge.

Using his hands to demonstrate, Jonesy began. "If I could peel away the skin and remove the top of the island, it would be easy for you to see what the inside is like. You've already seen the nine trenches of water - the pens - separated by concrete walkways, large enough for vehicles, heavy-duty cranes and hundreds of workmen. Facing the pens, enclosed in a mountain of concrete sculptured to look like natural rock, holding the picture of Der Fuhrer, is a myriad of cubicles, rooms, stairs and passageways.

"Consider, from pictures you've seen, the cliff dwellers from our own southwest. Now peel away a side of the mountain to expose all the rooms, walls, floors, ceilings and stairways making up the various homes and communities inside. If you can imagine what the inside of the Rock of Gibraltar must look like after the Nazis finished their honeycomb of tunnels, then you can begin to understand what's below. There are more rooms than I've had time to explore - some are locked - and places that I wouldn't go without pad and pencil to map my whereabouts. I think we should begin by exploring together until we get comfortable, then we can divide into teams until we're familiar enough so as not to get lost. I wish we had an artist with us."

"Tuck can draw in the sand." Billy Jim teased.

"Yeah." Tuck tossed down his hand in dismissal. "But, I don't know that I'm good enough for all of this," he explained. He did promise, nevertheless, if he found some paper and pencil, he'd try. He did not tell them about his journal.

VI
Respite

PALMETTO

Jonesy's tactical experience came in handy as they planned for the return of the Germans and plotted their meticulous search of the pens and everything underground. Like a good leader, Jonesy mapped out every move. "There cannot be the slightest hint anything is amiss or different about this island since the Germans left. We simply do not exist. Another thing, and this is important, if anyone sees or suspects something is askew - likely caused by an outsider for example - we need to know about it."

Base camp, including Tuck's hut, was struck and re-established on top of the ridge within sight of the airplane. The site was selected because of its location, camouflage and - as Jonesy, Billy Jim and Tuck knew firsthand - the Herculean effort it took to get there. By the time they were finished, the teepee was dismantled and its components scattered about to look as natural as possible. All those essential items, collected or constructed since the arrival of the Hamiltons, were moved to the ridge. As the group "backed away" from base camp, the sand was swept of tracks and there remained not even an ash of the ever-burning fire.

The one assignment Tuck despised was guard duty or watch. Jonesy had set up the schedule. "In order that no one be caught unaware as I had been, a sentry is to be posted atop the ridge, especially whenever anyone is underground. After sighting the sub, he is to make a mad dash down the ridge sounding the alarm. We can all share the watch while we're in camp." Billy Jim and Tuck were the logical choices, according to the General, as Billy Jim was now calling Jonesy. (Tuck was certain Billy Jim could get away with addressing the Queen of England, as Queenie.) "We can't very well ask Hannah to scamper down the hillside and I feel like I should be on deck at all times," Jonesy explained. "Consequently that leaves you fellas to be our eyes, ears and alarm system."

Needless to say, sitting up on the ridge with Jonesy's binoculars scanning the horizon, quickly became "dullsville". To Tuck it was a bore and challenge, especially when he would much rather be down below where the action was. Unlike Tuck, however, Billy Jim accepted the assignment with grace. He seemed able to put everything in compartments, knowing each would be opened in time.

"My turn down yonder will come. Till then..." he explained to Tuck, with patience.

After completing the first day of exploring the 'bunker', as they now referred to the underground city so as to differentiate it from the ridge, dome, base camp, lagoon, and point, they sat around the remaining embers of their nightly fire discussing what had been found.

According to Hannah, they'd found an industrial city constructed with the workers and the job in mind. "Ain't like no company town, I ever lived in and I've been in several," she admonished. "Usually they ain't no better than what migrant workers have to put up with. This here is a paradise in comparison." She looked at Tuck who registered his understanding.

Jonesy added his thoughts. "In addition to the work areas developed for the repair of U-boats, there are sleeping quarters, laboratories, dining halls, a galley and theater. Why, there's even quiet spaces set aside for entertainment and leisure such as hobbies, reading and music."

"All in all, it's like a kindly employer built a small, temporary hometown for workers he cared something about," Hannah pointed out. "Everything counted, boredom couldn't be blamed on the lack of nothin' to do."

To Tuck the only piece that seems out of place was the portrait of The Fuhrer, Herr Adolph Hitler, painted on a wall so it couldn't be missed from any pen. "It has to be at least ten feet tall, illustrating him with that lackadaisical Heil salute of his. And that Iron Cross hung around his neck. What an ego."

"Tuck," Jonesy said. "That's not an Iron Cross - it's the Knight's Cross, initially given only to exceptional submarine captains. It was the submariner's answer to the Iron Cross. In the beginning, there were probably not more than a dozen or so Aces. Those were captains who could claim the necessary tonnage of enemy ships sunk. As victories grew scarce towards the end of the war, almost anyone with a successful mission, of any kind, or simply returning, qualified. Except Hitler, of course. He had no love for his navy and I doubt he was ever on a U-boat. Did you know the average life expectancy of a U-boat crew was less than sixty days towards the end of the war? I don't think the leader of the Third Reich would subject himself to those kind of odds."

"Jonesy, how you see the operation down yonder when it was really churnin'?" asked Hannah.

Jonesy was leaning back against a stone with his hands resting in his lap. After a pause he said, "This is just a guess, but I can imagine how the city might blossom into action. A radio message would be received stating a U-boat needed repairs. After an assessment of the damages, an assignment to a particular pen would be made, depending on the needs. Then, as if on cue, the boat would bob to the surface and the pen bathed in fluorescent light. After the crew was whisked away, a devoted company of workmen would swarm over the sub like an army of ants, each with his own list of repairs to be made."

Hannah joined in. "Yeah. I can see what it might'd been like. I worked in a shipyard during the war. The graveyard shift. It'd be darker than sin outside, but bright as day inside with all them overhead lights everywhere. Weren't many shadows that way, which was good fer me, since I did lots of troubleshootin' at a bunch of different sites. Howsomever, most of the time it was so noisy you couldn't think straight. You jest had to set your mind on the task."

"I suspect it'd be like that down below, Hannah," Jonesy said. "Everyone with his - or her - own job to do and going about it in an orderly fashion. Overhead hoists and hydraulics would be moved into place. Divers would get their gear ready for underwater inspection and service. Welders would start highlighting the scene with flashes of electric arcs and cutting torches."

Hannah stood up and walked about, waving her hands like a traffic cop. "Just like us. When we'd be going full bore, we was a hustlin', bustlin', beehive of noisy activity. They called us a 'wartime machine'," she said proudly. "Towards the end, we was a turning out a Liberty ship every 24 hours." Billy Jim and Tuck smiled at each other, enjoying the duet.

Back to Jonesy who had sat up with his arms resting on knees. "Meanwhile, I imagine the sub crew would be hustled from their customarily cramped confines to a hot shower and clean clothes. Perhaps given a few pints of Bier or a taste of Schnaps before a traditional German feast for returning heroes. Finally a clean bed with fresh linens for a period of slumber, delivered from the smells and sounds of close quarters and too many shipmates. Free from the heavy odor of salt water and diesel fumes and the incessant rocking of the boat. Safe from depth charges, hedgehogs, planes, guns and bombs. Comfortable in knowing for at least that one night, there would be no awakening to the ear-splitting sound of the Klaxon and the gut wrenching fear accompanying the shout of 'ALARM! DIVE! DIVE! DIVE!'"

"And after the dancin' was done?" questioned Billy Jim, grinning at his Mother who was obviously enjoying her moment in the spotlight

Jonesy continued. "Well, finally, the boat would be repaired, made ready for another venture into the Atlantic, its sole mission: to kill convoys. Heavy machinery, hoists and hydraulics are pulled back into their nests. The clanking sounds of hammers and the rat-a-tat of the riveters are once more silent. Like candles on a birthday cake, the welding arcs and burning torches are snuffed out one by one until only the flood of fluorescence remains. There are no shouts of orders and instructions. The divers, their compressors shut down, have slithered out of dive suits and begun coiling black air hoses. Marine architects and engineers probably rolled up their charts, blueprints and schematics, stuffed them under their arms and walked away with closed briefcases. Machinists, shipfitters, electricians and ordnance experts have locked up their tool kits and placed them on nearby workbenches to await the arrival of the next U-boat." Then almost at a whisper, he said, "Slowly, as if the queen ant were dead, her followers would disappear from the hill in mourning."

Caught up in the spirit, Tuck jumped to his feet to offer his bit. "Let me try. The peace and calm Jonesy speaks of would be short-lived as a second wave would descend on the boat. Just like the *Nomad,* before we left on an extended trip - except more. Ship chandlers would arrive with an abundance of everything the sub might need, from aspirins to toilet paper. Hopefully, enough to last until met by a "milk cow" half way between here and Gibraltar. Then, if what I learned from my history lessons is correct, with a military discipline characteristic of the Prussian, ordnance, fuel, food, and damage control materiel would be in place and the boat declared 'shipshape'."

"At last," said Jonesy, now standing and almost dancing about. "The rested crew would march in crisp unison, from the ready rooms towards their replenished boat. The recorded sounds of a rousing Bavarian beer hall song would fill the underground cathedral. Workmen and crews of the other boats would stop work, cheer, salute and wave. Don't forget these were Nazi heroes going back into battle for der Vaterland. Anyway, caught up in the excitement of the moment, before they were halfway to the boat, I suspect the crew would break rank. Due to their youthful exuberance and because they knew what lay ahead, they'd no longer be marching. Instead, they'd swagger, swing their arms, skylark a bit and sing at the top of their lungs. By the time the record had finished, the crew would have disappeared below deck. Lines would be cast off, hatches closed and dogged. The whirring of electric motors would be heard followed by a hiss and a series of bubbles. Then, leaving only a small wash, the boat would be gone to carry out its next mission. The pen would wait in readiness for its next tenant.

"You know something?" Jonesy questioned laughingly. "When we get out of here, we could write an opera. It would be our answer to *H.M.S. Pinafore.* We could call it Der Fuhrer's Foolish Folly; a fugue showing his gradual demise through a sampling of all those that he sent to their death. We could present a serious picture while poking fun, showing him as a misguided buffoon."

This round robin, while not so dramatic as the first, became an almost every night event; allowing each to share what he had discovered during the exploration of the bunker. It not only gave each person a chance to voice his findings, but also provided an opportunity to fully discuss and remember things for possible use in the future. They could also make an on site visit if it was thought to be helpful to the group.

An example of this was Hannah's discovery of what might be a perpetual motion machine. Directing them down several halls, through a passageway and into what looked like a high school lab, she pointed to a contraption sitting in the center of the room. "It looks to me like they's captured the sun through these here solar panels in order to run the air compressor that drives that small motor there. Think 'bout that! The sun and the air are free. If they can run generators, automobiles, busses, trolleys, ships, trains and boats, think what that could do to our transportation!" Characteristically of her, she slapped her hands together to finalize her position. "Of course," she added with a grin. "Thet ain't gonna go set too well with the big oil companies.

"But looky here, they's even got a strange little non-return valve that, just through friction, suctions in a equal amount of air the compressor can deliver." Everyone looked at each other, shrugging their shoulders, not fully understanding or knowing what to say. "It's sorta like siphonin' gas or water, 'cept instead of a liquid they do it with air," Hannah explained.

"And that ain't all," she said, pointing to a corner cubicle. "They got a machine over yonder that cuts steel with some sort of powerful light. They's using a series of prisms, like them found in lighthouses, to magnify the beam so it's hot as a cuttin' torch. They might be using sunlight, but I think it's built around a big watt bulb. I tell you them Heinies are on to some really big things. With all the contraptions in one of the tippy-top rooms, with a rollback, roof I wonder if they ain't trying to control the weather. Might even be trying to harness the sun. At least they got all kind of weather instruments, gauges, and charts all over the place. Too bad they didn't stick only to their inventin' instead of trying to take over the world."

Billy Jim and Tuck nodded their heads in understanding as both had started fires with *Coke* bottle bottoms and magnifying glasses, but the information about the weather confounded them.

Seeing their puzzlement, Hannah spoke simply. "Weather's a concern to most everybody from mailman to farmer to the military. Jonesy, you know thet. Control the weather and you can control the world. Leastwise, influence it. Got something else for you to see." She walked towards a room filled with drawing boards illuminated brightly by sunlight and carefully positioned mirrors." The others followed closely behind. "This here's where the draftsmen puts down on papers what the engineers come up with, I 'spect. I ain't had time to review it all, but they's working on a strange ship design. This is one thing I don't understand. They's got a big, long bulge on the bow at the keel level. It almost looks like they's built a big torpedo shape right in the bow. It don't make no sense to me. A sailfish goes through the water easier than a whale. Seems to me it'd slow it down."

Hesitantly, Jonesy responded. "Hannah, when I was in Yokosuka after the war I saw a damaged Jap battleship in dry-dock with the same configuration. When I questioned it, I was told it helped the steering. Ensuring the prow traveled through the water more evenly or accurately. I guess the Japs or the Nazis have discovered something about the dynamics of water and hulls? Being allies, they'd share such information. "

"Don't know Jonesy. I'll be interested to see if it pops up in the future." Picking up a model of a submarine with vertical rudders at both ends. "Now, this here I do understand. Think what a sub or any boat far as that goes, might be able to do if it could sorta move sideways, even at high speed?" No one said anything.

Again realizing they didn't understand, she continued. "Just suppose you was trailing a sub so you could depth charge it. You has got to be close to over top it to make the hit. Now supposing about the

GHOST OF THE STREAM

time you are atop it, it engages both rudders and moves to the side out of danger. After all a sub has diving planes forward and aft. They's just rudders out to the side."

"A maneuver like that in marching is called oblique," Jonesy offered with a laugh.

Tuck, began using his hands like two rudders. His eyes lit up! He "saw it". "I get it! On a conventional ship, the rudder steers it by swinging the stern either left or right. It might look like the bow is turning, but it's really the stern that moves. I can understand how it might work. Might even make docking easier."

Billy Jim chimed in. "Yeah, I see it. Jonesy, you see how it might work, don't you?"

Jonesy smiled. "I see it. Certainly unusual, but just like a plane. It steers with its tail, but early planes had ailerons out in front of the pilots directing the nose up and down. Hannah, I know you were a troubleshooter during the war, but how is it you know so much about machinery and engines?"

Hannah threw back her head uttering a 'hah!' "When you're the only girl in a family of machinists and mechanics, it's a matter of survival."

Billy Jim spoke proudly of his mother. "Ma's even got her airplane engine and diesel tickets."

"Oh, yeah," Hannah added, "'nother thing. I stumbled on all kind of rooms we ain't yet explored. Up that there passageway," she said, pointing, "There's rooms, big ones, for everything: sleepin', eatin', cookin' and playin'. You name it."

Billy Jim and Tuck usually took turns on the ridge every two hours. Tuck grew to despise it with a passion and would become introspective at times in hopes of better understanding himself. It was quite easy for him to rest his elbows on his knees, lean his head into the eyepieces of the binoculars and gradually rotate 180 degrees from north to south. South to north. North to south. If an orangutan could identify a sub, he could do this, Tuck thought. While he was well aware of the importance of the job and wouldn't shirk his responsibility, it took every ounce of fortitude to stay at the routine. Luckily, he could search for the sub and at the same time think about other things. Tuck compared himself to disk jockeys, whom he thought could talk without thinking. He even daydreamed about taking out the U-boat, by himself, thereby becoming a hero. He backed away quickly for the very same reasons he gave Billy Jim

83

After running through his limited litany of subjects, he could usually count on memories of home to offer him a respite from his dreary task of coastal watch. Today was no exception and with certain homesickness, he allowed his mind to drift back...

When the courts had decided he should be taken from his parents and placed under the care of the County, Sam, the land overseer and unofficial "Mayor" of The Home, had driven into town and picked him up. The shiny, red Ford Model-A truck bounced along the rough, sandy path. Tuck watched Sam's steady hands hold the steering wheel loosely, yet in command as it twisted and turned in response to the hollows, bumps and rocks. "If you holds it too tight, it tires your arms and shoulders", Sam said. "But if you kinda ride with it, relaxed, be flexible you know, you remain the boss." Tuck knew he was talking for his benefit, but he was speaking so matter-of-factly it didn't appear he was preaching. Tuck liked that.

Still he paid little attention to Sam's remarks and turned to stare out the window. Caught up in his own world of misery, he was not in the mood for conversation or advice. What had happened? he wondered. Almost overnight, the world as he knew it had come to a halt. It was like a pleasant dream abruptly ending when you awaken. No matter how desperately you try to return and catch up with it, it rarely happens.

Tuck had been born to wandering parents who annually followed the farming seasons from South Florida to the northeast, mid-west and back. Seemingly victims of wanderlust and bent on self-destruction, they drifted from one crop to the next: from one labor camp to another. After his birth, he was told, both temporarily gained new directions and insight into the future. For awhile it appeared they might survive as a family-with-roots. Eventually, however, the "call of the road" and the lure of the temporary pleasures of life became too strong to resist. Both his Mama and Daddy lapsed into their world of stooped labor, sleazy farm camps and "passed by" humanity. When he was tiny, he was usually tucked away in some nearby corner of a juke or in a car or in a field crate at the end of a row of vegetables or trees. Thus his nickname "Tuck". If people accepted it as a play on words for one of Robin Hood's Merry Men - Friar Tuck - he did not explain.

Nevertheless, one day, years later, he was picking tomatoes for Rice Brothers Produce. The next, he was whisked away to a series of hearings with sugar-sweet ladies and fat men with wet, wrinkled shirts and tight collars. Despite his pleadings to return home, the court ruled he would be better off at the County Home. That decision ended his life

GHOST OF THE STREAM

as a "fruit tramp", made him a ward of the County and shut down his childhood, as he knew it. It also, forever changed his destiny.

He rationalized his Mama and Daddy would have been at the courthouse to see him off if they had been able. Just as well, he thought, no mush and no tears. Biting the inside of his lip and swallowing to repel the lump in his throat, he eased the emptiness he felt. He knew from experience tears would be next if he didn't, with all the strength he could muster, combat their arrival.

The old truck bounced hard a few times. Sam continued to talk. "You can let this get you down boy, or you can take ahold of it and get the best from it. Like the wheels on this truck, they just rolls with the bumps and ruts and been doing so for a long, long time. You can too. Use this next period to grow. Use it as a path; steppin' stones toward the future. Don't let this here experience drag you under. The short time you're here with us, measured against your entire life, won't be no more that a tiny bend in a long road. About like that." He snapped his fingers to emphasize his point.

What does he know, Tuck thought. He hasn't been uprooted from his family. He hasn't been passed around like a white-hot horseshoe by a bunch of do-gooders. How many times have I been moved anyway? Four? Five? It seems like I've been on the move my whole life. And here I am again, bouncing along a rutted, dirt road with everything I own in a gunnysack and a talkative, old driver, black as roofing paper.

The Home was one of three divisions of the County complex southwest of Miami. The other parts of the triangle were a hospital and old age home. Constructed during the 1920s, as a viable part of the real estate boom, it was built in the boondocks believing the cities would expand toward it. After the bust, the complex located ten miles from the nearest settlement served the "local's" medical needs and the County's burgeoning demands for housing the aged and dependents. On the western edge of the property was a potter's field, into which Tuck and most of the children were eventually initiated: usually with sheeted figures, rattling chains, moans and groans on moonless nights.

As the iron gates swung open, Tuck couldn't help comparing the landscape of the 100 plus acres with pictures he'd seen of old, Southern plantations. The picturesque Spanish style buildings, with their barrel tile roofs and many arches, nestled comfortably among the stately oaks, heavily laden with moss. There were also blossoming magnolias and ramrod straight, slash pines. The grounds were immaculate, indicating a lot of hard work, discipline and care. In the

PINE

distance, a playground and ballpark rang with laughter, shouts and cheers.

Braking to a halt in front of a building, resembling a mission, identified as "Office", Sam switched off the engine and turned to his passenger. "Tuck, I know you're down on the world right now and maybe for a good reason, but look at it like this here. You're at bat. No score. You can play like a good sport...maybe get a hit...maybe strike out. Or, of course, you can always say to heck with it, throw down the bat, walk away refusing to play. Most likely, with that last choice, you're apt to wind up a disagreeable young man and then, finally a bitter, old man.

"Tuck, what I'm trying to say, is just be yourself and do your very best. You've got lots of ability and there's a whole bunch of folks here that want you to become everything you can. And we'll help you." Sam smiled. "I'm kinda like a doctor. On call 24 hours if you need me. Forget the past, look only for today and tomorrow and discover for yourself just how much you have to offer, and in turn, receive. Son, I hope you'll play the game with every thing you've got. Who knows, you take a swing and you might even get a homer."

No one had called Tuck "son" in a long, long time. His throat tightened, but he managed a smile. Sam leaned over and opened his door. "Come on. I'll grab your things and we'll get you signed in."

Looking up from her typewriter, the squat, round lady smiled and asked, "Who do we have here?"

"E. Thom Fryer. Thom spelled with an 'h'", answered Sam automatically. "Howsomever, he goes by Tuck." He placed the *OK Feed* bag, containing Tuck's belongings, on the floor at his feet.

"How nice," said the round lady rolling a yellow card into her typewriter. "Does Tuck have an age?"

"Yes. Yes, Ma'am. "Eleven going on twelve," he stammered.

"Height?"

"Four feet, eight inches." He stood straight as proof.

"Weight?"

"Eighty five pounds."

Looking at him without waiting for answers, she talked and typed. "Eyes? Brown. Hair? Sandy...cowlick. Smile? Nice. Needs to use it more. Nose? One, with freckles." Grinning at Tuck, she pulled the card from the typewriter, marked the corner with a blue pencil and announced, "A-4." Tuck thought he might be grinning too.

"Ah, Miss Evans, I was wondering if we might put Tuck in one of the cottages. There's a vacancy in number nine." Then he gave the clerk - what was to become known as the "sugar cube" - a 14 carat smile.

"You know the rules, Sam Robinson. All new residents go to Compound A for testing, observation and evaluation." She paused. "But then it is the weekend isn't it?" Taking the card, she erased and used her blue pencil again. "Number nine, but just for the weekend. Now get out of here."

"Yes'um. Thank you." Picking up the sack, Sam took Tuck by the shoulder and guided him out the door. "A's a pretty nice place, but because there's little staff on duty now, it would be kind of lonely."

Lonely, now there's a word, Tuck thought. He had been alone most of his life it seemed. Even though he had been with people continuously since the day he was born, he still felt very much alone most of the time. He had played with the other children and worked with them side by side. He had accompanied his parents to the jukes and traveled with them during their town by town, state by state, crop by crop wandering. Still, even that kind of exposure did not quell or satisfy whatever was bottled up inside. He decided alone and lonely weren't the same, and he knew he would chew on that for a long time to come.

Still June, I think

I was feeling about as low as a fella can get when I entered The Home. Seemed like everything and everybody was against me. Regardless how far in the future I looked, I couldn't see anything but a black, bitter, void.

To be honest, I probably acted like a bonehead, as it would've matched my feelings at that time. Even got into a minor scrap and had to spend a week serving on the garbage truck. To add to my embarrassment a little ditty, in my behalf, was recited as we traveled throughout the compound:

Tuck is one of them dang Fryers,
Family of cheats, thieves and liars.
Now he's just your garbage man,
Bringing honor to his pappy's clan.

I have to credit a teacher, Mrs. Moser, with helping me overcome the urge to fight back. "Kill 'em with kindness. A laugh. A smile. A wave of the hand," she said.

It was one of the most difficult task I ever accomplished, but it worked. . Even developed a sly grin that says: I've got a secret and ain't telling. (I'll show you some day.)

Tuck was plagued with a feeling of not belonging...really belonging to anything permanent. An emptiness. A thing not complete. He knew something was lacking in his make-up. A character flaw perhaps. It was like not understanding a joke, but laughing anyway. Over the years, he struggled to understand without success. It was a longing to be a part of the whole, he believed.

By the time his Aunt Grace had "rescued" him from The Home, he was, thanks to Sam, on the road to a healing of some kind, but still confused and feeling like a railroad spike in a jewelry store. His Mama called it "at loose ends." He knew he should have been thankful for all the help he had received from relatives, friends and foster homes, but instead he was filled with resentment and contradiction. Greedy instead of being grateful. Selfish or self centered, he reasoned. He made a mental note to look up the word 'obnoxious'.

Living with Aunt Grace helped and once he had shared his feelings with her, comparing it to being locked out of the candy store, yet permitted to look through the window and watch others enjoying themselves. Neither could explain it, understand it nor cure it. He did believe, however, his grab bag of character traits: that resilience, that not belonging, that devil-may-care attitude and a lifetime of discipline, worked to his benefit and helped him survive to reach Mystery Island and would help in the future.

While he still had a long way to go to be a whole person, he knew living with Aunt Grace was the best thing that ever happened to him. She not only provided him with the emotional ties he lacked, she offered him a stability he'd never known and a home life he had never enjoyed. Simply stated, she loved him.

She even compassionately spoke of his parents as two people deeply in love with one another. She told of their weaknesses, the misery they shared and the battle of existence they fought each day of their lives. And because of the way she explained it, some of his bitterness towards them, melted away.

The bottom line, he thought, was that every young boy ought to have an Aunt Grace and a Sam to help him navigate the shoals of adolescence.

KNIGHTS CROSS

VII
Treasure Hunt

FLYING FISH

As Billy Jim set about to discover the very best way to kill the submarine, Tuck began his search for the treasure-trove Jonesy spoke about. He believed he understood Jonesy's lack of interest in searching for a hoard of riches, that we probably couldn't keep. After all, he'd just been through a horrible War and then lost to the world, living like a savage, for the last six months. What Tuck couldn't fathom was Hannah and Billy Jim's reluctance to even discuss the possibility of its existence or a hefty reward for locating it. He assumed all poor people wanted wealth. At least everything he had ever seen, until he went to live with his Aunt Grace, indicated money was the supreme goal, the staff of life. Without money one perished. Money to eat. Money to survive. Money to live. In his world of laborers, the poor, money was the essence of life. It was not a box of candy or a bouquet of flowers. This isn't to say one closes his eyes to his brother's needs, he thought. Regardless how poor you might be, there is always someone worse off. Many deserve our help.

Tuck learned from the Hamiltons, however, money doesn't mean the same to everyone. He had already spent thousands of imaginary dollars on a new house, with servants, for Aunt Grace, cars, fine clothes and a college education. He had spent a fortune to help upgrade the buildings at The Home. Then there was cancer to cure. Mrs. Bannerman to think of. But the Hamiltons said they would be happy with another boat. "Don't even have to be a new one. Just a good one," Hannah recorded when he finally got her to talk about 'if we had'.

He finally mused there would be time enough for all of them to decide how to spend it once the treasure was found. After bouncing ideas of exploration off Jonesy, Tuck began by mapping the bunker on scraps of paper he had found washed up on shore and a pencil he'd picked up from the plane. Over time, the group had refined the bunker with additional identification spots such as pens, offices, labs, machine shops and those rooms that were locked were labeled "secret".

"This cataloging," said Jonesy. "Allows us to keep tabs on each other and know approximately where everyone is at all times. It's imperative in the event a sub alarm is sounded. Again, the cardinal rule remains, if you use it, put it back. NOW! That way, we can get out in a hurry with everything where it's supposed to be. There can be no slip-ups about our being on the island. Our lives depend on staying alert and verbal cautions are to be welcomed reminders." He again reminded them to be watchful for an "uninvited guest".

Tuck eliminated obvious places not suitable for hiding, such as thin walls, spaces too accessible, too visible or subject to inclement weather. He thought the bunker was the most logical choice because of his imposed restrictions and its nearness to the submarines. It could easily support a secretive space, made secure and dry. The ridge was excluded from his list because of its construction. Basically it was a skin of terraced concrete, "wallpapered" with soil and vegetation. It could be neither secure nor weather proof; conditions he felt were absolutely necessary for the preservation of treasures - especially artwork and tapestries. The remaining parts of the island failed for the same reasons. Therefore, the bunker became his primary target for scrutiny, specifically those companionways, rooms and bulkheads demonstrating the characteristics he felt vital.

Day after day, he searched, in a well thought-out plan, consigned to paper. Like a builder initialing a blueprint once a section was completed, he checked off his drawings of the bunker after he was convinced a particular space could be ruled out. Each area was gone over with a hands-on approach. He looked for shadows; lighting and shading that might not fit in with its surroundings. He rubbed his hands - until the fingertips were tender - over any suspect wall or space, feeling for cracks, triggers, recesses, buttons and bumps. He looked for worn places, tracks, steps or stairs that seemed to go nowhere or ended at a supposedly blank wall. After defined searches, most areas were determined to be bogus or led to something else such as a back or side entrance.

Finally, his search was narrowed to three likely locations. The first was a narrow, cave-like opening beyond and above the end of the last sub pen - Zahl Neun. The stale, musty odor that he encountered as he eased up the stairs indicated the passageway had not been opened in some time. Thinking it an out-of-the-way staircase, unused and closed off, his adrenaline kicked in. Lordy, is this it? Tuck's heart rate and breathing increased as he neared the opening knowing that he could be but a few steps away from a fortune. The hair on his arms stiffened and he experienced a flood of excitement. Truthfully, he was a little fearful, too. And then there was that tiny kink in his armor that almost made him

GHOST OF THE STREAM

hope he would fail. However, regardless what he found, he wasn't about to turn back.

A random thought did race across his mind: surely this is the kind of stuff a submariner must feel making a torpedo run. Not certain of the outcome, but too committed to back off, he paused at the opening, playing his flashlight back and forth on the rough wall. By the time he worked beyond the simple lock hanging in a rusty hasp and opened the door, he knew it was a pipe dream. Disappointed? Sure. Relieved? Yeah. But this is only the beginning of my real search, he thought, keeping in mind the other two sites yet to explore.

What he had found was a large, curved room overlooking the nine pens from a head-on, vantage position. Each pen had its own station, complete with a huge desk and a padded, high back chair. At every station were banks of sound equipment, phones, control panels, power and light switches. Within easy reach was a file cabinet and racks of manuals, reference books, maps and schematics, each emblazoned with the Nazi swastika. Obviously the control center for the pens. From up here, everything happening in the pens below could be observed, Tuck thought, as he walked from one end of the room to the other. He surmised each pen was treated individually with its own "boss". Because of an inset type construction and a slanted, smoked glass shield, the control room could not easily be seen from below. He wondered if Gestapo tactics of spying were as far-reaching as Mystery Island? All of that aside, he did receive an unexpected bonus: an unlimited supply of notebooks and pencils. Since the area appeared abandoned, he felt safe in removing a few of each realizing he now had no excuse for not keeping a proper journal and making drawings as best he could.

Using a public address system, phones and multiple sets of signal light, traffic masters could control the comings and goings of every sub. Basically it was a manual system rather than electronic. Therefore, lighted display panels, such as those found in large train stations or utility companies, were unnecessary. Seated in one of the dusty chairs, he tried to visualize what the center might have been like during its full operation. It was difficult to concentrate because his imagining the last day of operation crowded out the picture in his mind. Instead of the usual shift changing, he visualized everyone, at hearing Germany had surrendered, tossing down his pencil, laying aside his note pad and standing up from his desk. After stretching and saying their few good-byes, they left the room, their hearts heavy. They had lost! Ten years of what? For what? There would be no returning subs. The War and the last watch had ended. Their only task now, was to pack their belongings and find a ride home to a crumpled

Germany. Tuck looked about the control room. It was a darkened, dusty relic of the past, occupied primarily now by some very busy spiders. Tuck wondered if the crew of the remaining U-boat had been given the task of destroying island and simply decided to "hang on" for awhile? Or was there something else?

After marking his drawings, eliminating one third of the possibilities, he went to relieve Jonesy who had taken to sharing the watch with him and Billy Jim. To give them additional relief, Hannah, too, would take a turn on the ridge almost daily. "Helps me save my mind for worrying," she noted, taking her seat beneath the chinaberry tree where McCoy had been buried. Tuck often wondered if they both pitched in to help because of his whining about guard duty. He hoped not.

The second suspect area also turned out to be a fluke, but it did reinforce the knowledge that rank has it privilege. By the labels on the records in one of the rooms set aside for music, Tuck supposed it to be an opera and waltz crowd. A small unassuming bar, complete with fresh, Cuban cigars, crystal glasses and fine, aged French wines stood amid comfortable wing chairs and sofas. The room was fitted with multiple speakers strategically placed to enhance the acoustics. A small, discrete library of moldy, leather bound volumes and current worldwide newspapers took up one wall. An old copy of *Der Spiegel*, lay alongside an Argentina paper with a date of November 10, 1945. The most amazing item he found was *The New York Times* dated May 3, 1946, just a month old, as near as Tuck could figure.

In addition to a passageway to their private beach at the northern end of the lagoon, there were showers, a steam room, dining halls and small conference rooms. A niche off the companionway to the beach contained a small elevator. Tuck's calculations indicated it would service the control room above, leading him to believe the traffic managers were members of the elite. If old movies he had seen were correct, he thought, it was a gentlemen's room and bet himself before the *Nautilus Scan* crew, no lowly, saltwater seaman ever enjoyed such opulence.

Another blue pencil job on his drawings brought into focus the last area he believed physically suitable for a counting house of treasures. And yet it didn't fit his guidelines of accessibility. It was too accessible, too visible. Again and again he reviewed his notes on the bunker. He stewed over every detail he could think of. He shared his findings, thoughts and ideas with Jonesy, Hannah and Billy Jim. "I've been over the bunker with a fine tooth comb. I think, if there is a treasure-trove, it must be in the area we call the 'lump'; that piece of rock containing the picture of Der Fuhrer." He knew Billy Jim wasn't giving him his undivided attention,

GHOST OF THE STREAM

as he appeared preoccupied. Probably working on some secret project to bring about the end of the U-boat, Tuck thought. Nevertheless, none were able to punch holes in his theories.

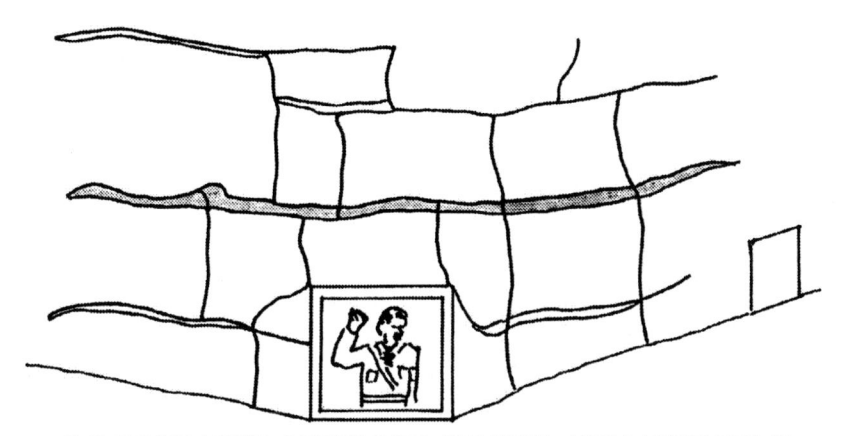

CAMOUFLAGED OVERLOOK: SHADED AREA / THE LUMP

Resisting logic, he began examining the massive block of what appeared to be natural stone. Like so much of the island's construction, it was sculptured concrete, most probably reinforced with steel. He just didn't see how the storehouse could be in such a conspicuous place. How would the loot be moved without everyone being made aware? Where was the opening? He spent hours going over every square inch rubbing the surface with his fingertips, but found nothing. Was it logical to have such a massive block taking up so much space when space was at a premium? Both Jonesy and he agreed it was not needed for construction. That is, it was not necessary for the structural strength of the island. The pens were built with a solid concrete wharf between each, supposedly on bedrock. Every wharf then supported several solid columns, which sustained the cantilevered roof. The ridge was free standing and constructed of much lighter material.

Since there didn't appear to be any opening, how could it be used, for anything? How could such a mass be moved? There were no tracks. No scrapes indicating it had been dragged. Was it a lump simply hiding an opening? Tuck challenged himself again and again. If it's not what it seems? What is it? Is it an illusion? If it's an illusion, how would Houdini see this thing? How would an inventor see it? What is it not? He also knew some of the best "hidden" items were out in the open where everyone could see them. He was reminded of the man who successfully stole wheelbarrows, because the guards were concentrating on the contents in each. He tried to envision the lump with himself inside. How did he get there? How does he get out? Does he need help or can he do it by himself? Receiving no answers, he decided to relieve whoever was on watch and think about something else. "For me to volunteer for guard duty, I must really be desperate," he said to no one in particular.

After a couple of hours on the ridge playing windshield wiper, looking north to south, south to north, he had calmed down a bit. Once more he tackled the problem of the boulder-like mass. It had become an obsession. Salt in a wound. He was satisfied he had searched the surfaces sufficiently. Because of the level of the water table, he had ruled out the ground beneath the structure. That left only the top unexplored.

Reasoning if there was something on top, such as lifting or moving machinery, it needed electrical wiring or hydraulics and a way to service it. And after being relieved, he headed for the operations room, which contained volumes on the construction and maintenance of Mystery Island. Starting with blueprints he tried to identify sites by drawings rather than words since all of it was in German. Any information on the lump was conspicuous by its absence, he discovered. It appeared to be the only site treated in that manner, giving rise to his belief there was something special about it. He had just begun thumbing through the first volume found in a bookcase labeled Konstruktion - Elektrizitat und Aufrechterhaltung when he heard Jonesy screaming "Submarine sighted! Get out! Get out!"

Regardless how they had trained for this moment - like the sinking of the *Nomad* - nothing prepared Tuck for the eventuality. It was as though his body existed elsewhere. He didn't remember being afraid. It was more like being in shock. Like he had just received unexpected devastating news and his brain couldn't comprehend. For a brief moment he was removed from the universe it seemed. The world and everything in it had stopped. He functioned in slow motion. His fingers suddenly had minds of their own, dropping and flicking items he was so desperately trying to put in proper order. Finally recovering, he slipped the books back into place and looked around to make certain everything was where it should be. After a quick turn around the pens, singing out the alarm, he scampered outside and scrambled up the ridge where he was relieved to find the others.

"I seen the sub when it first came into sight 'bout ten, twelve miles away." Hannah appeared nervous at first, but calmed down as she told her story. "At first, I was too scared to move in case they was watchin' me with their perryscope - like you warned us in the bunker, Jonesy." Jonesy smiled and acknowledged Hannah with a nod. "Anyhow, it just kepta comin' and I kepta watchin'. I figured it was doing 'bout ten knots. That meant, at the very least it would take an hour to get here. So I just sets and watched and waited without stirring. Sat like a stone frog, movin' just my eyeballs. Then 'bout four, five miles out, it began sinking. Afore you could say 'squat' it was gone. That's when I knew it was time to get ya'll up here. Did I do right, Jonesy?"

"You did it by the book, Hannah. Just the way it should have been done." Hannah blushed, happy knowing she had contributed. "In fact that was probably a good move to stay put as long as the boat was on the surface. I believe that should be part of the plan in the future. If we're out in the open, stay put." Billy Jim and Tuck nodded their agreement.

"Now, we go into phase two. I suspect the sub has already surfaced below and we'll just have to wait and see. Let's lay low up here and in the recesses until we can determine what their next move is. In the past, they have returned for periods as long as a week and as little as a few hours. Recently, it's usually been for no more than a day or so. They have never led me to believe they were searching for anyone or anything, so I don't know what they're up to. It's more like a brief, friendly visit with a neighbor and then they're gone."

Tuck was curious. "Jonesy how will we know what they're up to? They could leave tonight and we wouldn't know it. We can't very well waltz down there and take a look." Then a thought struck. "On second thought, perhaps we can. By the looks of the control center, it's not used by the sub crew and if it is, they go there by elevator not the stairway I located. If someone was stationed up there in the future we would know what they're up to. We won't be quite so blind. And, if we need to get out in a hurry, we can either take the elevator down to the first level, then scoot out the passageway to the lagoon or lay low in the stairwell."

"Let's explore that idea, Tuck. Any thoughts as to how?"

"I believe it's too late for this visit, but in the future we can be prepared and at the sound of the sub alert, one of us can be assigned there. There are lots of dark corners to hide in. Of course, he'd have to be prepared to stay awhile, you know water and food." As a afterthought, he said, "I'd better be sure the lock is not actually hanging in the hasp on the door and make certain the elevator works. I haven't tried it yet."

"I think hidin' in the stairwell be too risky," Hannah offered. "If"en they come at you from both ends, you gonna be trapped. Seems to me the control room has more risks than we need to take right now."

"Let's give that plan more thought," Jonesy said. "There is an unnecessary gamble. Perhaps we can lessen the odds."

"Well, I hope they don't stay long this time. I got work to do, if we're goin' to send that sardine can to the bottom." Billy Jim was still obsessed with sinking the sub.

Tuck had been so involved with his own project; he really hadn't stayed in touch with what Billy Jim had been doing. "What have you come up with, Billy Jim?"

But, Billy Jim was still on the subject of spying on the U-boat. "I can get in the control room right now." Billy Jim spoke nonchalantly. "Won't have to wait till next time. It's low tide. Alls I got to do is slip over the edge of the roof, swim underwater to alongside the spare sub, roll out and skedaddle up the stairs."

"Billy Jim, if the tide is really low, how are you going to get out of the water? The tides can be extreme here. How are you going to climb out if the dock is eight or ten feet above your head."

"Two ways, Jonesy. I already hung a rope over the side of the dock and as a backup, dangled one from the sub. One way or the other, I can get out, without bein' seen." Hannah smiled, knowing the ability of her son.

"Very inventive, but I don't want to chance our being found out just yet. Let's work on that plan after they leave. We'll be better prepared next time."

"Jonesy, how we gonna know when they do leave?" asked Hannah.

"As a rule they always collect some fresh fruit. If they stay longer than a day or two, they'll be swimming, picking up conchs and lobster in the lagoons. They'll be running around the beach like a bunch of boys just let out of school. Perhaps because of where it is and the effort it takes to get here, I've never seen them this far up on the ridge. That's why I selected it for us to live and hide. They might have explored it when they first got here, but no more. Again, I don't know for certain they have ever left anyone behind." He lifted his shoulders.

"That makes me wonder? How will we know if one of them is still here? And how will we know if he leaves with the boat this time?" Tuck ventured. "Of course, if he is here and chooses not to return we're still 'blind' so to speak."

"I suppose you're right. Hadn't thought of it that way. Regardless, when they disappear from the landscape, we'll know they're leaving, if history repeats. Let's continue our surveillance and once we see them surface and sail away we'll be safe until they return."

"Next time we'll be better prepared for them," Hannah said, slapping her thigh.

"Ain't good enough," Billy Jim remarked. "'Bout the missing seaman, I mean. We's lookin' in the usual haystack ain't we? Unless Jonesy can say for certain 'he's the one', we really can't be sure of anythin'. Think of all the choices. By this here time, the original one can be on board and a dozen more off loaded. If"en we can identify him and he goes back, we'll know he was here. So what? If we don't see him go, we still don't know if he's here or not or ever was. I 'spect if he returns there will be a scene of some sort. Somethin' between rejoicing and a one angry Captain." I can go on, but you see my point?"

Billy Jim, a mite pleased with himself, chose to go, using his plan explained earlier. Silently he crept through the underbrush and down to the dome's edge. Easing over the side and into the cool water he looked around a long while before taking a huge breath, then quietly sinking and swimming with a frog kick to the spare sub. Billy Jim gave no evidence he was anything but at ease with creeping into the enemy's camp. Again Lady Luck would have her way, the sub was still there, but activities indicated it was about to depart. Pulling himself aboard the spare sub, he crouched behind the gun mount and waited. After a quick scan of the pens, he determined there didn't appear to be any unusual excitement. In time, the U-boat dove and sailed away. Ever cautious, Billy Jim remained at his post for some time unaware he was being watched from above. Eventually, he climbed the stairs to the outside signaling the others the sub had gone.

"Ya'll learn it's easier to put toothpaste back in the tube than to git Billy Jim Hamilton to change his mind once it's made up", Hannah offered nonchalantly, dismissing the subject.

That afternoon Tuck was back at one of the stations in the control room, thumbing through the manuals and drawings, comfortable in believing their "visitors" were gone. He felt the secret might be in the room filled with electronics, but none of them knew enough about that field to be able to decipher anything of value. Among the drawings, he happened to catch the words, Der Fuhrer. Once again he came alive to the possibilities of success. Tracing the colored inked lines, he could see the electronic room was not only connected to the drawing tagged with the name of Germany's leader, but the gentlemen's room also. He saw a connection and decided to run it by Jonesy. Before he could get out of the chair he heard...

"Tok." A whisper so low, he wasn't certain he'd heard it. Then again, "Tok." This time he knew, and in spite of the hairs on his neck jumping to attention one by one, he assumed it was Billy Jim teasing and said so. Silence. Standing up, looking about, he saw no one and didn't understand how Billy Jim could've reached the spot where the voice came from without being seen. Tuck knew he could tune out the world when concentrating, but not this time. "Okay, Billy Jim, you've had your fun. You get a home free pass."

"No Beely Jeem, Tok. Can I come forward?" Tuck felt the blood draining to his feet and stammered, "Yes, yeah, I guess so." Looking like a novice trying to play the piano, he searched in vain, the desk and station for a weapon of any sort.

From the dark corner at the opposite end of the control room station, near pen Number One, emerged a small, scraggly youngster, seemingly of Boy Scout age. Still dressed in his navy uniform complete with its ribboned flat hat, he snapped to attention, saluted and presented Tuck his seaman's knife. "Herr Tok, I am deserter and wish to surrender as prisoner of war."

Flabbergasted, Tuck hesitantly took the knife. Then smiling mostly to himself, told his "visitor" to stand at ease. Quickly thinking he should make it official said, "I hereby accept your surrender and place you under the protection of the United States of America." He sat down heavily to think. Finally, he said, "I guess we should put something in writing." He wanted to offer him a chair, but thought differently. After all he was in charge and didn't want to lose his edge, if he had one. After several deep breaths he took one of his pads and began his questioning, trying to keep a straight face. "Name, rank, age and serial number?"

"Oberhaus, Dirk. Seaman apprentice. Thirteen. Fourteen next month. Zwel- zehn-vier-drel!"

"Two, ten, forty-three? Yes?"

"Ja. I mean yes. Sir!"

"Number of your U-boat?" No answer.

"Where are you from? No answer.

"What's your mission?" No answer.

Standing tall again, he spoke. "Name, rank and serial number, all I required to give, Herr Tok, Sir. Geneva Conference 1864."

Stifling a smile, Tuck replied, "Okay, Dirk Oberhaus, I think everything is in order. Have a seat." Remembering a John Wayne western, Tuck pulled out a chair with his foot. Dirk sat. "Now that the paperwork is out of the way, we can visit. Nothing we say will be entered on the paper." He tapped the pad with the eraser end of the pencil. "How do you know my name? Why is it that you speak very good English?"

Dirk hesitated. Squinting and squirming, he looked around the room, not certain he should answer. "I will not be shot for talking to you? Off the cough. As friends?" he added.

"No firing squad, I promise." Tuck tossed his pencil on the desk as confirmation the official part of the inquisition was behind them. "It's off the record. But you must be honest with me. You know the word honor?"

"Yes, I know. Everyone on U-522, I mean *Nautilus Scan,* speaks English not so bad. It was part of Master Plan. I do not know details, but something important for us to do in the States after the war. I know your name from listening at you and Beely Jeem talking in the tall trees. Your German, how do you say 'pricked my ears'? There are German soldiers working in the fields and orchards in your country? You are friends?"

"Yes, I am friends with them and we can be too. Dirk, the war is over and as soon as we get back to the States, we'll get all of this sorted out. I don't believe you can be considered a deserter or POW. Nevertheless, you will not be harmed while under my care. I will protect you with my life." Tuck thought that was rather extreme and wondered if he had sealed his doom with that statement.

"You must promise no turn me over to Beely Jeem or the airman. Beely Jeem cut my throat - with my own knife - then put me on his hook for fish. Airman is a warrior, killing is his business. Both them believe all Germans are Nazis. That not so. All Nazis are German, maybe. I not know, but I know not all Germans, Nazis. The giant woman, I think okay."

"No Billy Jim, no airman, but you must promise me to stay hidden until I can arrange your safety. Understand?" Dirk nodded. "I'll keep your knife for the time being."

"I know this place goot, I find you easy. Not you find me."

"We'll devise a plan. What does Dirk Oberhaus mean? Knife over house?"

"It is a protection signal, not warning or fear."

"Why did you leave the boat? Are things not so good on board?"

"We lose a few almost every good port. Some come back. Some do not. The Kapitan not care as long as he has hands enough to run boat. Oberleutnant has iron in his drawers. No funny stuff." Tapping his temple, "He born Nazi, to Nazis, by Nazis."

"But you picked this drop-off. No town. No people. Why?"

"One day, I see a glass boat on lagoon. Two kids, like me, diving up crabs and lobsters. Having fun time. Seemed like nice place. Quiet. Peaceful. Plenty food and water. I decide to stay. Much better than sailing with no future. Maybe much more lucky than my great uncle, Diederdom, who left Germany for the States in 1912 on board the *Titanic*.

Tuck blanched, but recovered quickly. "So what do you do at these other ports?"

"A little salvage work, maybe. Moving big-shots Nazis from place to place underwater. Kapitan says they just ahead of hangman." He indicated hanging himself. "Many times not underwater. Most people not care who going anyplace. Biggest job, most money, moving drugs to Cuba and Central America.

"And it winds up in New York, yes? Tuck questioned.

Dirk offered no explanation or comment. "Island university paid us for a while to look for Lost Atlantis. Crazy professor with much money to fire. Maybe get to States one of these days. We been off Key West and Miami. Looks okay through periscope. Manual says tall, pointed structure, in Miami, County Court House."

Tuck smiled. "We have a saying in my country: 'It's a small world.' The name of one of my neighbors, a government official, is on that pointed building."

After a pause: "We be friends in States, Tok?"

"Of course, but tell me, why does the boat keep coming back here? Surely you can get food elsewhere.

"Only reason we come back here is for repair. The sub, in pen nine, is now our 'milk cow' for spare parts." Tuck smiled at the irony "Sometimes we close anyway, so we stop for fresh food, parts and relax. Not need stay long time

. One of these days we never set foot on this place. I knew the times coming back getting short, so I jumped ship. Now I under the protection of US of A."

"Dirk, how well do you know the island? I mean can you stay hidden until I can square everything? Food and water is no problem."

"I watch Beely Jeem swim in and hide on other sub to watch my boat sail away. He is very brave, but foolish to do that. With gun, I could kill him. Easy. I be very scared to enter enemy's camp alone. He never knew I here. I have watched and listened to all of you for long time. I can hide, okay."

Tuck was dismayed at knowing they had been watched so closely, but did not miss the irony that Dirk had done the exact same thing as Billy Jim. "Yes, Dirk, you can hide well. Are you alone?"

"Yes. By myself."

"Are there any guns here?"

"In armory!" He said excitedly. "You want me to get you gun?"

"No. And promise me you will not get guns. It will only complicate things."

Dirk's look told Tuck he didn't understand.

"Confuse. Verwir'ren, I think."

"Okay, Tok, I understand. No guns. We are friends, Yes?"

"Yes. Friends. For the time being, I want you to go to the airplane up on the ridge. You know where I mean?"

"Yes. I been there, some times."

"Get inside the plane at night. There is a compartment under the middle seat where the bombardier would arm the torpedoes and fire a machine gun. Stay there at nights until I come for you. I suspect you can stay ahead of us during the day. Do you understand that I'm trusting you?"

Dirk nodded. Tuck was impressed, in awe really, with Dirk's conduct. He seemed mature for his age and had an ability to handle and understand things. His demeanor demonstrated a control that Tuck rarely felt. He's someone to emulate, Tuck thought, especially his composure. "Do you have a family, Dirk?"

"Yes, we are - were - eight: Oma, Opa, parents, older brother, two younger sisters. Opa, Papa, brothers dead. All killed in war. Others...don't know."

"Were you a 'Hitler Youth'?"

"Ja. From age six. No choice really. It was expected of all loyal Germans. Families might not like losing children, but what Hitler want, Hitler got!" Tuck thought there was bitterness in his voice. "And most thought there was something goot about what was planned. It just went verruck along the way."

"Crazy?"

"Yes, crazy. No more made sense."

Knowing something of separation, Tuck sketchily shared his childhood experience and continued, "What was it like? The Youth Movement, I mean?"

"Quite good. It was like all time fun in beginning: playing war, spies, Secret Service. Then came lessons, drills, marching and all together work projects."

"Work projects?"

"Like your Civilian Conservation Corp. At first, I very proud to be chosen. Not know soon everybody be chosen. No choice no honor to be selected. Time came when we no longer go home - went to camp cabins instead. Very soon family replaced with friends our own age, soldiers and instructors. They became family and soon you involved in studies and projects and you forget old family." Tuck could see how it happened and he was sorry for Dirk's lost childhood, but could, in a fashion, relate.

For a period both just sat observing the other, mulling over what they had just learned.

Believe it's still June

Comparing our childhoods sent my mind and memory reeling. I can hardly believe so much has happened to a little kid from Kendall in so few years. I've never dwelled on my life as a " fruit tramp", but since Dirk and Billy Jim and others have asked about that life perhaps talking about it will serve some purpose. (Like getting my mind off the treasure hunt.)

Most questions center on our personal lives. First, migrant kids grow up fast...in every respect. Since most members in a family live in one or two rooms, a tarpaper shack or under a tarp stretched between trees we learn quickly about the human body: how it looks, sounds and all of its functions.

Our toilets are usually the woods or an outhouse complete with a Sears and Roebuck *catalog. For baths it's usually a nearby pond, lake or stream. If we're lucky the camp might have a garden hose hanging from a tree limb - but no stall. There is always the admonishment not to use too much water or the rent goes up.*

The furniture a camp supplies is sparse: usually because the families before made off with the "good stuff". (Of course they're not planning to return because the owner will make them pay for it or have them arrested.) A table might be up-ended crates with a sign- board for a top. The chairs would be citrus or vegetable crates (lugs). A bed could be a 2x4 frame with small mesh chicken wire stretched across it. The mattress: a blanket or ticking of sort. Naturally there is always the possibility of bed bugs. Many houses have no flooring. Magazines, newspapers and rags help keep your feet off the raw earth. Rats, dirt and despair are constant roommates.

Children are not young very long. They develop their independence and toughness early. Bad manners or no manners are the norm. Petty crimes are expected: after all ain't the "man" out to get what he can without fair pay? The Golden Rule – "do dem furst". Formal education is secondary to everything. We see our future to be no farther away than the end of a row of vegetables or the last tree in the grove. Produce is our calendar. (I notice I have slipped into first person. Have I really escaped?)

Early parenthood – most often without a marriage - is prominent; thought to be a "way out". Unfortunately it becomes a life sentence to continue as before. We seem unable to learn a basic truth: a person that cannot provide for himself cannot properly care for a child. Children cannot raise children. Consequently older women become "mothers" again or for the first time, because the younger women are needed in the fields. It's an unbroken cycle. Kids know their grandmother better than their mothers and many times don't know their fathers at all.

Transportation is the lifeblood of the next job. Most migrant groups have excellent mechanics in their midst. Good enough to make a living and stay in one location. My dad is a good mechanic and responsible enough to always have a decent car or truck. "Gotta be in so and so on such and such a date. No excuses." It's a way of life! A mind set! (Can you imagine - while on the road - crawling underneath a disabled car, dropping the oil pan, disconnecting a piston rod, putting the pan back, adding oil and continuing?)

We're thought of as "passed-by humanity". Easily labeled as gypsies, trailer trash and so forth. We do, however, provide a service that most Americans will not do: stooped labor. And it costs us our dignity, sense of worth, our health and keeps us on the very edge of hell. I'm not making excuses because we continue to make bad choices. Perhaps there's a middle ground?

There seems to be a universal belief that migrants have no feelings. Nothing could be further from the truth. Oh, they may not be as visible as the movies indicate – flowers, candy and glittering gifts – but they're very real.

I wish I could convey to you a scene I saw not long ago. A young nigra girl was dragging her dead dog home. Her heart was broken, her cheeks bathed in

> *tears. Coming to meet her, on the run, was her Mama with her arms outstretched, ready to wrap her hurting child into the care she knew so well. It wasn't the dead dog being dragged unceremoniously home and it wasn't the thoughtless driver that didn't stop. It was her "chile" hurting beyond understanding, beyond comprehension and needing a mama's comfort...a mama's love. The only thing she had to give.*
>
> *Lordy, I'm perspiring, emotionally spent. I may return – there's more. I may not.*

Tuck went to Jonesy with his findings about the treasure hunt. He tried to act as if nothing out of the ordinary had taken place. Explaining his findings, Jonesy answered, "You're extrapolating." Tuck's quizzical look came from not understanding the meaning of the word, plus not knowing if Jonesy had somehow found him out.

He bluffed with, "What?"

"Extrapolating means reaching conclusions by imagining the results based on what you know or observed."

Tuck exhaled softly. It was a new word for him, but he took it to mean he was on the right track and became more comfortable as he continued showing Jonesy the drawings he had found and explaining his thoughts about the lump. Jonesy agreed it might be governed by electronics and controlled in the gentlemen's room. But that was as far as he'd go. Tuck thought Jonesy wanted him to solve his own dilemma.

Before he returned to the search, Tuck sought out Billy Jim for his thinking about the possibility of a Nazi being on the island. "If I find him. He's mine," Billy Jim remarked, deftly throwing his knife into a nearby tree. "He'll be as dead as Henry Lee if I have my way."

"No trial by jury? No justice; just revenge?"

"Call it what you want, Tuck." He retrieved his knife, flipped it into the air and stood looking up at it, without moving, until it dropped point first into the earth between his feet.

"What if he's as pitiful as Jonesy was when we first found him?"

"Jonesy is one of us. Big difference. Why all the questions, Tuck? You find yourself a stinkin', little Hun?"

"Just wondering. I have a lot of time to think while I'm searching for the treasure and on watch." After a thoughtful pause, he asked Billy Jim another question. "Do you know what the C.C.C. stands for?"

"I give up, what?"

"I don't know either. Just wondering."

Again, in his puzzlement, Billy Jim shook his head. "You wonder too much, Tuckster."

Tuck returned to the "drawing board" with difficulty, thinking about Dirk and how he was deceiving his friends. He excused himself believing it was in their best interest at the time.

Outlining the three structures, the lump, gentlemen's room and the electronics room, placing each in proper perspective, he could see a common thread connecting them. Having stepped off the dimensions, it was obvious the lump was a mass of greater proportions than could be explained by its use. It appeared to house only the elevator and a small portion of the passageway to the lagoon. Growing weary, he decided to extrapolate in comfort by taking his homework to the gentlemen's room. Settling himself in a very comfortable chair complete with footstool, he lay back and thought about the removal of a single bar of gold.

This is what he came up with. A U-boat making a clandestine run to Brazil, for example, calls in a need for repairs or fuel. Through codes, the traffic manager knows it is a ruse and what the sub expects. By taking the elevator to the gentlemen's room, opening the safe, so to speak. "Wait a minute," Tuck shouted. "That's it! There's no treasure room. In the beginning the Nazis weren't planning to stash loot. No need. As conquerors of the world, they would have everything. So the only secure place they needed here would be used for payroll, expense money, secret documents and so forth." Okay Tuckster, he thought, the treasure-trove and the safe might be in the same place, but the safe wouldn't be large enough for all the loot they'd supposedly taken. Reassuring himself to search for the safe but not to expect it to hold the treasure, he picked up where he'd left off with one exception: be on the lookout for new construction!

He believed the manager would eventually be responsible for preparing the shipment to be placed on the sub. Those privileged to the operation would very likely be included in the "membership" of the gentlemen's room and could be summoned quickly and quietly. Even something as large as a piece of artwork could be crated, identified with any kind of a stencil and given to the ship's chandler for placement on the sub. He closed his eyes and began visualizing the transaction step by step.

After some time of playing a gentleman of class, he was comfortable with his description of what could have happened with the exception of the actual "grand opening".

Again he ruled out everyone enjoying the gentlemen's room was in on the project. It would have to be a very select few as secrecy was of utmost importance. "Then Tuck, where's the weakness? Where's the 'loot'?" he said aloud. If in fact, the lump was the safe, and it could be opened by a switch, wouldn't the switch be concealed? And wouldn't the opening to the treasure room be in an out-of-way place? Of course the $64 question was how? If he could answer the where, the how would follow.

In the end, he decided the "where" must be above the lump. Taking the elevator once more to the control room, he began his search in earnest. He reasoned if the electronics they had discovered could change the earth's gravity, it could move something like the lump with ease. Believing the switch would be more difficult to find, he began again looking for the evidence of an opening. Since there were no need of wires, he also concentrated on finding an antenna.

Initially, he thought the lump might be lifted as a bell might be or the outside box lifted away from an inside box. Neither proved feasible, as there was no room above the lump for such a lift. Additionally the lump could not be lifted in secret. Finally, he settled on a door opening inward, perhaps hinged at the top or a slide-in-the-wall panel. Even if he found the switch, he was not sure it would be operative. Perhaps the best solution was to be in a position to observe the operation the next time the U-boat arrived. In his heart, he knew he couldn't wait and began thinking about an area where the entire lump could be opened in secrecy.

"Talk it through, Tuck," he said. "There's an answer, you just have to find it." He sat down in a thick padded chair overlooking the pens scribbling notes as he thought. "Okay, I'm a traffic controller of subs. In addition I'm in charge of payroll and contraband distribution. I received a coded message from a U-boat to prepare a shipment. What do I do? Would there be paperwork of any sort? Probably not. It wouldn't help me if there were. A map of what sub went where in South America might provide a paper trail, but wouldn't help me locate the treasure. Because of the distrust among the Nazis during the last years of the war, someone would want to know who took what and when. Find the records? Find the gold? Possibly? Okay, what's next?

"The master would set into motion what needed to be done. He summons a conspirator to prepare a shipment. The aide leaves the control room, takes the elevator down to... Oh, my gosh!" He yelled. "That must be it!" Jumping up from his chair, he grabbed his flashlight and took off at a run for the elevator. The control panel contained three buttons: 1, 2 and door open. He stabbed button one. While the car moved downward, he began pecking and tapping on the walls of the elevator. None appeared hollow or moved when he tried sliding them. The door opened and he grabbed a chair, stood on it and lifted the ceiling panels but saw only the lift cables and shaft above. He stamped on the floor and found a solid footing.

What he was looking for was a way into the lump from the elevator. It was the proper height, location and afforded the security and secrecy he felt necessary. If you press an elevator button and it doesn't come to you, you assume it's being used elsewhere, he thought. Well suppose it was being used to collect a shipment or prepare payroll. "Great, Tuck," he said. "You believe you have the 'where' and 'how'. Now what?" He didn't know and stabbed the number one button. Except for the door closing, nothing happened. It was then, he realized, he was still on the first level and needed the control room, so quickly he pressed number two. For a brief period there was no response and he became concerned. He looked about. After a few seconds of nothing happening, the atmosphere in the car changed from excitement to a controlled calm charged with anxiety. Rapidly his mind raced like the wind through a canyon!

He believed they were, with the exception of Dirk, alone on the island, but still he was an intruder and quickly imagined being trapped in the elevator with Dirk or someone else controlling his destiny. He was consumed with a sense of urgency, certain the door was about to open to a fate he could only imagine. Driven by fear, he admonished himself for trusting a Nazi. Suddenly, instead of the car moving upwards, it moved down. Down very slowly. He exhaled a breath he had been holding. Fearing he was about to drown, he was desperate and dropped to his knees searching for evidence of leaking water, but found none. While he was aware he might be on the threshold of something deadly, his mind also told him it might be something of value. Regardless, he wanted out! Now! But he also wanted to continue. He was a moth to the flame, a lark to a berry patch.

Common sense prevailed and he began pounding and kicking on the elevator walls, screaming and yelling as loud as he could. He didn't care who heard, even a sub full of Germans would be better than plunging into a watery cavity, locked in a phone booth sized coffin. The adrenaline flowed. He screamed with a sense of urgency!

"Help! Help me!" he cried. "Dirk, if you're there, get me outta here." Again he beat his fists against the walls knowing he faced certain death. Driven by fear, he punched control buttons. Over and over, he rammed his shoulder against the panels and stomped the floor. He hollered! He screamed! He begged for release! He remembered a playmate that had died in an abandoned refrigerator. Suffocated! Buried alive! He imagined how she must have died, fighting for a tiny taste of fresh air. He recalled how he wound up on the bottom of a pile of buddies during a football game. The pressure on his chest was tremendous. He couldn't breathe. Could not get a breath! He was in a body cast of fear. Every muscle, emotion, thought and nerve ending hurled his body and mind towards a paralysis. He panicked and with all his might squirmed, pulled, punched and dug his way to freedom. Tuck knew the entire episode was mental, but it affected him physically and emotionally.

For a brief period Tuck was resigned to the inevitability of death and it wasn't until he nearly passed out that he realized the car had stopped. After inhaling and exhaling several times, he calmed down a bit and, after surveying his situation, began acting like a rational person.

Although he believed the elevator had malfunctioned, he did think it strange the drive motor continued whirring. If he were entering the water, the electric motors would short out. He didn't think the box he was in, had traveled but a few feet before stopping. Everything was still, save his pounding heart and heavy breathing. Perspiration poured down his forehead and into his eyes. Wiping his face, he searched the four walls. Nothing unusual. The lights were still on, but no water was seeping in around his ankles. Perhaps he had only imagined moving downward, he thought. Almost as a natural selection, he pressed the door open button. The lights in the car blinked. His heart jumped. He heard a hydraulic pump kick in. Very slowly, the side panel, hinged at the top, opened into a honeycomb of cave-like rooms, dimly illuminated by the elevator light. The stale, stagnant air and pungent odor escaping through his opening the door, made him gag; hinting the room had been sealed for some time.

Playing his flashlight around the rooms he looked for a light switch, but finding neither a switch nor bulb, he assumed there was no electric power. In one wall just outside the elevator, there stood a huge safe complete with large hand wheel and a set of tumblers. His excitement heightened! The rooms appeared to be an addition as they were unfinished and illustrating sloppy block laying. An afterthought he supposed. He began roaming from one room to the next waving his light about, his mind and body tingling with excitement. As before, he wanted to run, but didn't want to. It was like a dream you wanted to end, but would have been disappointed if it had. The walls dripped of drama, evil and wickedness. The mood was dark and vile. Initially all he saw were stacks of slatted crates, heavy-duty ammunition boxes, wooden trunks and aluminum tubes of various sizes. However, the darkness began to fade due to the opened elevator door. The rooms began to glitter and sparkle from the beam of his light reflecting off opened chests of jewels, gems, pearls, diamonds and coins. Treasures and riches beyond explanation!

Bolstered by his new-found wealth, he let out a scream his great grandfather, Mantooth, would have been proud of. "Yu-yu-ya-ya-yea-yea-YAAAA." He dashed from one crate to the next, touching and fondling one piece after another. He even dug his hands into the chest of coins allowing them to slowly slip and fall through his fingers as though he might be washing his hands. Draping himself with necklaces, bracelets, jewels and gems, he imagined himself an overly decorated Christmas tree. "This is better than any pirate treasure," he screamed to no one and everyone. Continuing his search, he dashed about from chest to chest and room to room. Filling one room was a collection of golden framed paintings, tapestries, carpeting and fine clothing. Another contained antique firearms, knives, weapons and a brass cannon. A giant size Nazi banner, made of fine wool, covered one entire wall of another.

As he picked his way among the breathtaking hoard of treasures he could never have imagined, he learned he'd need tools to open many of the crates and boxes to discover their contents. While he worked his way towards the elevator, he backed away from one of the smaller halls and bumped into something causing a clatter. Thinking it might be a valuable vase or precious antique, he turned around making a grab for what he had hit, at the same time shining his light in its direction.

"Yeowee!" he screamed, jumping back, tossing the object and his light into the air. Wiping his hands on his pant legs, he picked up the light. The blood rushed from his head as a threatening blackness encompassed his consciousness. He grabbed at a table to steady himself. There on a golden high back chair, sat the remains of the most macabre idol possible: a fully dressed, skeleton, in a German officer's dress uniform, minus the skull and cap he had blindly grabbed in the dark.

Upon closer inspection he observed many of the bones had collapsed when he bumped into it. The brightly colored uniform, now with little form, drooped loosely over the chair. An empty pant leg was draped haughtily over the arm of the throne. Standing beneath it, rested an old dried out boot with its toe turned slightly upward. It contained the bones of a foot and the larger leg bone, sticking up like a spoon in a cup. Around what remained of its bony neck, was draped a monocle and a heavy golden chain containing a pendant fashioned in the shape of a three cornered billowing sail. It was about two inches wide at its base and three inches high. Bouncing it in his hand, he estimated its weight equal to a large hen egg. In the center was a scroll of either white gold or platinum and yellow gold on an emerald background, surrounded by twenty-two diamonds, each the size of a green pea. It was a simple design, but it's mere size and workmanship made it far and beyond the most beautiful piece of jewelry he had seen in the room. Perhaps the dead man had agreed, he thought. Tuck knew it violated Jonesy's rules, but he wanted to take it as evidence and after replacing the other pieces, put it in the hip pocket of his jeans with a reminder to replace it when he came back for the inventory.

Tuck was surprised at his calmness or was it more of a letdown, he wondered? After all he had experienced every physical and mental emotion on his chart. He had assumed once he found the treasure, he would experience all sorts of feelings, joy, jubilation, exultation and excitement. Instead, what he really felt was satisfaction, a feeling of success. Triumph. Like an excellent term paper or that he had run a good race and won. Perhaps the anticipation of the hunt is more exciting than the find itself. In any event, he was quite pleased with such a secured future and began thinking about all the tomorrows.

In his exuberance, he had lost track of time and knew he should be getting back to the others. Stepping into the elevator he expected to return to the surface by simply reversing his mistake going down. He surmised the Nazis had rigged the elevator to react to a combination of one minus two equals minus one, or in this case, the bargain basement. While he waited for the mechanism to respond, he scolded himself for initially not bothering to look below the lump, simply because it was below the water table. I should have realized a problem of underground water would not have fazed the architects of Mystery Island, he thought.

After a few seconds of standing in the car, nothing had happened. No pump noises. No whirring drive motor sounds. Once again he became alarmed. More than alarmed. He was flat out scared. Scared to death. Again he felt that common chill accompanying fear, like the earth was closing down on him. Now what, he thought. He wondered if the Nazi, sitting on the throne, was a victim of a faulty elevator, or something worse. Perhaps a warning to other thieves crossed his mind. "Yuck," he cried, but walked over to the skull and illuminated it with his light. There between its eye sockets, slightly above the bridge of the nose was a hole the size of a small caliber bullet. Turning the head with his foot he saw a sizable hole where the bullet had exited. So much for the faulty elevator theory, he thought and wondered what lay ahead for him at the elevator landing. That is, if he ever got to the landing.

Stepping back into the car he quickly punched in a combination of floor numbers followed by a "door open". Nothing. Before the images of a ghost settled in, he tried another. Once more, nothing.

"Wait a minute," he said. "I'm trying to close the door in order to move the car." Does a "door open" cancel out a command to move?" he wondered. He tried a different combination of numbers and waited. Silence. "The reverse of open is close, but there's no close button. Now what?" he cried aloud in exasperation.

He pulled down on the door down. It was locked in an open position. He searched for hidden buttons, levers and switches. No luck. Finally it dawned on him. In his agitated state, he had failed to recognize the control panel was different. There was no "door close" key. Of the few elevators he had been in, all had both open and close choices. Why not this one? He thought. Perhaps it's a safeguard to keep the elevator from closing and leaving while someone was in the vault. So, it must be controlled from down here. A simple extension of the switch wires would do the trick. But where to put the switch so it's handy and not too obvious was the challenge.

He cast about for a large box. Finding one, he dragged it in the elevator. Standing on the crate, he pushed away the ceiling sheathing atop the control panel. His light found two wires that extended across the car and disappeared into the movable partition. He jumped down and searched the edges of the wall. Presto! There it was, a small toggle switch embedded in a seam that he was certain controlled the closing of the door. Replacing the crate, he flipped the switch and stepped back into the elevator. Immediately the door swung down and locked into place. He did his mathematical button pushing and amid the familiar sounds, the car began its brief journey to the surface. The door finally opened. There was no Dirk. No Nazis. Relieved, he exited; flopping down in the first chair he came to in the gentlemen's room and knew what it meant to be "a limp noodle". He was exhausted, mentally and physically.

To recover from the excitement of finding the treasure, Tuck walked the ridge to the airplane. Quietly, he tapped on the plane's belly and whispered. "Dirk. It's me Tuck."

No response. After several more tries at both sides of the plane, he climbed up and looked into the cockpit. "Dirk, you in there?"

"No, I over here." It was Dirk just coming up from the point. "I go for a swim."

"Whew, I'm glad to see you". Initially, he wondered if Billy Jim had found Dirk and was holding him someplace or something worse. "I just want you here tonight, in case I need you. Okay?"

"I be here."

At first no one believed he had found the treasure-trove. Mostly they just passed his information off as a joke with a "yeah, yeah" and continued at their tasks. He supposed he did sound like the kid who cried wolf, trying to explain all the rigmarole he had gone through. But, what the heck, he was so happy for everyone, he just wanted to share his good news. In any event, he decided on another way to introduce the subject.

They were holding their usual nightly review. Billy Jim told he had located the armory, busted the lock open and reported what he had found. "'Bout anything we need is in there. Small arms, all kinds of ammo, rifles with scopes, grenades, floating mines and explosives. Jest tell me what you want to take out that sub and I'll get it fer you." Tuck threw a couple of sticks of wood on the fire until a small blaze appeared.

Hannah said she had collected and prepared conchs for tomorrow. "They's soaking in lime juice this very minute. Be tender as cotton candy for tomorry's supper."

Tuck tossed more pieces of wood on the fire until Jonesy said he thought it was bright enough. "Don't want to advertise our presence, now do we?"

"What did you do today, Tuck?" It was Billy Jim with a smirk on his face.

"Oh, my usual, hunting for fame and fortune," he teased. "Jonesy, do you know when the Geneva Convention agreement was signed?"

"No. It has been revised since its original signing, I know. Why?"

"No reason. How about the C.C.C.?"

"Civilian Conservation Corp. Why all the questions, Tuck?"

Before Tuck could evade an answer, Hannah sat up and stared at whatever was reflecting from the fire in the sand at her feet. Taking a small stick she raked at it and it moved almost snake-like making her jump backwards. Jonesy and Billy Jim became interested also and moved for a better view. By this time Hannah had picked the pendant up with her stick so all could see. She sputtered, "Glory be. Would you look at what I found?"

Jonesy glanced at Tuck who had not moved, but was grinning; looking like he'd swallowed a light bulb. After a brief explanation, it was only then they were convinced Tuck had indeed, found the treasure-trove.

Everyone knew the jewelry had to be replaced and decided tomorrow would be an ideal time to inventory the treasure and explain how the elevator worked.

As they began their tour they agreed the four of them together, could gamble thirty minutes in the bunker. "But, no longer," Jonesy cautioned, setting his watch. After a closer look at the gentlemen's room, and the private entrance to the lagoon, they entered the elevator for a ride to the second level and the control booths. Tuck imagined they might have felt the same as he did, when he stepped for the first time into the car and pushed a button. He assured them he had "done this before", but didn't think he offered much comfort, especially to Hannah and Billy Jim who, like himself, had limited experiences with elevators and escalators. He detailed exactly what he was doing and without delay he was showing them a bird's-eye view of the sub pens, as a traffic manager would have seen them. He also scanned the room for a glimpse of Dirk, his mind still unsettled that he didn't get to explain his presence at last night's gathering. Satisfied Dirk was not in the control room, he hurried the group along for the best was yet to come. Again, he explained the combination used to reach the treasure house. Magically, the door opened and they were staring at a cache of treasure none of them had seen outside a museum or "pretties" displayed in the *Sears and Roebuck* catalog.

After a preliminary inspection of the chambers and a look at the horrendous watch guard on the golden throne, they set about making a hurried list of what they had found. The cylinders held rolled up artwork of the Old Masters according to Jonesy. They did not attempt to remove them for fear they might be damaged. The heavy ammo cases contained gold bars, while the slatted crated housed framed masterpieces. The lighter cases were filled with currency: Swiss francs, counterfeit US dollars and British pound sterling and Reichmarks.

Jonesy told them the Swiss francs were the only thing of value. "They wisely didn't steal any monies from their allies. The lira and yen issued by those governments are as worthless as their own money."

Even though Jonesy reminded them the treasure wasn't theirs, each was already engaged in how they'd spend their share. Tuck asked Jonesy what he thought about a picture of the Der Fuhrer wearing the Knights' Cross he didn't earn, marking the location of stolen riches.

"Perhaps lies begets lies or fact is stranger than fiction," he said, walking away.

"How 'bout many a truth is told in lies?" Billy Jim offered.

THE PENDANT

Is it still June?

Marvel of marvels. I met my first Nazi. It wasn't like I thought it would be. I suppose I thought he'd be a composite of all the editorial cartoons I'd seen during the war. Maybe a Hitler look alike. Little paintbrush moustache, lock of hair over one eye and an arm perpetually extended in a Heil salute. By the same token, every Jap would have slits for eyes, buck teeth and wear oversized, black horn-rim glasses with thick lenses.

By contrast, Dirk was a kid like Billy Jim and me. He appeared more mature and self-assured, but there was no apparent animosity between us. Just two teenagers getting acquainted at the first day of school. There was a thread of similarity in our childhoods, but some madman didn't force mine. And my country wasn't decimated. No sirree bob, I was the luckier of the two. I hope we'll continue to be friends once we get to the U.S. of A. Meanwhile perhaps he'll help me with my German.

VIII
Target: U-boat

"This here's the forward torpedo room and crew's quarters," Billy Jim said, undogging the hatch so they could look inside the dim compartment. "One just like it all the way aft. No torpedoes in either one. Must have used them before the war was over or transferred them to other boats. Anyway, the biggest weapon on board is the deck gun and there's plenty of ammo for it." Billy Jim was walking Jonesy and Tuck through the spare submarine, identifying the various compartments and components while Hannah was on watch.

"Movin' along." They walked slowly aft from the bow while Billy Jim kept at his running commentary, stopping briefly on occasion. "This here area's a little nicer so I 'spect it's for petty officers and chiefs." Pulling back a curtain, he announced, "Officers' quarters. Wardroom. And this nicest pigeonhole, is for the Old Man." Across the passageway, Billy Jim laid his hand on the radio console. "It's probably the only radio on the island. Over yonder is the sonar."

It was obvious he'd been here before, studying the layout. Jonesy and Tuck were impressed with his knowledge of the U-boat, as they followed him from stem to stern, watching him point out the many cubicles, cubbyholes and compartments. "Thet's a sea cock, used to scuttle the boat if necessary," he said, nudging the large valve with his shoe. "There's three on board. Open 'em and it's, 'Hello Davy's Locker.'" He was in rare form today, doing a mock, comical dive with hands over his head. "I 'spect there's a time bomb on board to hep with the sinkin'."

While still amidships, he called over his shoulder and pointed as he spoke. "Control Room - the brains of the boat. Directly above is the conning tower, you know, the pilothouse. Above that is the watch deck or bridge. Ya'll probably know that the entire structure above the deck is known as the 'sail'." They moved further aft. Touching a familiar looking engine and pointing at another, he continued. "Diesels. Over there, air compressor and then the electric motors complete with batteries. Another torpedo room and crews quarters at the stern.

"Oh yeah, there's also an inflatable raft stored back yonder, but don't know if it's any good. You know how wartime rubber was."

One after another, they ducked and stepped through hatches, crabbing by tubes, pipes, levers, valves, wheels, cranks and gauges, each with a specific purpose and familiar to every hand aboard. Many were labeled with words Tuck recognized and could interpret: "Sprechen Maschinen or speaking tube to the engine room. Wasser - water - gauges. Kommandant would be the commander. Here's an interesting one," he said pointing to a brass plate. Unterseeboote. Almost self-explanatory: Under - sea - boat. Submarine." The name Krupp, Germany's largest armament and munitions maker, was also prominently displayed.

There was the occasional photograph of a girlfriend, family, landscape or home. Billy Jim stopped and stared at the photo of a child taped to a locker door. She appeared to be about eight years old. Resting her cheek on her folded hands, she gazed into space with a pleading, far away look in her eyes. In a child's hand, she had written, 'Ich Liebe Sie, Vater, Brigitte'. The picture brought a lump to Billy Jim's throat remembering a baby sister lost.

A dog-eared chart, illustrating many entries and an equal number of corresponding erasures, lay on the plotter in the control room. Here and there was a discarded hat, shoe, book, letter or towel; all left behind, in what appeared to be a hasty departure.

U-923 SPARE SUB

The sub, a late entry into the war, was cramped, dark, smelly and wet. It stretched the imagination to see how fifty men could be squeezed into such a tiny space and expected to do their jobs with speed and proficiency. Tuck and Jonesy had already cracked their heads a half dozen times and barked both shins trying to maneuver, at a slow walk, the maze of hatches and bulkheads. Jonesy finally admitted, "Imagine doing this tour on the run. If I were a regular crew member, I'd be a permanent patient at sick bay." Tuck, rubbing his knee, grinned and shook his head in agreement.

Back in the control room, relaxing on one of the stools used by those controlling the sub's movements, Tuck reflected on what it must have been like underway. "Can you believe the conditions of this thing while at sea? Inadequate ventilation with hot, sweaty, unwashed men sharing bunks. Two toilets for fifty men. At best, after a couple of weeks out, nothing to eat but canned food and hard, moldy bread."

"That bread was called 'white rabbits'," Jonesy offered. "Because it would become so hoary with mold."

Tuck and Billy Jim giggled. Tuck continued to - extrapolate. "Then add to all of that discomfort by throwing in regular depth charge attacks, the fear and stress of torpedo runs, flared tempers and contrary equipment. You have to wonder why so many volunteered for such hazardous service."

"But they did, Tuck, 40,000 brave, reckless, young men went to sea under these conditions. And three fourths never returned." For a long moment, Jonesy stared pensively.

"Maybe the excitement of that devil-may-care atmosphere and the 'glamour' associated with the U-boat, was the draw," he added. "Fighter pilots have that image. Of course, a good Captain could make the difference between a dedicated crew and one that is undisciplined."

Tuck had been aboard the U-boat but a short while, but he could already feel or imagine the mystique. He thought of the last skipper, Captain Wilhelm Buchholz, according to the log on his desk, and envisioned him roaming the decks. He wanted him to be another Captain Bannerman, quick with a word of encouragement or a "thanks" for a job well done. A knowing smile or a comforting pat on the back, would be his customary behavior towards a frightened seaman, as they waited out a barrage of depth charges. Such a skipper would have been regarded as a "jolly pirate". He would have had the respect and admiration of his crew and in turn they would have followed him to the death. And many probably did.

"Billy Jim, I'm astounded you know so much about the boat, but I wonder why you've gone to all this trouble. After all, this isn't the sub you're after, is it?"

Billy Jim looked at Jonesy with that crooked smile and glint in his eyes Tuck had come to recognize as, 'chain pulling time'. "Why, Jonesy, I thought you'd learned by now what I'd come up with. Mortal combat. We's gonna tie a couple of them mines from the armory to the bow. Ma can run any diesel ever built. I got you on the helm, Tuck on the throttles and me up on the bridge givin' directions." Billy Jim walked around the control room, gesturing with both hands, in full charge. "We get lined up on the other boat, then it's full speed ahead for a ram. I'll be able to get off pretty easily and once Ma gets the engines running properly, she can jump, too. Naturally, I hope you and Tuck can set the course and speed and get off, as well. But in the end, it's gonna be one heck of a blast! Kerboom! Kerboom!" Intertwining his fingers, Billy Jim twisted his hands as if trying to pull them apart. "Both subs tangled together in a mess of metal, explosions, smoke and fire, sinking with all hands on board. They won't know what hit 'em. Nothin' left, but a little hair, teeth and eyeballs. Pretty neat, even if I do say so myself. What'cha think Jonesy?"

Jonesy started sputtering and backing away from Billy Jim, bumping into a gauge measuring wasser depth in meters. Putting his hands to his mouth, his eyes the size of half dollars, he tried registering his protest, but all he could get out was, "You... You..."

Tuck couldn't stand it any longer and let Jonesy off the hook. He took it well and Tuck thought he saw another little breakthrough in Jonesy's normal reserve. Jonesy managed, "Well, I never..."

Billy Jim was enjoying it all and the twinkle of success in his eyes indicated they would again see his unusual sense of humor. "Okay, Billy Jim. You've had your fun. What have you decided? Or have you given up the idea of destroying the sub?"

"Jonesy, to answer your question, the more I know 'bout the sub the better plans I can make. Dress rehearsal, you know." He climbed up the ladder through the conning tower, indicating they should follow. Up on the bridge, pushing aside a tattered tarpaulin rigged by lookouts against salt spray, Billy Jim threw up his hands, jumped back, exclaiming! "What the dickens is this here?" There stood Dirk, holding a spanner wrench at the ready. Visibly shaken, at being discovered, he seemed to wilt, with a look of fear stamped across his face.

Dropping the wrench, then saluting, he mouthed, "I am Dirk Oberhaus, Beely Jeem, a prisoner of war under the...the sansuwary of..."

Quickly, Tuck stepped between Billy Jim and Dirk and finished the sentence. "Sanctuary and protection of one Tuck Fryer." Putting his arm around Dirk's shoulder, he could feel his entire body quivering. Tuck spoke softly and with confidence. "Everything is okay. You have my promise, remember?"

Between chattering teeth, Dirk replied. "I remember, but do they know?" pointing towards Billy Jim and Jonesy.

"What the Sam Hill is going on?" asked Jonesy, completing his entry onto the bridge. Briefly, Tuck told them of finding Dirk and of his guarantee of safety. "He was suppose to stay hidden until I could clear it with everyone." Addressing Dirk he asked why he hadn't stayed in the plane as planned.

"You not come for me. I think you forget. The plane so small I not able to move. Then I see Beely Jeem go into submarine many times and think he finished. I come in here for safekeeping. Fine warrior I make, I so scared I wet myself."

Billy Jim was red-faced. He addressed Tuck through clenched teeth. "You makin' one big mistake, mister!"

Neither Tuck nor Jonesy was surprised at Billy Jim's outburst. While Jonesy made an attempt at accepting Dirk, Billy Jim said to keep the dirty, little Nazi out of his way, or else.

Out in the open, the air was sweet and the bunker cool. The ceiling looked like a giant, lime colored umbrella, a sharp contrast to the atmosphere aboard the U-boat. With a cutting edge to his voice, Billy Jim finalized his tour. "Since it don't appear I have any volunteers, I'll figure a way I can do the job by myself if I have to."

"Do you really feel like you have to do this Billy Jim?" Jonesy asked. "I mean, you don't even know these fellas, so you can't hate them. Look at Dirk, he's just a kid. You might hate what they did to your brother, but they were only following orders like so many others; me included. I'm certain, I killed innocent civilians in many of my bombing runs. Don't you imagine the victim's families hated me for what I did?"

"But we didn't start it. They did!" Billy Jim protested, stabbing a finger at Dirk who still stood at attention, in soiled pants, against the bulkhead. "We got involved 'cause we had to. And we finished it, or will when we take care of this one final piece of business." He looked with disdain at Dirk. "Besides don't thet prayer we recite in school say 'Deliver us from evil'? That's all I'm doin'."

Jonesy shook his head, wanting to touch Billy Jim, but refrained. "Son, there's a thin line, very thin, between removing evil and vengeance. I wish you'd reconsider. Let's put that energy to work getting us home. If this boat can be used, let's sail away on it. You said Hannah could run the engines. We can use their charts and logs and 'dead reckon' to the west and find some piece of the Florida peninsular. Can't be too far. Or how about the raft? We got the compass from the plane and I can compensate for it's gravitational pull. We can forget Mystery Island. And Billy Jim," Jonesy added almost at a whisper, "Do you recall the Lord reserved vengeance or revenge for Himself?"

Softening his approach somewhat, Billy Jim replied. "The raft might be a possibility, but we can't use this thing," indicating the sub. "Too many parts missing. Plus, since we don't know how to submerge, we'd have to blow away a chunk of the roof to get it out. No, we first need to take out the other sub or at least the crew. Then we can decide how to get home." He slapped the spray shield of the bridge. "Maybe, we can capture the other one, you know take it over." Tuck felt a small tug of enthusiasm, hoping Billy Jim was giving thought to something other than destroying the *Nautilus Scan*.

The next day Tuck found Billy Jim dog paddling around the spare sub. He waved him over, shouting, "Come on in, Tuck. Water's fine." He was wearing the goggles from the dead airman's helmet as a dive mask, explaining he had waterproofed them, almost, with the sticky gum from a banyan tree. "Biggest problem is sharks. They musta come here to eat the garbage from the sub when it's docked."

Tuck knew that Billy Jim was aware of his fear of sharks and the thought crossed his mind that he may have been pulling his leg, but he had no desire to challenge him. He was also reminded Billy Jim might not want him to see what he was doing underwater. Between dives down the side of the sub, Billy Jim said he was refining his idea, but was through going inside the sub. Again, Tuck didn't know how much was "smoke" and how much was fact.

"Vere do ya got your dear little Fuhrer stashed?"

"He's sitting in the gentlemen's room," said Tuck, still fearful Billy Jim was determined to do away with him. "Not bothering anyone."

"Don't matter none. Right now I gotta go relieve Jonesy." Using the line hanging over the dock, he climbed out of the water, walked past Tuck and headed in the way of the ridge. However, he abruptly turned, put his finger to his lips and with his head motioned Tuck to follow.

They walked the dock to the stern of the U-boat, carefully climbed aboard and entered through the rear hatch. Dripping wet, Billy Jim motioned Tuck to follow quietly, and pointed to the water he was leaving on the deck. As they stole along the passageway, Billy Jim retrieved a marlinespike from the overhead where he had hidden it earlier.

Like cats they made their way toward the voice they both now heard. Just before the radio room, Billy Jim stopped indicating to Tuck he should listen. Finally, Tuck nodded.

The first indication that Dirk knew he had company, was when he felt the pointed end of the steel spike under his chin, pushing his head backwards. Flicking the toggle switch, silencing the radio, Billy Jim raked the earphones from Dirk's head. "Hello mine little Kraut or is it Agent Kraut?"

Still looking forward, towards the console and telegraph key, Dirk pushed a switch with his knee destroying the radio. A light gray tendril of smoke arose from the console as the acid did its job on the electrical components. Dirk slid his chair backwards trying to rise, but Billy Jim placed a firm hand on his shoulder ordering, "Stay!" With the spike pressing hard against his chin, he asked what he thought his friend, "Tok," would think of him now?

"I am just a young boy, like yourself, homesick for his family. I was trying to see if I could talk to Germany."

"Certainly, you were and I'm Herr Joseph Goebbels, your Minister of Propaganda," Tuck said, stepping from behind Billy Jim. "How many more of you are there on the island?"

"I by myself. Regardless what you think you hear or believe I doing, I under the protection of the Geneva Convention as a POW. Signed 1864."

"Yes. That we agree," said Tuck. "But, I heard the word 'vertreter' and the last two numbers of your serial number. Could that be for 'Agent 43'?"

"Perhaps, before, but not now. I go to the States with you. No longer be a Nazi." He almost spit out the words. "I really change." Tuck thought Dirk was either a very good actor or telling the truth. He did not appear frightened nor was he perspiring.

"Another thing. You knew when the Geneva Convention agreement was signed, but none of us did. Neither Billy Jim nor I knew what C.C.C. stood for, but you did. How do you explain that?"

With a hint of humor or sarcasm, he answered. "Maybe we better educated!"

"Or better trained and rehearsed." offered Billy Jim. Anyway, as of right now, I'm placing you under *my* protection. I will keep you safe until I decide what to do with you." He was emphasizing *I*. "Right now, I got just the hidin' place for you. It's a special room, out of the way, provided by the Nazis for when one of their own went bonkers. You can scream, bash your head against the wall and no one will stop you."

"Tok, will you not help me?" Dirk held his hands outstretched, begging. "Out of sight, Beely Jeem kill me."

"Dirk, you deceived me. What do you expect from me now?" Dirk dropped his hands.

"It is true, I sent here as agent, but after watching and hearing you, I not want to be agent any more. I want to go to the US of A. I was not telling the other sub anything of use, only making my report of small talk. In my heart, I really desert when I first surrender."

"Yeah, and we're 'spose to bleve you. Just what did you say to the other boat? Weather's fine. Wish you was here? If I know you, you've been sneakin' around, watching our goings on and probably even listenin' to our nightly talks." Billy Jim looked at Tuck. "Probably knows about the treasure and wants a share. Then soon as he knows its location, we get hammered and he calls his buddies for a pick up."

Tuck eyeballed Billy Jim with a furrowed brow as a caution about saying too much.

"I not know of any treasure," protested Dirk. "I not want anything of the Nazis." This time he did spit. "Tok tell you of nice treatment to POWs at his city. Soon we get to States I go to work. To school. I be good citizen. You wait and see. You be proud you save me from going back to South America." Dirk paused. "One thing does ponder me. How did you know I was here? I heard you say you finished with sub."

"Simple," said Billy Jim. "When I was here on one of my earlier trips, to see what I could use, I noticed the radio was warm. That surprised me 'cause Ma and me had earlier tried it out and found a couple of tubes missing. Then just today when I was showin' Tuck and Jonesy 'round, I touched the radio and it was again warm. You was my first suspect, even if I didn't know for sure, you really 'zisted. I kept watchin' and gave you enough rope... Today, when I was diving, I heard you key the transmitter and knew it was a perfect time for Tuck to see what you's really all about."

"Very clever, but it will serve you no good. Before I changed mind to become a US of A citizen, I give my Kapitan full report. Now that he knows, he will take care of you unless you allow me to help. If I not destroyed the radio, I could send new message. Maybe I fix crystal radio to transmit correction." Tuck could see Dirk was struggling and recognized that he, too, might react in the same manner in order to buy time or stay alive.

"That won't work, Dirk," said Tuck. "You could send almost anything. I would never be able to interpret what you're sending in Morse code, especially in German. Any other way to contact them?"

"I afraid not. But my heart is pure." He placed his hands on his chest, which did nothing for Tuck and Billy Jim.

"Ain't that convenient. If pigs could fly, they wouldn't bump their butts. A full report, huh? That's amazin', since I ain't finalized my plans," Billy Jim answered "Now be a good little Nazi and put your hands behind you so I can tie 'em." Tuck could only stand and watch, but did ask if it was necessary. Having tied his hands roughly, Billy Jim then crammed a hunk of towel into Dirk's mouth preventing him from yelling. "No sense upsettin' Ma and Jonesy till I know what I'm going to do with 'Dirt' here." Manhandling him to his feet, Billy Jim pushed Dirk towards an underground brig located at the northern end of the bunker. Tuck followed silently. Before ensconcing Dirk in the archaic prison, Billy Jim demanded his clothes.

Dirk drew back, raising his voice to protest his treatment loudly. "Not allowed by Geneva Convention. This cruel and inhuman. I be very cold without uniform. Without uniform, can be tried as spy! Shot, maybe hung!"

Walking away they could still hear Dirk shouting. "Come back! Tok! Beely Jeem! Not fair treatment of P-O-W!"

Billy Jim, with Dirk's clothing over one arm, led Tuck outside into the sunshine. "Don't know how much the little snitch was able to tell, but it wasn't a whole lot. I snipped the antenna lead as soon as I learned the radio was workable. As of late he's been talking to hisself. Now, I really do have to go and relieve Jonesy."

"Wait, Billy Jim," Tuck said, touching his arm. "What are you going to do with the uniform?"

"Me? I ain't gonna do nothin'. But you are. You gonna put it on and go a hummin' and a singin' and a whistlin' that little Kraut song you know."

"Ach, Du Lieber Augustin?" he sang aloud in an untrained, but pleasant voice. "Oh, You Dear Augustine?"

"Thet's the one. I want you to keep this hat on and your head down and traipse all over this here island in hopes if there is 'nother Kraut out there, he'll recognize the music and contact you."

"And if he contacts me?"

Handing Tuck a pistol, "You take this here Lugar outta your pocket, put it into his gut like this and bring him to me."

Still fearful Billy Jim was determined to do away with the sub, and perhaps Dirk, Tuck agreed to go along with Billy Jim's plan. He also decided to see if he could help him or stop him.

After his search for the treasure, Tuck had a good understanding of what was available on the island and in the bunker's armory. With Billy Jim's way of thinking and determination burning in his mind, he made his way to the gentlemen's room with his notepad. In one column, he began listing ways of destroying a sub filled with seasoned warriors, presumably well armed. In another column he noted his thoughts about the success of each. All of the ideas such as scuttling, fire, explosion, combat and trickery were almost carbon copies of those he had first shared with Billy Jim. As before, they fell short of victory for various and obvious reasons.

He wondered if there was some way of getting everyone off the boat, as Billy Jim suggested, and take it over themselves. After much thought, Tuck could determine no way of ensuring everyone would leave. Even a diversion on the far side of the island would not guarantee everyone's response. And anyone left aboard would have to be dealt with, probably face to face.

Tuck looked at his page. He had listed dogging all outside hatches, save one, and flooding the hull using fire hoses. Then he envisioned a bunch of guys that had feared and fought drowning their entire time aboard the sub, only to survive and die dockside like frightened rats in a barrel. Any surviving through the escape hatches would have to be shot while in the water. He knew gasoline and fire could be used, as could hand grenades and other explosives. It was too much for him and he tore the pages into small scraps.

Although it was never stated, Tuck believed everyone understood if they could not be coaxed off the sub, the entire crew would have to be destroyed. For containment reasons the sub was the logical place to do it. Any surviving members would be far worse than anything they could imagine. He saw them facing a vicious assemblage of ferocious savages, seeking revenge by any means. And he doubted the four - or five, counting Dirk - would prevail against fighting men trained to handle fires, leaks, explosions, gunfire, bombs, depth charge attacks and hand-to-hand combat under the most adverse conditions. He knew they would guard, protect and fight for their home like a mama lion with a lair full of cubs. Plus they had experience on their side. Whatever they did and how they did it, had to be accomplished while everyone was aboard and below deck. So it had to be silent, swift and complete with no mistakes or loose ends of any kind. His mind kept coming back to trickery of some sort. But what?

At this point, Tuck was exhausted. He put his pencil and tablet on the table at the side of his chair and made final his decision. He would not help Billy Jim with his plan of destruction and instead work towards changing his mind. He felt if they could come up with a better plan, something safer, something that might somehow satisfy whatever was driving Billy Jim, they might encourage him to join them. He knew he needed help and would be well served to have Hannah and Jonesy and, hopefully, Billy Jim as counsel. He wished he knew whose side Dirk was on or if he'd remain neutral. Meanwhile for the next couple of hours, Tuck, dressed like a German sailor, walked the island singing over and over, the only German song he knew. In time he was making up additional lyrics that made no sense whatsoever: "Ach, Du Lieber Augustin, Augustin, Augustin, alles das heim. Alles das heim."

During that night's get together, Tuck outlined his thinking. Walking around the fire and flailing his arms about, he shared with them each point he had considered and his ultimate reasons and decision for rejecting it. He completed his remarks by confessing: "I believe it's madness for us to take on the sub and its crew in combat. We will surely bring on ourselves injury and possibly death, while doing something that might prove unnecessary. I'm convinced, in my own mind, that we are flirting with death...our deaths, if we try to destroy it. As I said, every solitary soul must die in order for us to survive. Otherwise any survivor will want to kill us for what we have done to their shipmates. Finally, there will be no limit to what they will extract from us - or the manner in which it is extracted - as revenge. Not one of us will be excluded from the punishment. Surely, there's another way: trickery, direct honest approach, and any other method save murder." For a moment he stood silent and looked at each of his friends, one to another. "Now, I've talked long enough and I'm willing to listen to anyone about anything." Tuck sat down, emotionally drained

For a slow motion minute, no one said anything. Tuck then did the unthinkable. He betrayed Billy Jim by telling Hannah of their capturing Dirk using the radio. "Perhaps we can ransom him?"

Once more it was midnight-in-a-cemetery quiet.

At last, Jonesy, stirring a stick in the sand, broke the silence by backing into the situation. "Tuck, you've done a very good job thinking this through and bringing it to us. For that we're grateful, but I don't know where we go from here." He explained to Hannah Dirk's surrendering to Tuck in the control room. Then the three of them finding Dirk on the sub and at this point he had to allow Tuck and Billy Jim to complete the saga.

After Hannah walked about, shaking her arms, slapping her palms, screeching, hollering and moaning about betrayal and not being included, she was, at last, satisfied with Dirk's whereabouts. Feeling responsible for Hannah being deceived, Tuck tried to smooth over the potholes. "Hannah you must recognize we, as men, have a code of honor to protect our womenfolk. It's a thing we feel very strongly about. We're born with it. On occasion it's better not to tell everything you know, especially if it might cause harm. I saw my Daddy do something once that I thought Mama ought to know about. But after thinking about it, I decided it would only hurt Mama if she knew. So I didn't tell. Same thing here, it would have just caused you to worry if you knew about Dirk." Hannah engulfed Tuck in a hug just as she had done when she believed Billy Jim was lost.

Both Jonesy and Billy Jim recognized Tuck's role in calming Hannah. "At times like these, crucial times, me thinkth the lad hath a tongue of silver," Shakespeared Jonesy to Billy Jim.

The talk returned to the taking of the U-boat. "You assume the sub can or will be taken only at dockside. Ain't there no other way?" It was Billy Jim's turn at bat. "Seems to me we ain't looked at all the choices."

"What do you have in mind, Billy Jim?" Jonesy asked. Hannah just sat and stared as if contemplating, in depth, all that she had just listened to.

"Nothin' concrete," he replied. "But I don't think Tuck's is the only answer either. There must be more selections than what he's talked about. You got any ideas? Any thoughts 'bout what Tuck told us? Ma, you been awful quiet."

"No son. It just seems to me, it's a no-win situation, howsomever we look at it. I think Tuck might be right about the cost bein' too expensive. Maybe it's something we can't afford. You thinkin' there's any other way, Billy Jim? If so, now's the time to get it said."

"It's too early to set it down just yet, but yeah, I think there's other ways possible."

Jonesy stood and stretched. "Billy Jim, if you have additional thoughts or information to what Tuck has outlined, you need to tell us. Now's the time."

"Criminy, Jonesy, you gave Tuck time to work through all his ideas. Ain't I allowed the same courtesy?"

Tuck smiled at Billy Jim. If he were a cat, he thought, he'd be licking his paw and smoothing down his whiskers right about now.

"We don't have to make no decisions tonight," Billy Jim said. "Why don't we sleep on it and see if any other ideas surface. I promise this, if we's stuck with Tuck's list and nothin' better presents itself, I'll go along with ya'll." Those words were sounds of jubilation to Tuck and he was certain all three of them were happy with Billy Jim's concession. But in his heart, knowing of Billy Jim's adamant dislike for the Nazis, he wondered...

In time everyone agreed - Billy Jim being lukewarm - to mount an effort to save the sub and its crew by negotiation. Their reasoning: the war was over and perhaps if they could meet with them, get to know each other, they might be able to get home safely...all of them. If that didn't work, another option was to try and trick them out of the sub or force them out. It was a shot in the air, but as Tuck believed, anything was an improvement over Billy Jim's desire to take out the sub and its crew.

GHOST OF THE STREAM

Since none of them knew what Billy Jim had in mind and he remained closed mouthed, Tuck decided to observe his activities. Not wanting to act suspicious or appear distrustful, he also decided not to tell Jonesy or Hannah of his intentions. Meanwhile, the four of them began formulating their plans in order to be ready to spring into action the moment the sub surfaced.

Billy Jim's plan for Tuck to walk the island, dressed as Dirk, had produced no results, so he had quit. "Probably your singin'," teased Billy Jim.

"Okay, here's what we have." Jonesy was holding court on top of the ridge so all could be present and everyone a lookout. "Because of available water, fuel hoses and electrical lines, the sub usually docks at Pen Seven. At least in the past, when we've checked, that's where it's been. We'll consider the forward end of the pen as our 'conference room'. When we're through here, Tuck and I will move a desk and a few chairs to that area and set them up in the shadows by the lump. When the sub arrives, we'll station lights so as to be able to illuminate the entire docking area, as we deem necessary, and at the same time we can remain in the darkness. An element of surprise, if you will. We'll have to move a microphone for the public address system down to the conference area. Can you hook it up, Hannah?" Hannah said she believed so. "Any questions so far?" Jonesy was finally very military it seemed.

Billy Jim had a look of confusion. "Jonesy, I understand about you wantin' to talk to them Nazis and how you're settin' up the meetin' place. But what'cha gonna say to make them want to accept your plan? Seems to me they's doing quite well without any help from us. Can't they just swarm out on the deck, armed to the teeth and start shootin'? If so, it's good-bye peacemakers? There's got to be more."

Jonesy showed a hint of aggravation, but kept it checked. "Billy Jim, I'm just outlining the physical layout. We'll have to prepare a script and what part each will play. You'll see when we get it all together. For example, I have Tuck down here with me because he speaks a little German. We will have rehearsed what we're going to say and how we're going to say it. You and Hannah will be hiding in the control room armed with a couple of those high powered rifles, with scopes, from the armory. Tuck and I will be armed also. We can keep them bottled up in the sub indefinitely, if we do it right. Just think about you shooting a squirrel. It pokes its head from a nest or hole in a tree and you shoot. Same thing here. The men can only get out one or two at a time and if necessary you and Hannah can pick them off with ease. You can keep the entire sub at

127

bay with a couple of rifles. Think about it. We four can keep an entire sub bottled up with just rifles! We can even tie open the two main hatches to keep them from submerging."

He was incredulous. In what could only be described as mock disgust, Billy Jim threw his hands down to his side and said simply, "My gosh, he's play actin'. And he don't know a thing 'bout huntin' squirrels." Then with his very best Sergeant York imitation he slowly said, "Jonesy, ya gotta let the critter come outta hit's hole, afore ya shoots hit. Otherwise hit falls back in hit's hollow and ya gotta climb the tree to git hit."

Tuck smiled, waiting for Hannah to pull an imaginary pipe from her toothless mouth and add with her molasses voice, "Ats rite Alvie."

While Hannah stood watch, Jonesy began pulling wires and moving amplifiers, for the public address system. Billy Jim and Tuck had collected a supply of small arms and ammo from the spare sub and the island armory. They had test fired each of the weapons, adjusted the scopes and sights and placed them, along with a supply of grenades, at strategic spots in the control room in front of each of the pens. "We'll make final adjustments when the sub gets here," Billy Jim explained. A supply of water, coconuts and fruit was stashed about in the event anyone was detained for an indefinite period.

Tuck stood watch while Jonesy directed Billy Jim where to stage the lights and identify corresponding switches. Hannah completed the public address system by hooking up the amplifiers and mikes. "Nothing to it," she said, twisting a couple of wires together. "It's just a low impedance system."

Between their normal routines, watches, the planning and rehearsals of their own offense, life returned to whatever they could make it - with the exception of checking on and feeding Dirk. Once they had agreed to try and talk to the Nazis, all of them stayed busy. There wasn't much time for Billy Jim to do anything more on his project and little need for Tuck to scout out his activities. Tuck had, however, determined Billy Jim had put together some unusual items: an exceptionally long piece of line or cable along with several buoyed crates that floated just beneath the surface. They were stationed out from the stern of the spare sub and barely discernible. Billy Jim would not discuss them and since Tuck had no boat, and because of the possibility of sharks, he didn't want to swim out and investigate. He was destined to continue to watch and wonder.

Obviously, things were greatly improved between Billy Jim and the other three. Their feelings of togetherness, while still tender to the touch, were improving daily and the usual banter and camaraderie was returning to its earlier level. Because of their feelings for Hannah, Tuck and Jonesy were happy about the change of heart and that Billy Jim had become a valued and vocal member of their planning sessions.

It was Billy Jim who thought of breaking holes in the glass shielding the control room in the event they had to shoot from there. He measured distances, rechecked and sighted all the gun scopes from where they might be used. He even offered to see if the deck gun on the spare sub could be made usable...just in case. And probably his most valued contribution was playing devil's advocate as Jonesy and Tuck prepared their script to be used in the negotiations with the Nazis. He would challenge them with sample questions and answers, making suggestions when their responses didn't suit him. "You really bleve this...or that? If'en you was in his shoes, how'd you answer? He constantly questioned them about their final goal? And kept reminding them if it was unrealistic. Relentlessly, he probed like a doctor on the western frontier, trying to remove a bullet from the good guy. Only the "clink" of the slug dropping into the metal dish was missing. .

Billy Jim made their presentation better. The thought occurred to Tuck that Billy Jim did not have to spend his life aboard a fishing boat, if he chose otherwise. He also wondered how much of Billy Jim's turnabout was due to Hannah interceding in their behalf? Regardless, they were pleased to have him on their side.

During this period, Dirk did something to improve his standing with Billy Jim. One night while Billy Jim was on watch, an arm wrapped around his forehead and he felt a sharp point on the carotid artery on the right side of his neck. "Please not move. It is Dirk, who departed your escape-proof prison. Salt infected lock closes hard, but opens easy. I come in peace to prove my going to US of A right thing. I not help you kill my shipmates. I not stop you if that only way. I leave you with this: I could plunge knife in your throat and toss lifeless body in Gulf Stream never to be found. Think about that. Do not follow. I watch with interest. Now where is uniform? I am looking a disgrace."

"In the gentlemen's club." The knife was removed and Billy Jim was able to turn his eyes enough to see that Dirk was wearing a long sleeve shirt – upside down. His scrawny legs were pushed into the sleeves while the shirttail was tied around his waist. He looked like a baby with droopy diapers. In a blink he was gone, a shadow disappearing into the night. A ghost. Billy Jim was visibly shaken, but as embarrassing as it was he knew he had to divulge what had happened. He did so with trepidation, but never again mentioned anything about his plan...if there remained one.

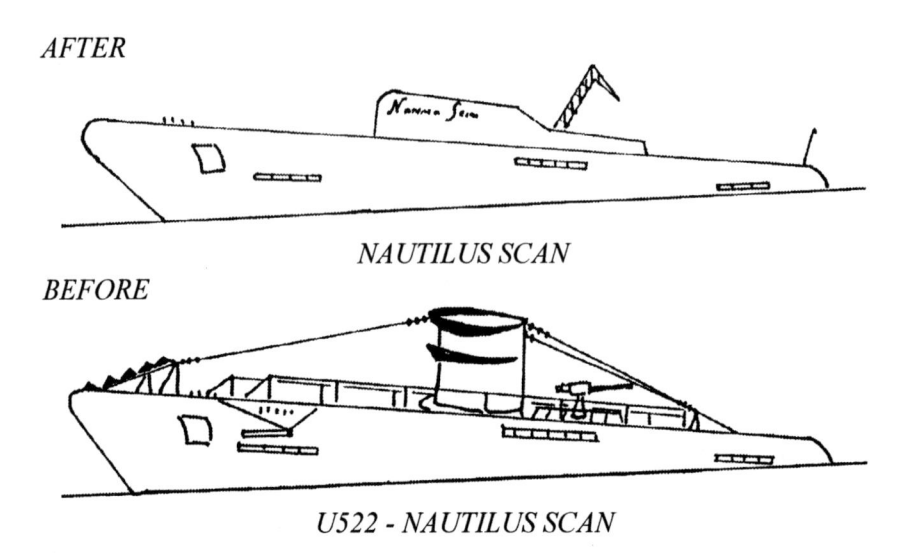

AFTER

NAUTILUS SCAN

BEFORE

U522 - NAUTILUS SCAN

For nearly a week they watched and waited. Then one day, on the horizon, the quarry appeared. Like a well-trained drill team they scrambled down the sheltered side of the ridge and raced for the secret passage into the gentlemen's room. Hannah and Billy Jim stepped into the elevator and rushed to their stations at each end of the control room giving them a panoramic view of the pens. Jonesy and Tuck dashed into the bunker and took their seats at the conference table. Having manned their stations, they waited in heart-pounding silence. Tuck wondered what Dirk was up to. No one, but Billy Jim had seen him since his escape. Unknown to any of them, Dirk, now properly dressed, had found himself a box seat to watch the opening performance in secret.

Tuck, nervous and looking around, noticed Jonesy had again cut his hair and beard and trimmed the ragged ends of his pant legs. He began to feel like he did when he had to make an impromptu speech in front of Mr. Plott's fifth grade class. Each passing second – as measured by the giant solar clock on the wall facing the pens – added to the pressures he felt. Even though it was as quiet as a feather floating on a whiff of air, to Tuck each movement of the giant second hand took on the noise of a pile driver. Katoonk! Katoonk! Katoonk! Tuck's fears puffed up with each stroke like a hand pump filling a bike tire.

Jonesy stage whispered, "You're doing fine. Remember it's just a game. A play."

"Yeah, right", Tuck answered, but instead he found his brain beginning a new game of ping-pong. He scrambled and unscrambled his practiced words like a decoder might. Katoonk! Can I do this, he wondered? What if I make a mistake? His mind was a swing: back and forth, back and forth. Katoonk! If I were a car, he thought, I would be shifting gears, no, stripping and grinding gears. He realized each movement of the second hand of the clock now matched the beat of his heart and he tried to slow down both. Katoonk! Katoonk! He could actually feel the light chop of his body, mind and soul increasing into ground swells of disproportionate size. The more he envisioned what was about to happen, or what he thought would, the more excited, anxious and unsure he became. Katoonk-katoonk! His palms and upper lip were sweaty, and as usual, when nervous, the corner of his mouth began twitching. He knew he was going to throw up. The "katoonks" were closing in on each other.

Over and over he rehearsed what he was to say. He toyed with the switch on the microphone until he realized the clicking sound could be heard over the speakers. Katoonk-Katoonk! He looked over at Jonesy and was amazed at how relaxed he appeared. Was this what the military had prepared him for? He wondered. Forming a "V" with his fingers, Jonesy gave him the "victory sign", growling a few lines of Winston Churchill's famous "We will fight...." speech. Tuck knew this was probably the greatest single moment in his life. Katoonk-katoonk-katoonk! He had never confronted anyone with a gun. He had never even been in a serious fight, save the minor fracases kids get into. Now, they were writing a chapter of life to which none of then knew the ending. He finally told himself if Hannah and Billy Jim were as cool as Jonesy, he could certainly muddle through somehow. He looked about for Dirk, hoping to see that he was truly on their side. He prayed the "pounding" of the clock would stop, but the second hand continued to march along to the beat of its own drummer. Katoonk-katoonk-katoonk-katoonk!

At last! The first sign of the sub's presence was a deluge of boils followed by a roiling explosion of bubbles, as water was forced from the ballast tanks causing it to surface. The top of the periscope appeared, revolving as suspected, until it stopped; pointing towards the picture of Hitler. In a few seconds the conning tower and deck were safely above the water line. At the final moment of surfacing, the sub actually rocked slightly. Tuck thought of a fishing cork bobbing to the surface. After the excess water ran off, they heard the clank of a hatch opening. A head appeared above the crown of the bridge. It looked about, but seeing nothing amiss, disappeared shouting something down into the control room. As a white cap appeared above the blast shield, Jonesy looked over at Tuck and pointed a finger. Show time! He mouthed. Stage fright, be gone.

Tuck thumbed the microphone, took a breath and spoke slowly and as clearly as his shaky voice allowed. "Achtung! Achtung, *Nautilus Scan!*" In the same instant, the sub was bathed in lights, Hannah flipping the switches on cue. The white cap quickly dropped from sight. They could hear muffled voices, understanding but one word: "Kapitan". Tuck continued. "Wo ist der Kommandant?" For a moment there was no response. Then a voice, but no head.

"Ich bin der Kommandant."

"Guten tag, Kommandant. Wie heissen Sie?"

"Ich bin Frederick von Stecken. Fred."

"Ich bin Thom. Tuck. Sprechen Sie English?"

"Ja. I mean, yes. I speak English."

"Kapitan, let me turn you over to our leader. He is Lt. Jones and can fill you in on the details." Tuck gladly handed the mike to Jonesy, who gave him a "thumbs up". He felt both relief and exhilaration. A soggy noodle came to mind.

Jonesy spoke with confidence and ease. "Kapitan, I am Lieutenant Taylor Jones of the U.S. Navy. My friends and I, find ourselves guests on your very remarkable island. We wish you no harm. Neither do we want to be harmed and have taken the precaution to arm ourselves with weapons from the other U-boat and the small armory here in the bunker. We can and will shoot anyone coming on deck without our permission." On that signal, Billy Jim rapid-fired his rifle harmlessly into the water near the sub. "Do you understand?"

Tuck imagined the Kapitan automatically ducking his head, but probably would not have been surprised, nervous or upset. "I understand. What is it you want of us?"

"First, you can send out four men to tie up the boat, hook up the electrical and fresh water, but only four! They are being watched very carefully. And Kapitan, I must caution you, anyone outside the boat will be in the cross hairs of several very fine and very powerful German made guns. So please no tricks. There is no reason for anyone to be hurt."

The seamen appeared, rather hesitantly, and began their duties including the placement of a gangway. Jonesy told the Kapitan of their plight and desire to communicate.

"Lieutenant, what do you suggest?"

"I suggest, Kapitan, you and your executive officer come ashore and we discuss how to best serve the needs of both parties."

"I will agree to come ashore, but I think it best to bring my Number Two and permit Number One to stay aboard. If this is satisfactory, we will join you immediately."

Jonesy looked at Tuck, who shrugged, not seeing anything wrong. Tuck remembered during rehearsal, asking Jonesy who could speak for the crew and was told he believed the highest-ranking officer. If that were the case, the Kommandant would rule regardless who was with him. Jonesy told the skipper and his Number Two to come ashore and be seated at the table and chairs just off the bow of the sub. He added, "Kapitan, in the spirit of our reaching an agreeable solution, please come unarmed. You will be searched."

Within minutes, the Kapitan and his mate were rapidly climbing down the side of the conning tower. For a moment, they stood at the gangplank, shading their eyes while looking about. Finally they walked to where Tuck and Jonesy sat. The mate was youthful looking, of medium height. Smooth complexion with blue eyes and blond hair. He had about him a stiff military bearing and gave the impression he would not sit down if he thought it might wrinkle his trousers. Remembering what Dirk had said, Tuck wondered if this was the gent "with iron in his shorts." He was a pleasant fellow, quick to shake hands, bow and click his heels. Tuck imagined him getting his start in the Hitler's Youth Movement at a very young age. And even to this day he cannot believe the Third Reich lasted only a few months beyond a decade instead of the promised thousand years.

On the other hand, the Kapitan was preceded by his "presence" to the meeting place. There was about him a countenance that would be apparent if he were in a room of a hundred people. He wore soft sole boat shoes, baggy, khaki colored pants, and a white turtle neck sweater. The sleeves were pushed up on his thick forearms, the right one displaying the tattoo of a well armed, angry shark. On his hands were leather gloves with the cuffs turned down and fingertips removed. The traditional crumpled white cap, favored by U-boat captains, sat atop a head of copper hair, neatly trimmed beard, even, white teeth and sparkling blue eyes. About his neck was the Knight's Cross, which Tuck felt with confidence, he'd earned. He was assuredly the type of sailor Hitler would detest in his dislike of the navy

After introductions were made - the mate was Otto Huff - Jonesy asked the Kapitan what his intentions were and future plans. Leaning back in his chair, he verified what everyone hoped might be his answer. "We wish to go home. It's been a long, long time. We have tried the transition to South America without success. The Caribbean Islands are becoming for the tourists. This island is no longer of interest to us. It was a life preserver at one time, but its usefulness is no longer. We are tired. Weary. All of us, to the man, want to return to Germany and help rebuild...our country...our lives."

"What's keeping you from returning?" Jonesy asked. "We've been here long enough to see you leave and return many times. I'm surprised you didn't see our smoke, an ash or footprints. In the beginning, not knowing you were here, we made no effort to hide. In fact, you could say we were quite careless." Other than shaking their heads in unison, neither submariner showed any emotions at hearing that information. Jonesy made a note of the contradiction.

"You always go south." Jonesy continued. "You always come back. If you want to go back to Germany why not just strike out to the Northeast?" Jonesy was curious and so was Tuck.

"Money. It takes much money to operate the *Nautilus Scan.*" At those words the Kapitan smiled rubbing together his thumb and first two fingers. "Diesel fuel is quite expensive and we are getting only small jobs in marine research and salvage, if you understand what I am saying?" Jonesy looked at Tuck, but neither said a word about the treasure they'd found. Jonesy again scratched a note on his pad.

Otto Huff, finally spoke in a staccato manner. He sat ramrod straight, both feet firmly on the floor, a hand on each knee. "Why are you interested in our plans? We are of no concern to you. The war is over. You have no jurisdiction over us. We are not criminals. We were simple sailors doing the job required of us. Why are you questioning us? We should be inquiring of you. This is our island. It belongs to Germany. Must I remind you these are international waters. You are the trespasser!"

The Kapitan rested his hand on Otto's arm. "Bitte. Ruhe."

Jonesy looked to Tuck for an answer. He mouthed, "Please. Quiet! Told him to shut up."

"Forgive us. We have been under much strain recently," the Kapitan explained. "We were speaking of our going home. Our crew is anxious and is looking to us for a solution. Because we can no longer rely on the milk cows for fuel and supplies, we cannot go directly across the ocean from here. The distance is too great and our range too small, so we must take baby steps. First we go south to Brazil then cross the Atlantic to Africa at the shortest distance. From Africa, we hupfen, springen? The Kapitan looked at Tuck to determine if he understood.

"Hopscotch," Tuck answered.

"Yes, we would sail across the South Atlantic to Africa, then hopscotch up the coast to Gibraltar, Spain, France and finally to Deutschland." The Kapitan's face lighted as if remembering fondly, his homeland. "All of that takes more money than we can accumulate."

"So are you stuck over here?" Tuck asked, but recognizing the Kapitan spoke of Germany as he thought of Florida: love... home...love of home.

"Tuck. That's an unusual name. How do you come by it?" Tuck told him and he nodded his understanding. "We have such a word: 'falten'. It means to fold or crease like in a blanket." Tuck told him of the similarity and asked where he learned English.

"It was taught to those of us thought most likely to occupy the United States after we had conquered you." He shrugged his shoulders, his mouth poised in a pointless grin. "Many of our instructors were educated in the States. Some of the botanist trained at the University of Florida - where they have a very fine College of Agriculture. Jonesy and Tuck smiled at the irony, but neither saw any sense in pursuing the subject, except to congratulate him on his use of the language. The Kapitan then paid Tuck a compliment. "You are the first American I've met to correctly pronounce 'von' as 'fun' or 'fawn'. Tuck smiled.

Continuing, he was relaxed and spoke with ease. "I suppose we could surrender to the U.S. and get a plane ticket home, but we would like to return in our U-boat, or what's left of it." He pointed to the yellow vessel at dockside that held little semblance to the U-boats seen during the war.

Jonesy said he thought that was reasonable, but suggested they may not want to display the Nazi flag. "Perhaps the German merchant banner would be more in order. How much money do you think it would take for fuel and supplies? In fact, how many of you are there?"

Before the Kapitan could answer, Otto spoke up. "Quite many more than you, I think. Thirty eight to what?" he asked, twisting his torso as though looking about. He smirked at seeing nothing.

Jonesy dismissed Otto and returned his attention to the Kapitan, whom he was now calling Fred. "Suppose I could get you help crossing the Atlantic from here, will the boat make it?"

"With minor repairs and major supplies, yes. The old *U-522* - the new *Nautilus Scan* - can make it. What do you have in mind?"

Jonesy hunched forward to make notes, speaking while he wrote. "I'm certain we still have sub tenders in the Mediterranean and the Atlantic. I think it's possible, with the help from our navy, we can make it happen. Too bad there isn't a radio on the island," he added without a hint of their knowledge of the radio on the spare sub. "I could make some calls and get the ball rolling. I assume you can use a Number 2 fuel?"

Fred said yes to the diesel fuel and told them radios were restricted because directional finders could hone in on the island. "Radio transmissions would have been a dead give away and we didn't want that." Jonesy did not look up from his notes and Tuck continued to stare into space as if thinking. "So while we were here, we listened more than we talked and any communications was by short range transmitters. We do have a radio on our boat."

Jonesy knew he was standing on a teeter-totter, but proceeded in order to establish what was known and unknown. "We'll have to work on that. Perhaps there is a radio on the spare boat. Do you think we might use that?"

"I doubt that radio would work. We have stripped so many parts." Both Jonesy and Tuck wrote 'Radio - lie.'

Otto jumped to his feet. "Kommandant. I protest! We do not need the help of this U.S. Navy. There cannot be more than a handful here. We will not be held hostage by so few. If we use their help, it is like we are giving up. Surrendering . We should tell them to, how do you say it, pack it in and go about our own business."

The Kapitan had had enough of Lieutenant Junior Grade Otto Huff. Without raising his voice, he said in clipped words, "Oberleutnant zur See, return to your station." Tilting his head to both Jonesy and Tuck, he said, "My apologies. Some habits and attitudes die stubborn deaths."

Otto seemed neither embarrassed nor hurt. He gave Tuck the impression he'd been in this position before. However, at the time, Tuck didn't understand its full meaning. Straightway, Herr Huff marched toward the U-boat, walked across the gangway, climbed the conning tower and disappeared. Watching him, Fred said only one word. "Youth." He pushed his cap to the back of his head giving him a rakish look. "Where does this leave us, Lieutenant? Or may I call you Jonesy?"

"Certainly. Yes, by all means. Fred, I do have a problem with using your radio because of the instability of Otto. I feel it could be dangerous for any of us to go aboard your boat. Nevertheless, I don't want to keep your men bottled up any longer than needed."

"I thank you for your consideration for my men. Don't concern yourself about Otto, however. He's of the old school, but I doubt he would go against my orders. Lieutenant, Jonesy, it would be helpful to have some fresh fruit brought aboard. Perhaps some of my men, under guard of course, could be sent to harvest enough for a meal or two?" Jonesy raised his hand in protest.

"Kapitan, I think it's time for Tuck and me to get together with our people, tell them what we've discussed and reach a conclusion agreeable to all of us. If you agree with this and go back aboard, we will try to have a decision by tomorrow morning. I must caution you, however, the same rules apply. No one on deck without our permission. We'll try not to keep you any longer than necessary."

"Then I agree to your plan." The Kapitan stood, squared his cap, saluted, shook hands with both Jonesy and Tuck and went aboard the sub.

Handing his rifle to Jonesy, Tuck went to collect a supply of fresh fruit. After several trips he had stockpiled two stalks of bananas, and three large buckets filled with mangoes, oranges, limes and guavas. Within minutes, upon their notification, the two sailors assigned the task were outside retrieving the food. Neither looked comfortable in doing his duty.

Jonesy ordered everyone to the control room. While Tuck, rifle in hand, watched the sub, Jonesy briefed Hannah and Billy Jim about the tail of the tiger they held. Tuck would like to have sat in on the review, but his guarding the sub was more important at the time. He knew there was an escape hatch aft and he didn't want it used. Therefore, it was imperative that he continued walking the length of the room in order to observe the bow and both sides as often as possible. He did hear sketches of the conversations.

"Jonesy, you's told us a lot, but what does it all mean?" asked Hannah.

"In summary, Hannah, I believe it boils down to this: apparently, the Germans don't know about the treasure. Properly used, this could be our best, maybe our only, bargaining chip. They lied about the radio on the spare sub and indicated no knowledge of my presence. If that were the case, why leave Dirk here? Those two things alone tell us they're not being completely truthful, therefore, making everything suspect.

"They did offer for us to use the radio on their sub, but under the circumstances I don't believe we can safely do that. And without a radio, I don't see how we can get the Navy involved. It would be a piece of cake if we could. We do have the Swiss money that could send them on their way. Of course, they'll wonder where we got it and under the circumstances, it could get rather hot around here."

"At first, I thought there was a chance we could get Fred to take us home before he heads for Germany," Tuck contributed in passing. "Initially, I really liked him. He seemed like a reasonable fellow, friendly. But now that he lied, I don't trust him either."

"What about crazy Otto? Sounds like the kind of nut to just start shootin'. We sure can't trust him. Can we?"

"Billy Jim, the Kapitan doesn't appear concerned about him, but I feel the same way as you. I've seen his kind crack under too much pressure. He is experiencing the defeat of something he believes in quite strongly and won't give up too easily. We need to watch him closely in my opinion. Very closely. Like, Tuck, I was taken in by Fred's friendliness. Now, the bottom line; I don't trust either. Like the judge said, 'You lied to me, so everything you say is suspect'."

"Jonesy, you promised the Kapitan an answer in the morning. What'cha gonna tell him?"

"I don't know, Hannah. When you think about our situation, it's rather glum. Even though we may appear friendly with the Kapitan, I don't know how we can use it to our advantage without putting all of us in harm's way. I wouldn't feel comfortable on the sub, knowing that the four of us could be taken hostage very easily. We don't know if there aren't more mavericks, like Otto, on board. If that's the case and we give up the treasure to show our good faith, I suspect we - and anyone else opposing Otto - will find themselves dead."

Jonesy was exasperated and the disappointment showed in his facial expression. "I'm afraid I misread the entire scenario. I believed with a promise of help through the Navy, that they'd jump at the chance to put all of this - the island - and the war behind them in a desire to get home. Now we may be fighting for our lives whether we want to or not. When on watch be very, very alert. We can still contain the crew in the sub, but we can't hold them forever. I think those not on guard should sleep in the control room tonight. We'll be together and have an opportunity to continue our dialogue until we have an answer. Let's keep the lights up bright and stay on the ball." Again, he praised Billy Jim for his foresight in punching some gun ports in the sight shield. "It might prove to be an insightful precaution."

The next morning another supply of fresh fruit and coconuts was delivered to the sub and Tuck announced it: "Frech Frycht!" Not feeling, but wanting to sound peppy and upbeat, Tuck used a favorite "sunshine" greeting he often received when he was picking fruit with the POWs: "Guten morgen, mein lieb klein Sonnenschein." He expected to see the smiling face of the Kapitan. Instead the boyish face of Otto Huff, wearing the Kapitan's hat, appeared over the rim of the bridge. Tuck's heart sank. He turned and hurried back towards the table and chairs.

Without preamble, Otto told of the change in command during the night. "The Kommandant and a few of his faithful have seen the wisdom of relinquishing the control of the boat and I have assumed command. Therefore, in the future you will negotiate with me and only me."

Jonesy asked to speak to the Kapitan in order to ascertain his health and whereabouts. "Without that knowledge, there is nothing to negotiate. These proceedings are over until such time we know the Kommandant is safe and unharmed." Jonesy then spoke softly to Tuck telling him he wondered if they were playing some sort of game. Loudly to "his men" he told them to hold fast and maintain their vigilance. Laying down the microphone he walked away from the table. Stopping, he retraced his steps and picked up the mike. "Tuck, pull the plug on the electric and turn off the fresh water supply. Then help me tie back the hatches and secure these cables to the sub. It will deter them from trying to submerge."

Less that two hours later, Otto called from the protection of the bridge wanting to talk. Jonesy was Gibraltar. "You know my conditions, Herr Huff."

Another voice called out from behind the blast shield. "Lieutenant. It is me, Fred. I'm afraid Herr Huff has the upper hand at the present. He has about half of the crew contained and is determined to take the boat to Paraguay for a new front. A Fourth Reich, if you will. He is determined regardless of my arguments against it. "

Covering the mike with his hand, he asked Tuck if he thought half of the crew could operate the sub? Tuck reminded him Otto had said there was 38 of them. "That's only twenty or so men, but since they won't have any wartime duties and each man can be enlisted to operate the boat, I believe they can." Tuck whispered. "Based on the information Billy Jim gave us during the tour of the spare sub, I think it's possible." At an attempt of light-hearted humor, Tuck reminded him Billy Jim only needed four people to ram the other sub. Jonsey grinned and nodded his head in agreement.

Jonesy keyed the microphone. "What's your position, Fred?

"Er, Jonesy. I'm afraid, I'm holding down the bench right now. Just a few klopfens up side my head, but big time embarrassment. I'm okay. What will you do, Lieutenant?"

"That's what we're trying to figure out. Actually, we have an unusual situation. As you probably know from your reading current newspapers, your military no longer exists. It was disbanded as part of the conditions of surrender. The war criminals have been tried by a tribunal in Nuremberg and I doubt Otto can be found guilty of mutiny or any other crime. It's like a parting of the ways between not so friendly friends. There is no one to judge him of anything. In the end, I guess he has as much right to the sub as you do or anyone else as that matter. I think it might be looked upon as the spoils of war."

Silence.

Jonesy continued. "If Otto and his gang want the sub, will he allow you and your men off? And if he allows you off, what guarantee do we have that he won't pull out of here and torpedo the bunker? Otto?"

More quiet time. "He's thinking, Jonesy."

"Lieutenant, I have decided. We no longer have any use of this island. It is too expensive to keep returning; and for what? I give it to you. Our new responsibility - our duty - lies in South America. Unfortunately, I cannot allow any of the crew to stay behind. Everyone is needed to operate the boat as well as to help establish our new mission. We will prepare to leave tomorrow morning. Perhaps you will allow us ample water, fresh food and any remaining fuel for our voyage?"

"Fred. How do you feel about all of this?"

"What choice do I have? Perhaps it is best I stay with the boat and try to reach Germany from down there. I do thank you for your friendship. Alles Gute."

Tuck said, "Auf Wiedersehen." Pulling Jonesy away from the mike, he asked, "Do we really want Otto and his gang or anyone as far as that goes ashore, especially since they are all suspect? Wouldn't that be like the chickens inviting the fox into the hen house?"

Jonesy whispered, "My feelings exactly. So it's like before: us against all of them. I think it best to stall them until tomorrow."

Billy Jim, who said he needed some real air, excused himself and left the control room. Jonesy said he was a walking zombie and Hannah just nodded her acknowledgement. Both fell into deep slumber. By the time Hannah relieved Tuck at midnight, he too, was exhausted; announcing he was ready for burial.

Accordingly, Tuck was surprised and aggravated when he was awaken just a few hours later under very unusual circumstances. The gruffy voice said, "Aufstehen". He felt several quick jabs against his back. "Auf!" Brushing away the cobwebs of sleep, he recognized the uniform standing over him along with a menacing rifle. "Ve haben der otters. Kommen." Again he felt a poke of the rifle barrel against his ribs. "Bewegung!"

Taking the elevator to the gentlemen's room, Tuck saw Jonesy and Hannah seated on a sofa, but no Billy Jim. He was again nudged by the gun barrel to join the other prisoners. Facing them was the new Kapitan of the submarine. With his foot on the arm of a chair, leaning on his knee, he menacingly waved a chrome plated, nine millimeter German Lugar at them. With a sneer he announced, "Your stumpf, alt frau, told us of the treasure. We wish to take it with us and you will help us. Ja?" He put the pistol barrel under Jonesy's chin forcing his head up and backwards, then clucking his tongue indicated a shot.

Hannah was weeping softly and looked miserable. She twisted her mouth towards Tuck's ear and whispered. "They grabbed me from behind during my watch. Told me they had the boy and I best tell 'em about the treasure if I ever 'spected to see him again...alive. I thought they meant Billy Jim. Lord God I was scared...and helpless...and useless. But they was meaning you. It wasn't till after I blurted out what I knowed, that I sensed they'd tricked me. Like you said, they didn't never even know about the treasure. Dirk hadn't told them, if he knew. It was a bluff, but by then the damage was done. I'm so sorry Tuck."

Tuck touched her hand and told her it could have happened to any of them. "The truth be, I don't believe they have Billy Jim. Wouldn't he be here if they did?" Tuck shrugged.

"Be quiet, please," said the new Kapitan, waving his pistol. "We have the matter of one of our men to settle. Who will tell me of Dirk? We know he is here because we had many broadcasts from him. Who vill speak up?" Again he waved the pistol like his wrist was limp.

"I will tell what we know of your Agent - 43," Jonesy said. "He pretended to be a deserter and was accepted as such, including our protection. However, he was found out, put into the padded cell, but he escaped. I have not seen him since. Perhaps when he sees you are in command of the situation, he will present himself."

"No doubt, he will. A rising star of the Fourth Reich." Otto announced with a sneer.

Unknown to anyone in the room at that time, Dirk had presented himself once more to Billy Jim with an offer to help. "Number Two is playing you like violin, with the Kapitan waving the baton. I participate many times, but no more. I go honest now."

"Wha'cha going to do about it?" Billy Jim asked. He did not fully understand what Dirk was telling him.

"I not know, but being Nazi agent this long time after war, not right for me. Maybe watch and see. Maybe can help on inside." With that, he again disappeared as quietly as before.

Billy Jim continued his preparations, still confused, but more comfortable with Dirk. The only thing he could make of Dirk's riddle was that both the Kapitan and Otto "were on the same team", he said out loud.

"The same band, playing the same song! That's got to be it!" "Tuckster; where you at when I needs ya?"

There was no shortage of bodyguards and they walked about in a threatening manner while Otto outlined their plan. He looked at Tuck. "I understand it is you who knows the most about the treasure, therefore, we will count on you heavily. I do not expect any tricks or you, all of you, will pay dearly. I make myself clear. Ja?"

Everyone nodded. "Goot. We stay on schedule. Load the boat, depart as planned and leave you as we found you - except a little less rich." He laughed a silly little giggle like he had found the plumb in his pudding. Tuck felt a great emptiness in the pit of his stomach as he saw, once more, his future changed drastically. The only hint of satisfaction was the fact he had forgotten to replace the pendant when they had inventoried the treasury. Finding it in his pocket last night, he had stuffed it under the console before going to sleep.

Jonesy, quite aggravated, spoke. "Let's get on with it, then. What do you want from us?"

"First we will broadcast for Dirk to appear. Then you will show us how the elevator works, take us to the riches, which we understand is underground, and then you will help us carry the treasure to the sub."

And that was the way it happened. Except Dirk did not appear even with the Kapitan and Otto broadcasting for him to return. Mostly the crew worked in silence except for an occasionally gasp at finding something special. A bit of skylarking did take place, supposedly because they had nothing to gain individually. Their roles were looked upon, by Tuck, as little more than pack mules. Nazi burros.

To the trio's great disappointment, Kommandant Frederick von Stecken, again wearing his own cap, eventually joined in the transfer of the treasure. He explained his duping them quite simply: "How do you call it? Friend and foe, both the same. We play you for suckers. Gestapo training." Even though they knew of Fred's deception beforehand, they were still hurt, but had no idea how their current situation could be reversed. Since no one ever mentioned Billy Jim, all, except Tuck, feared he was being held prisoner elsewhere: perhaps as a wild card to be played later in this deadly game. No one mentioned that Dirk had not shown up. With hope of all hope, Tuck prayed he had really changed and was with Billy Jim.

As they worked, making trip after trip to the sub, Otto and Fred told them what little they knew of the treasure. "Lots of time we heard many high ranking Nazis use this place as a way station to shuttle their stolen goods to South America. If we ever transported anything, we never knew. However, it could have been labeled anything, 'state documents', 'embassy', 'diplomatic' and would raised no questions. After the war, we spend days and nights searching, but never find." Jonesy gave Tuck full credit for locating the treasure trove. Fred acknowledged Tuck with smile and a two-finger salute. "Danken, mein Sonnenschein."

"When you came along," Otto said, "And wanted to help us return to Germany, we thought that very strange. The victor is assisting the vanquished? We never heard such rubbish. But you see, I was wrong. You help now in many ways you not know." He threw back his head with a mocked laugh. "You give Fourth Reich mission a wealthy start."

"I don't suppose you've heard that the Allies are helping to rebuild Europe and Japan?" Tuck asked. "Bet you don't know of the Berlin Airlift or the democratic type governments in place in Japan, Italy and Germany? You both make me sick. We were concerned about getting you home and all you could think about was betraying our trust and trying to continue a losing battle on a new front. You stink."

"That's enough, Tuck." Jonesy placed his hand on Tuck's shoulder.

"Yes, that's quite enough," said Otto, placing his hand on his holstered sidearm. "In the New World Order, you could be shot for such insubordination. Yes, we have heard of the things you say, but it is nonsense. Propaganda! All of it!"

Jonesy changed the subject. "How'd you get out of the sub? We thought we had all the holes covered."

"Simple, really." Fred laughed. "We grease up few of the smaller men, equipped them with underwater breathing apparatus and with a little push, ease them out the aft torpedo tubes. After quick swim underwater, to far end of bunker, it all downhill sailing from there. Unwrapping their weapons from the oilcloth, you peoples are collected."

Then came the disclosure the trio we had been waiting for. Otto bragged, "You really believed you could hold off thirty-eight warriors of the Third Reich with a boy, an old woman and what, unstable airman at best? I often wonder how we could have lost a war to the kinds of you." Not one betrayed their feelings at learning that the Germans did not know about Billy Jim.

Hannah stood up, put her hands on her hips. "But, you did lose. You little pimple. You lost to a bunch of peoples just like us. Simple folks, black, white, red and yellow, rich and poor, educated and uneducated. All pullin' together for a common good and we booted your high and mighty butts right off the face of the earth. It cost me a son, but you lost your country, your citizens, but most of all, you lost your honor!" Jonesy reached out and gently pulled Hannah back down. "And don't you go ajudgin' Jonesy's ability by how he looks. Underneath all that hair and them raggedy clothes is more man than you's ever be!"

Otto stared at Hannah in contempt. "Not quite off the earth, my dear Frau. Today Paraguay! Tomorrow the world!" He did his Heil salute and clicked his heels. A few of the crew followed suit. "We have survived and we will again, reign supreme. But, it is too much for me to argue with some Dummkopf Oma. We must ready our boat." He saluted, Fred. "By your leave, Kommadant. I will tend to our getting underway." Fred returned the salute, but to Tuck there seemed to be lacking a spirit seen earlier.

By the time the U-boat was ready Tuck, Jonesy and Hannah were again seated at the conference table, still under guard, saying little as they watched the crew ready the *Nautilus Scan* for sea. All felt like failures, causing Tuck to suggest Mystery Island was really 'an isle of intrigue'. Even though they had discovered an unusual island, solved a real treasure hunt, shed light on what happened to Flight 19 and tried to direct a U-boat back to Germany, they felt at a loss. So many pluses adding up to a big fat zero. At least Fred had confirmed they were quite accurate as to the use of the island and as far as they were aware, all of them were still alive. Once Billy Jim was collected, wherever he was, hopefully they could regroup, and without fear from the sub, plan their escape, perhaps on a gigantic raft. Hannah had mentioned earlier that she already had plans in her mind of a large platform of logs with a rudder like the early Mississippi River barges. "If'en they ain't too heavy we can use the wings standing on end, as sails. Can drag thet rubber raft behind as a lifeboat."

Before long, the activity at dockside increased. Seamen were scurrying about disconnecting electrical wiring, water hoses and anchoring cables. Several hundred pounds of fresh fruit was stashed aboard. Fish, lobsters and conchs - which had been easily collected from the existing pens - were stored in the passageways in numerous watertight containers. Lines were cast off and finally everyone on deck found a hatch in which to disappear. The Kaptain was about to leave the bridge and go below.

Suddenly everything changed!

"Kapitan! Kapitan! Bitte. Nicht schiessen. It is me, Dirk. I have something to tell. You must not do this thing. I been with the Americans and they can be trusted. They tried to help me when they thought I jumped ship. They treat our men very good in US of A. Until they know I be agent, they accepted me as friend. You must take boat to US of A."

The Kapitan didn't know what to think. "Ich verstehe nicht."

GHOST OF THE STREAM

"Bitte. I make you understand. They are honorable people. Close down motors, come ashore and let me tell you we no need to go anymore to South America. I believe we go to US of A." Dirk stood in front of Hannah, Tuck and Jonesy, his arms spread at his side, palms opened. He turned his body slightly and pointed to the three. "I stake my life on they do right thing."

A single shot rang out. Dirk spun around, falling, face forward on the cement floor at the feet of the three he had just defended. A large pool of blood quickly formed around his upper torso.

Rising to his feet from behind the blast shield enclosing the crane, stood Oberleutnant zur See Otto Huff, holding a smoking rifle. "Little traitor. Schwein Hund. Better he dead than live a life of lies." Jonesy dropped to his knees, beside Dirk, and felt his neck for a pulse. Looking up, he shook his head.

"The Kapitan looked at his Number Two and screamed, "Mein Gott! You are such a fool! Go below at once! Ready the boat!" The Kapitan momentarily disappeared from sight as he yelled again into the control room. At the same instant, Otto Huff dropped his weapon, causing it to discharge. With both hands, he clutched at his throat from where now appeared the handle of a side knife and a quickly growing splotch of blood. Tuck, without a doubt, knew who threw the knife and strained to see where it came from.

Once more the white cap of Kapitan Frederick von Stecken appeared above the rim of the conning tower. It was only then that he saw the bloody body of his Number Two stumbling toward the open hatch from which he had emerged. Showing little concern for his fellow officer he once more acknowledged, with a slow shake of his head and look of shame, the body of Dirk now lying on a growing maroon disk. Suddenly, as he lifted his cap in farewell, another booming voice was heard. Surprised, he dodged and half-ducked from sight, seeking protection behind the steel of the conning tower.

"Kappy-tain I suggest you do not 'smerge! We've mined your vessel and it will blow if you engage the propeller shafts." It was Billy Jim, on the other submarine! Somehow he had moved the microphone there and his voice reverberated throughout the bunker like an echo in the mountains.

Jonesy, Tuck and Hannah jumped to their feet! Hannah screamed, "Billy Jim!" running, arms outstretched, towards her son. Shouting his commands, Billy Jim stripped away the canvas cocoon from the anti-aircraft deck gun and swung it around until it was pointed at the conning tower of the *Nautilus Scan*. Stepping into the shoulder bars, he cocked

145

in the first round and sighted down the barrels. through the eyepiece. Needless to say he took everyone by surprise.

Clearly the Kapitan, caught off guard, was flabbergasted. "Well, well. So there are more of you. Dirk's report was incomplete." It was all he could come up with. The unbelievable was happening and he could not comprehend it. He shouted muffled orders below, then addressed Billy Jim. "Do you expect me to believe you, a child, can stop this submarine from sailing?" Once more he looked down and screamed.

"You can count on it, Kom-man-dan-tee. You 'smerge, you'll bleed. Bleed bad. All of yous." Billy Jim remained calm, carefully pacing his speech and activities. He was doing his best to provoke the Kapitan into action. Tuck could feel he wanted a reason - more than he had - to destroy the sub.

"Where did you come from? We thought there was just the three. Perhaps, you'd like to explain."

"Yes, Kappy-tain, I'll tell you what I want you to know. With two cables, we've attached a contact mine, we found in your armory, to each of the propeller shafts. You engage either engine, forward or reverse, and you'll wind those mines into your hull like a yo-yo. If you don't understand yo-yo, try fishing reel. In other words your next billet will be Hades instead of South America." Billy Jim kept using the term "we" to indicate there were more than one. He did his Mother, Jonesy and Tuck proud. Tuck hoped Dirk had had a hand in it also. Looking down at Dirk, Tuck didn't see how anyone could survive the enormous loss of blood now congealing around his stilled body.

"I do not believe you. What proof do I have that you are telling me the truth." Obviously, he was trying to buy time in order to figure out what to do and at the same time talk to the men below deck.

"Kappy-tain, We have 'spended our supply of patience. If you dive, you'll have all the proof needed. You have till the count of five to close down the motors and begin leavin' thet sub. Hands on top of your heads. Do that and no one gets hurt. You get your island back and we'll borry your sub for a run to the U.S. mainland. I 'spect the Navy will be here afore dark." Billy Jim continued to slowly swing the gun in an arc covering the entire conning tower, but mainly kept the barrels pointed at Fred.

"One final question." It was the Kapitan. "How do you expect to get the submarine out? You cannot dive it and without diving you'll rip the tower off getting out of the pen. Have you thought about that?" Again, he yelled orders below.

GHOST OF THE STREAM

"Yes, we have, Kappy-tain. We've placed explosives on the roof of this bunker in order to blow away a section big enough to allow us to sail through. If you'll look aft, you'll see a fuse hanging down at the end of the pen. Now that's enough. One...Two...

The Kapitan made his decision. His last. "Number One, DIVE! DIVE! DIVE!"

That said, Billy Jim fired on the sub, raking it with armor piercing 88mm shells. He riddled the conning tower until it looked like a sieve. It was little more than a series of bullet holes held together by a few strands of metal. The entire bunker smelled of cordite. Satisfied, with that target he replaced the empty magazine, lowered the barrel and began strafing the hull and deck and continued until the sub disappeared from sight. The last remaining evidence of the U-boat was a copper haired body floating on the bloody bubbles from a leaking hull. Floating just beyond his extended arms was a crumpled white cap so cherished by U-boats captains of note. Hannah said it appears he's reaching for it.

The three gathered around Billy Jim congratulating him for his insight and thanking him for their deliverance. "No telling what they had in store for us," Jonesy said, pointing to the dead Captain.

"Billy Jim your bluff saved the day."

"Weren't no bluff and I 'spect we need to get out of here. Fast."

Before any of them could move, they heard a muffled explosion followed by the surge of water into the pens. Tuck saw Billy Jim hold up two fingers and shout. "Get to the ridge!" Each began running for a passageway out of the bunker. Tuck chose the original stairs he had found into the control room; in order to retrieve the pendant he had squirreled away there last night. He hoped he had time. Then another explosion. In a matter of minutes all were gathered atop the highest spot on the island.

Looking down, they saw the wounded sub had surfaced, the deck with its ragged conning tower barely awash. It looked like a floundering whale struggling to reach the surface for a breath of air. It was impossible to tell if anyone was making an attempt to escape. Instead, with the little movement it had, the sub turned towards the bunker. "They're trying to return!" Tuck screamed.

In quick succession, with bow at a slight upward angle, the sub released a final torpedo towards the pens. The loss of the weight of the torpedo allowed the bow to rise even more while the stern, obviously taking on water from the explosions, began dragging the hull downwards. Still it eased silently, slowly forward. The additional weight of the treasure in the after crews quarters compounded the problem until trimming the vessel became impossible. Finally, trying to keep the boat afloat, the last of the water was blown with a loud hiss. Still no survivors were seen.

Leveling slightly, the sub edged forward ever so slowly towards the bunker, like a wounded animal returning to its den. Eventually, however, the blue-green Gulf Stream, flooding over the conning tower, wrapped the *Nautilus Scan* in its watery, unforgiving arms. At that same moment the bunker and pens were blown apart! The cantilevered roof collapsed into a massive fireball sending red-orange flames high into the ice blue skies.

Soon one explosion followed another, in sequence, an indication, the entire island had been mined. Jonesy screamed. "Grab as many stems of coconuts as you can and head for the lagoon! I'll get some twine. Quickly! Go! Go! Go!"

Standing in the shallow water of the lagoon, Tuck had tied but two branches of coconuts to his belt when the remaining parts of the island ruptured like a volcano, sending flames, smoke, debris and himself high into the air.

IX
Voyage's End

After what seemed like several minutes, Tuck bobbled to the surface, shaking his head and gasping great gulps of air to fill his parched lungs. It took a few seconds for him to get his bearings as he looked down from his undulating, swirling aquamarine crest into the valley of water below him. Obviously, he was riding the surge from the island blast, but had no idea where he was in relation to where Mystery Island once stood. It had simply vanished. Melted away like a burning candle. He saw nothing but water, sky and acres of floating waste.

COCONUT PALM

He remembered what had happened and recognized he was back where he had begun just a few weeks previously. Providence, it seemed, had once again delivered him.

With a touch of irony he remembered Jonesy had said the U-boat became his "ghost of the stream". It appeared the island had now become Tuck's "ghost". An island that "didn't exist", had disappeared. He shook his head in disbelief.

He hollered for Hannah, Billy Jim and Jonesy, but received no answer. Perhaps we will drift together once the surge subsides and the waters calm, he thought. He was thankful to still have the coconuts for they provided floatation and in the future, nourishment. He was moving rapidly on his water-world roller coaster, spinning, dipping, diving and hanging on for dear life. In time, the ocean settled to its normal flow and according to the sun, his steady course was west by northwest. He was grateful that he did not appear to be out in the Gulf Stream itself. A course to the northwest, he knew, was certainly more favored than one influenced by the Stream.

At dusk, he was still frustrated and confused. However, he had "been here before" and believed he would continue to survive. That belief gave him strength as he focused on the reception with Aunt Grace. He remembered Hannah, Billy Jim and Jonesy and hoped they, too, would be safe until rescued. As he prepared for the night, he climbed up on the stems of coconuts as far as he could. He believed any sharks in the area would be deep in calmer waters. With a somewhat settled mind, his body half in and half out of the water, he drifted with the currents and winds.

After a day such as he had just experienced, he was weary and exhausted and was certain the others were too. His lips and throat burned with dryness, but he decided to wait until morning to open one of the coconuts. He reached and felt his pockets. His knife, wallet and the pendant were safe and secured. His eyes suffered from constant saltwater baths, his body itched and scratched from the dried salt. Oh, how he longed for a shower, a clean, steady bed...and the loving comfort of his Aunt Grace. "You're spoiled, boy. Been living in the lap of luxury far too long," he scolded himself in the manner of Captain Bannerman.

Something touched his leg! He recoiled and pumped his legs, trying to put distance between himself and the attacker. He tried to pull more of his body higher upon his bed of coconuts, but they simply sank deeper from the added weight. Whatever it was, wasn't going away, but it was causing him no harm either. In the dark, he gambled and reached gingerly for whatever it was. To his relief and surprise, it was a palm frond with another stem of coconuts intact. He grabbed hold and tied them together with the others. The thought struck, they might have been Billy Jim's or Hannah's or Jonesy's, but he hoped not, for they would need them. Running his hands over the stem as best he could and finding no line attached, he assumed they did not belong to his friends. Grateful for the increased size of his island of tropical nuts and a frond for shade tomorrow, he was able to pull his body up out of the water slightly, nestle his head on his arms and sleep.

At first light, after seeing no one, he began searching for anything that floated in hopes of constructing a raft of some sort. Perhaps, he thought, if he could salvage enough flotation, he could survive his drift. After all, he reasoned, he had the coconuts that would provide him with water and nourishment. Many men had survived on less. Mystery Island and its electromagnets were no more, so the likelihood of planes and ships finding him was a real possibility. He was certain he had not come this far only to die and said so aloud.

By the end of the first day, after paddling and kicking wildly about chasing treetops and trunks, he had accumulated enough debris to fashion a sizable raft. He began by piling the heavier limbs and trunks on top of each other, creating a platform. Then interlacing the branches, fronds and smaller limbs into each other he created what looked like a crude natural shelter. Finally, he was able to rest with his entire body out of the water and protected from the sun.

After another uncomfortable night of trying to sleep on a swaying, dipping "bag full of doorknobs", he greeted the dawn with an empty heart, tired body and agitated mind. Nevertheless, with the rising sun came peace and beauty and it lifted his dampened spirits. Things really do look, feel and seem better in the light, he thought. The sky was cornflower blue and had dusted itself with puffs of snow white clouds. The air was fresh, crisp and crystal clear. To the west, he was certain he could see land on the horizon. That meant no more than fifteen miles. He slid from his perch and began the laborious task of kicking and steering the raft westward. Because of its size, it was a daunting chore, but he kept at it with the same determination he used in reaching Mystery Island. Kerthunk! Kerthunk! Kerthunk!

After hours of kicking, dreaming, imagining and continually seeing a shoreline just over the horizon, the raft bumped into something. He climbed aboard quickly to investigate. It was his old companion from yesteryear: the hatch cover from the *Nomad*. The explosion must have shaken it loose from where he had placed it as a threshold to his hut, he thought. Smiling at the strange chain of events, Tuck said, "Welcome". After pulling the cover aboard the raft, he returned to the water and continued kicking.

Tuck had seen the sea's temper change more than once during the past few days. How many days, he could no longer remember. Five? Six? Seven? He didn't know and was reaching the point of really not caring. He was wearing out plain and simple: an empty seashell whose inhabitant was moving elsewhere. The football brown skin, he hesitated to think of the word flesh, was stretched tightly over his frame. He believed when he was found; they would think him a mummy. "No, more like a burlap bag of wire coat hangers," he jokingly croaked. Where he could once see great distances, he now saw only what his dim, clouded vision allowed. His lips were swollen and split. When he tried to speak, only incoherent, guttural mutterings came out. Lifting his limbs or head took more energy than he had.

The muscles in his neck throbbed continually, causing his head to droop forward when he tried to rest and relax. He was aware of having to hold his chin up with his hands in order to search the sea. Days went by that he failed even to open a coconut. He was used up, worn out, wasted and ready for the scrap drive...except the War was over and there were no more scrap drives. Ain't even good junk, he thought.

There were also periods of deception and hallucination. One minute the air would be filled with the sounds of darting terns, the clumsy splash of diving pelicans and the screeching chatter of sea gulls squabbling over the same morsel of food. He would blink and the scene was gone, replaced with silence.

More than once he imagined himself at the helm of the *Nomad* docking at a port familiar to him: moving about the cabin, looking over the sides, glancing towards the stern and bow, twisting the wheel, working the throttle and gracefully easing the yacht into its berth. "Okay, Matey, make her fast," he called out.

After a few more days under the cruel, hot sun, he envisioned himself as a piece of burnt toast. Eventually he would crumble and blow away like so much sawdust. He knew he would be dead and welcomed it as a relief from his misery. His body, now as brown and wrinkled as a dead leaf, carried cuts and abrasions caused by the drying salt rubbing into his flesh like sandpaper. His leafy lodge, having lost its foliage, now looked like a poorly made basket carelessly tossed on trash pile of tree trunks, limbs and roots.

He thought of his few short years with Aunt Grace and wished there had been more. He thought of the Hamiltons and Jonesy, but his strongest image was that of Captain Bannerman - perhaps because he was at sea. Nevertheless, he was certain he was in his presence and looked forward to being with him again. It was then he saw the Captain or thought he had. He raised his body forward; lifting up his arms as a child might reach for his loving father. "Captain, help me. I need you. Please help me." The Captain made no move in Tuck's direction. He simply nudged the raft with the side of his shoe and was gone. "He didn't see me," Tuck said, flopping back against a limb. "Didn't even look in my direction. Left without ever acknowledging I existed." He whimpered from down deep in his throat and soul remembering once again the final words from *Hiawatha's Departure:* "Thus departed Hiawatha!...To the land of the Hereafter! No!" screamed Tuck. Frightened he dragged himself to a more erect sitting position. "Not me! Not yet!"

Tuck thought it strange, but in his state of mind, he took Longfellow's words and Captain Bannerman's visit as his wake-up call. He accepted them as "a sign", an indication that he wasn't going to die. Tuck had always believed in a Higher Power and throughout his life had prayed, without much concrete proof. However, he resolved he would not give up and would hold on to his life as long as he could.

With nothing left but a little faith and a lot of hope, he opened his last coconut using his fading strength. After drinking its milk and eating the semi-sweet meat, he slumped against the hatch cover, letting his right hand trail in the cool water. As best he could, he continued his vigilance, searching the horizon much like he did while watching for the U-boat. More than once he thought he saw a boat or ship only to have them quickly fade away like an ice cream cone on a hot Florida day. Regardless, one

GHOST OF THE STREAM

image continued. It did seem to be heading his way. Because he had been fooled so many times in the past, he continued to pay it attention, but without much excitement. "I'll wait a few more minutes for a better view," he mumbled. "A few more minutes before trying to stand and wave my arms." He closed and opened his eyes periodically in order to better judge its position to the raft. He squinted with one eye closed, then the other to focus for a better view. After one of those "sightings", he determined it was time to stand and wave. He removed his hand from the water, placed it in his lap and felt his chin fall forward to rest comfortably on his chest. I'll try again in ten minutes, he thought.

For the second time in a several weeks Tuck awoke in a strange place and, looking at the needles and tubes, made a mental note to be more careful where he passed out in the future. This time he was in the Special Care Unit of a Savannah hospital. Hovering and fussing over him were doctors and nurses, interns and volunteers. They told him how lucky he was and said that he was being treated for malnutrition, exposure and dehydration. "But, we gonna get you well, honey-pot," he was assured, more than once, by the syrupy-toned voices with warm Southern accents.

Eventually, he asked one of the Candy Stripers, about his age, how he got there. She told him a yacht called the *Storyteller* had picked him up. "It was in all the papers. You're famous. The crew reported they found you about twenty miles out, floating on a pile of tree trunks along with a gray hatch cover."

Tuck smiled thinking of his incredulous journey with the cover and was amazed. Others would be flabbergasted...well almost. "It must be over five hundred miles from Miami to Savannah."

"I guess so," candy girl said, smoothing out his bedcovers. "Anyway, the Coast Guard was called and 'viola' you've been here, with us, ever since."

"Do you know where my clothes are?"

Miss Candy, whose name was Pamela, giggled. "You had on no more clothes than what you were born with. Naked as a jay-bird." Then, as if to ease the embarrassment, she whispered, "You were wrapped in a sheet, however."

"But, I had on pants, a shirt and shoes when I was on the raft," Tuck protested.

"Maybe you can take it up with the Coast Guard," Pam said, pulling the sheet up around his chin. "They would know how you were dressed when you were picked up. I know how you were attired when you arrived here, because I helped prep you." She smiled and Tuck blushed.

After a couple more days of being poked, tested, stuck and drinking as many milkshakes as he wanted, he was transferred to a private room where the media circus began. There surrounding his bed, along with Aunt Grace who had flown in from Miami, were newspaper reporters, radio newscasters and doctors to handle the medical questions. Everyone wanted to learn how he survived over a month at sea after being shipwrecked. Questions flew from all directions. Tuck answered each one as carefully, completely and truthfully as he could. Eventually the questions slowed and the interest wound down. The doctors took that opportunity to temporarily close the inquisition ordering everyone out so he could get some much-needed rest.

Although the media reported his story, the critics pooh-poohed the tale because no such island appeared on any known nautical chart. The stories of Mystery Island, the Hamiltons, Jonesy, Dirk and the wrecked Avenger, were taken at less than face value, attributing them to his very active imagination. The low gravity area, as well as the U-boat and the treasure-trove were discounted for the same reason.

"Preposterous!" said one radio announcer. "Along with this cock-and-bull-story, he wants us to believe he was able to save only the hatch cover after having his hands on millions of dollars of Nazi loot. That's just too convenient, isn't it? Why he can't or won't even tell us what happened to the *Nomad*. He should try peddling his make-believe nonsense elsewhere. Gimme a break!"

If only I had that pendant, Tuck thought. I know I, all of us, held a real piece of jewelry in our hands at one time, just as I know that I didn't dream up the entire Mystery Island experience.

Nevertheless, he did have to admit his "judges" did an excellent job of shaking his confidence and, at times, making him doubt himself. He reached the point of questioning everything he had reported. Had he imagined the complete journey on the hatch cover? Was it possible - a coincidence - to have been reunited with it after the island disintegrated? Did I imagine the whole thing and had, in reality, been on the cover the whole time? He thought. Could anyone survive that long without food and water? Was he hallucinating? Had it been an illusion after all? Without the pendant or one of the others stepping forward to corroborate his story, he would remain a paradox - or worse - a laughing stock.

His rescue did create a lot of news and the attention didn't die until one by one the exploits on his journey were publicly destroyed or disclaimed. The missing Hamiltons were blamed on a rickety old scow. "A fast tide coulda sunk thet old bucket of theirs," volunteered a fishing crony.

"There was a Taylor Jones on Flight 19 and he was called 'Jonesy' by his friends," recounted a reporter. "A fact Tuck could have learned from all his reading. Didn't he say one of his proudest moments was when he received his first library card?" After a pause, he continued. "There's an archive of U-boat records in Cuxhaven, Germany. A registry of sort. Their records of each sub are quite accurate, if not yet complete. My paper has already contacted them. If there were submariners by the names he gave us; von Stecken, Huff and Oberhaus, they will be able to confirm it. Also they will know the whereabouts of *U-522*...if such ever existed." He smirked at his audience.

There were no real disclaimers for the treasure-trove, the low gravity area, or the electromagnetic field. Consequently, they were neatly labeled and filed away under "Devil's Triangle" for use in the future.

Eventually the "shrinks" - the psychologists - really did a number on his believability when they delivered the coup de grace. The group of sanctimonious intellectuals, was lead by a white coat with a Vandyke beard, which he stroked periodically and looked towards the ceiling to stress his near godly prowess. Looking Tuck over like he was something less than an amoeba, he began his dissection of his lengthy travels. "Ahem. The entire episode can be explained as delusional, or more precisely as 'dissociative disorder'". The doctor went on to explain: "It is a psychiatric phenomenon in which the sub-conscious mind is able to make the conscious mind believe something is happening when, in fact, it is not." Stroke. Stroke. "It is similar to a person becoming mentally removed from an event and observing it much as a moviegoer watches a film.

"Additionally, I took the liberty of checking the young man's background. Ahem... It appears he spent his first years as a member of a migrant family who had a poor work history and constantly stayed just one step ahead of the law." He rolled his eyes. "Not surprisingly they were referred to as 'fruit tramps'. He also spent some time in a home for wayward children – in other words a reform school - where he continually had trouble with authority. So he knows how to live by cunning and deceit and is no stranger to law enforcement." He sneered. Aunt Grace squeezed Tuck's arm, smiled at him and shook her head ever so slightly.

"It was the means of survival for the lad," offered another white coat. "So strongly did he perceive in his mind, the island and all the happenings, they became reality. He may not even recognize he is being untruthful. Lying."

Vandyke, who seemed to have lost interest in Tuck, continued talking to the ceiling in mellifluous tones as if appeasing the gods of psychiatry. "Thus, his imagination became a means of his survival." Stroke. "He was able to bear up under tremendous stress and pain because his mind was telling him he was elsewhere. Actually, it is little more than a superior level of self-hypnosis." Patting himself on the back, he finalized. "I dare say, ahem, I'd be able to reproduce the same results under laboratory conditions given the opportunity."

Tuck was so happy to be released, he resisted asking Vandyke why he didn't just say self-hypnosis an hour and half-hour ago?

In time, Aunt Grace and Tuck returned to Miami. Having been dragged through the proverbial briar patch, Tuck was numb, and just wanted to put all of it behind him and rest at home. Not quite so easily done, however. The fact he had been branded a liar was more than he could handle. The term, "them dang Fryers" kept coming to mind and played like a stuck phonograph record. Day after day, with nothing much to do but get well, his mind kept dredging up and dragging back facts he could no longer ignore. He so wanted to make "Dr. Vandyke" eat his words, plus salvage a bit of his family's name. He explained to Aunt Grace that it was like a dog bringing back his favorite old bone time and time again. She understood and agreed they needed to clear the air if possible. "I'll make some calls," she promised.

Tuck began wading through the facts as best he could, writing them down, then re-writing them in proper sequence to see how each fitted with the entire escapade. One troubling spot was when the Coast Guard transferred him, from the yacht *Storyteller* to the hospital. He had been unconscious and had to rely on hearsay as to what had happened. According to the Candy Striper, Pam, he had arrived without his clothes, wrapped in a sheet. She didn't know what had become of his clothing, but promised to find out.

She did. With the help of the head nurse on duty at that time and the hospital administrator, it was determined Tuck did, in fact, arrive in the same state in which he was born. The whereabouts of his clothes remained a mystery, and the Coast Guard assured them they received no clothing at the time of their picking him up. It was unlikely he undressed himself, Tuck thought, so it stood to reason, his clothing and his possessions remained aboard the yacht. The raft would not have been salvaged and would have soon broken up into small pieces of driftwood presenting no danger to shipping.

The last time Tuck could recall having the pendant with him, it had been in a pocket of his jeans. In the other pockets were his knife, wallet and handkerchief. He didn't think the nature of wet jeans would allow the items to slip out unnoticed. His best guess was that the clothing, along with their contents remain or, at one time, were aboard the *Storyteller* by chance or on purpose. He imagined he was stripped of the wet, ragged clothes he was wearing and put to bed. The clothing might have been tossed in the wastebasket, but surely the knife; wet wallet and pendant would have been heavy enough to attract attention. If the items had been found, even after he had left, they could have been turned in. The thought that a boater would steal from someone he rescued did not set well with Tuck. A disservice not usually found among seamen and boaters. He likened it to charging a fee for a volunteered tow. A modern pirate, he thought.

The more he tumbled it over and over in his brain, the more convinced he became. The crew of the vessel that probably saved his life, had extracted a very handsome reward for doing so. He was confused about what to do and finally shared his feeling with Aunt Grace asking her if he was being selfish or ungrateful in wanting his belongings. She assured him he wasn't and together they proceeded to find them.

The first stop was the Coast Guard base at Miami Beach, Aunt Grace had visited while keeping tabs on the search and rescue efforts launched on behalf of the missing *Nomad*. The jovial Commander Dietrichson, looking every inch a Southern Colonel overseeing a 1000-acre cotton plantation, greeted Aunt Grace with a hug. He took Tuck's hand in both of his, warmly telling him he had followed the reports of his exceptional travels.

"What can I do for you?" he asked, motioning them to chairs in front of his desk.

Tuck reviewed, as best he could, the happenings since his rescue then explained his belief that his belongings might be aboard the *Storyteller*. "I wonder how we might go about finding out, without accusing anyone of anything or appearing boorish?" he asked.

Dismissing his concern with a smile and a wave of his hand, he picked up a thick file and flipped through it's dog-eared contents with his thumb. "I don't think we have any fear of appearing ill-mannered or embarrassing the owner of the *Storyteller*.

Aunt Grace and Tuck looked at each other not understanding, but appreciating the word "we".

Thumping the folder in his hand, he said, "Commodore – self-proclaimed I might add - Commodore Peckensniff" is well known to us. In fact when we learned it was he, aboard the *Storyteller*, who found you, his file, as a matter of routine, ended up on my desk." He smiled at

Tuck and winked at Aunt Grace, which reminded them both of Captain Bannerman.

"If he has your treasures, as I suspect he does, he'll be most happy to return them to you. No questions asked nor answered. Without betraying any confidential information, Commodore Peckensniff is a merry rogue who delights in living just within, and sometimes just outside, the law as it suits his need. He is both a source of vital information for us as well as, at times, a boil on our bottom." He laughed. "Out of necessity, he is tolerated...up to a point." The Commander's facial expression changed and by his smile they knew he was an ally and had come upon an idea that needed to be explored. If he'd had on a red suit, he could have been Santa Claus, Tuck thought.

Punching a button and picking up his phone, he asked a few questions and made a request Tuck and his Aunt could not understand. Having received his answer, he spoke clearly so they might hear. "Regardless. Tell him to stand by. We'll be there in fifteen minutes. And, Lieutenant, use the words 'national security, ATF and drugs' to press the need for us to meet." Grabbing his hat and the bulky folder, looking like the cat that had just dined on the family canary, he motioned for them to follow. After a brief drive to a nearby marina, he braked to a halt alongside a gleaming, silver cloud colored yacht with lines singled and engines purring. It wasn't until they made their way up the gangway that Tuck noticed the vessel's name: *Storyteller.* His heart jumped around inside his chest.

Beneath the crystal-blue deck awning, the Commander greeted the owner, with arms extended, graciously. "Commodore, it is so good of you to see me on such short notice. I apologize for any inconvenience I may have caused, but wanted you to meet some dear friends of mine." He then stepped aside allowing the Commodore to fully see Aunt Grace - and Tuck.

The step forward the Commodore was about to take was aborted. The hand that was about to be offered went, instead, into his coat pocket. The other hand fidgeted with his ascot that didn't need any fidgeting. The color drained from his face and he did a quick, little jig, stumbling about and gulping loudly.

At that very moment, as part of his continuing education, Tuck recognized he knew the meaning of "body language".

The Commander was about to burst and after letting the Commodore stew a bit, finally spoke. "Commodore Peckensniff, I'm certain, like all of us, you have been following the exploits of this young man. Please allow me to introduce you to Tuck Fryer and his aunt,

GHOST OF THE STREAM

Grace Gregory. I believe, of course, you met Tuck during your rescue of him. Naturally, he is most grateful and wanted to thank you personally." After a lengthy pause - time enough for the Commodore to relax a bit - Commander Dietrichson added, "And pick up his belongings."

Once again pushed off balance, the Commodore danced his little jig and stuttered. "Well, yes, certainly, er. Ah... Except I don't have any of the lad's possession. I'm sure you're aware, Commander, we transferred the youngster just as we found him with the exception of wrapping him in a sheet to cover his nakedness. He was in terrible condition and I'm surprised he survived."

"Yes. Yes. I'm assured you are surprised, but I want to show you something." Laying the opened portfolio on the deck table, Commander Dietrichson allowed the Commodore to view some photographs. Pointing, he said, "These were taken by the Coast Guard helicopter when we picked Tuck up from your vessel. This one shows him as he was being transferred. You can see, he was wrapped in a sheet. Later we discovered he had on only his birthday suit. Tuck came to me, wondering what might have happened to..."

"Er. Ah. My dear Commander," Commodore Peckensniff interrupted. "What in the world would a young, shipwrecked boy have on his person that I would want or find interesting enough to keep?" He pointed to himself with both hands. "No, we transferred him just as we found him."

Once more the Commander, very much enjoying himself, his voice dripping with molasses, pointed to another photo. "But, Commodore, here's a body shot of Tuck in the hospital. Taken as a precaution, you know, in the event the Medical Examiner might need it." Turning the photographs in order to give the Commodore a better look, he asked, "How do you account for the fact that Tuck is wearing what appears to be a white, one piece swim suit? He's badly sunburned everywhere except where his tee shirt, pants and shoes protected him from the sun."

Pointing to another picture as if by accident, "Why, would you look at that? There's another shot of your boat taken at some other time. Incidentally, why are all of these smaller runabouts alongside the *Storyteller*?"

Again stammering and stumbling about, while searching for an answer, the Commodore, delighted for a change of subject, finally responded. "What is the date of that...? Oh yes, wait; now I remember. As I recall they were fishermen, in a tournament of some sort. They were looking for dolphin and hailed us to see if we had seen any schools or weed lines."

"My. My. That's certainly a coincidence and I'm delighted you weren't involved any more than that. Would you be surprised that some of those very same boats were later caught tossing frozen 'bricks' of marijuana over the side and their crews are now awaiting trial?" Both Tuck and Aunt Grace strained to look over the men's shoulders, but mostly they stood wide-eyed, unable to fathom the scene unfolding before them.

The Commander, seeing the Commodore squirm, grinned and put a bigger hunk of bait on the hook. "Kind sir, is it possible someone in your employ, say a steward, found the possessions and decided to keep them for himself? Since I'm convinced the items are here or were, we can arrange to have the vessel searched, but I hesitate to delay your departure any longer." He placed a kindly hand on the Commodore's shoulder.

Commodore Peckensniff was visibly relieved and jumped at the offer. "Why, I never thought of that, Sir. If you will please excuse me, I'll ring for the stewards and learn what I can. Please rest yourself on the after deck. May I offer you some refreshments?"

"No, thank you," said the Commander. "We don't want to delay you anymore than we already have. We'll just take the property and be on our way." The Commander nodded at Tuck, giving him a "thumbs-up", signaling things would be set right after all.

In no longer time than it took the Commodore to open a safe and return on deck, he explained. "One of the stewards did have the items." He handed the Commander a wallet, knife and the missing pendant. "The steward had taken them from the lad's clothing before he disposed of them. He will be terminated, I assure you. And, young man, I apologize for any inconvenience and anguish this matter might have caused you."

To the Commander, he said, "Had I known of this, I would have contacted your office immediately. I would've wanted to know how I might find the lad in order to return his, ah, trinket. The steward told me after all the publicity, he was afraid to come forward. He was also worried that Tuck might be harmed or duped by the unscrupulous." Not one to toss in his cards easily, the Commodore did say to Tuck if he ever decided to sell the "bauble" he would like to have first refusal, reminding him, after all, he had saved his life.

And that is how they got the pendant back!

Beginning or end?

Keeping a journal was more difficult than I thought it would be. But I enjoyed doing it and will probably continue. One final entry. I asked the Coast

Guard Commander if he could explain Commodore Pecksniff's selection of his name, remembering it was self-proclaimed.

"So you read Dickens? Yes, Pecksniff was a Dickens' character hypocritically professing high moral principles. I suspect our friend chose it for two reasons: he wanted to flaunt his knowledge of literature, assuming it had a certain sound of aristocracy. Then not wanting to appear a plagiarist inserted the 'en'."

"He couldn't have selected a more appropriate moniker," I responded. "Blame it on the butler, indeed. Would you care to venture a thought as to how he came to name his yacht Storyteller?"

"Perhaps another time," he said smiling. "Now get out of here. Go! I've serious work to do."

A trip to The Miami Herald, *which photographed the pendant, produced a written promise of an in-depth retraction with copies being sent to all wire services, involved radio stations and the Savannah hospital.* "Regardless what we do, Tuck, you'll be inundated with requests for information. You'll be interviewed and make appearances on radio talk shows everywhere," the editor told us. "Every treasure hunter in south Florida will be scouring the Gulf Stream for your Mystery Island. Who knows, I suspect you'll even be hired as a consultant." The editor grinned at the prospect of the gold rush he imagined.

Tuck asked if the sub wouldn't be protected as a wartime gravesite. The editor said no, reminding him the incident happen a year after the war. "Incidentally, we heard from Germany's U-boat archives located at Cuxhaven at the mouth of the Elbe River. It's director, Herr Horst Brelow, was anxious to help, confirming the names you gave us, but no final information on *U-522.* Their records do indicate its last destination was the South Atlantic. And just so you'll know you were in the hands of a pro. Dirk Oberhaus was actually twenty years old and a top youth agent."

Getting up to leave, Tuck said to Aunt Grace, "It's finished. That should put a cork in 'Dr. Vandyke' and his 'dissociative disorder' theory."

The editor leaned back in his chair, flipped his pencil in the air and laughed. "Finished? Why, son, it's news. It's started all over for you. Just you wait and see. Besides, you don't know for certain Oberleutnant Otto

Huff is dead. If not, he's going to be like a nest filled with smoked hornets and he just might want to extract his pound of flesh."

"Thank you, Mr. Davis," Tuck said, smiling. "That certainly puts my mind at ease."

"Auntie, have one stop to make before we go home." Tuck announced. "Your bank." Pulling the pendant from his pocket, he added, "This should go into your safe deposit box."

"Why certainly, son. We can have it appraised and insured later."

"There'll be time for that, but I want to have something notarized first."

"Sure. Patty can do that for us."

After the notary had completed Tuck's request, he handed the envelope, containing the pendant and letter, to his Aunt. "You should read that in private before putting it in the lock box. The Commander helped me with it." After closing the door of the safe room, Aunt Grace read:

I, E. Thom Fryer, do hereby give and bequeath the jewelry known as Pendant Isle de Intrigue *to my Aunt Grace Gregory, for her kindness, love and care.*

E. Thom Fryer
July 21, 1946

That night, at home, Tuck was finally able to tell Aunt Grace, in great detail, of his unusual experiences, but only after she registered her complaint about the pendant. "Tuck, I appreciate your gesture, but I can't accept it. It's yours and your future. I'll keep it for the time being. Eventually though…"

Tuck placed his finger on her lips and shook his head. "Somehow, somewhere, I know Billy Jim Hamilton is alive and well. He will survive no matter what's thrown at him. I hope Hannah and Jonesy are too." As an afterthought, he said, "If the Hamiltons are alive, I'd like to help them get a new boat."

Aunt Grace nodded. "That can be arranged."

"You know just before the island blew up, with things happening so fast, we didn't get a last chance to go back and check on Dirk. For my own peace of mind I have to believe he was dead." He then added thoughtfully, "I really do think he changed and I'm convinced he helped Billy Jim in some way to prove it. He had ample opportunity and the guns available to take us out anytime he chose."

"Tuck, I, too, hope your friends are safe. They sound like good people, all of them." She touched his hand. It felt warm and good. "You know, in my heart, I never gave up. I felt all along you'd return someday". She bent over, pulled the covers up to his neck and kissed his forehead. "Goodnight, Tuck. I hope you know how much joy you have brought into my life. I'm so happy you're home."

Tuck was glad also. He slid down in his own, clean, comfortable bed. He felt vindicated, satisfied in the same way he had after finding the treasure: he'd succeeded at something. It was more rewarding – more valuable - than the riches. In the darkness he said, "Auntie, thanks for being there for me...and just being you. You don't know how much I love you."

HATCH COVER

About the Author

Bill Pearce, a native of the small settlement, Kendall, south of Miami, Florida, was a teenager in 1946, the time period of the story. An Eagle Scout, Florida history buff and Korean War Navy veteran, he is intrigued with the German U-boat activities, especially those in the South Atlantic. ***Ghost of the Stream*** is a melding of his education and varied experiences.

Like many youngsters of his age and locale, he enjoyed hunting and fishing in the Everglades and spearfishing in the Keys. He witnessed oil tankers burning on the Atlantic horizon and learned - along with the rest of the world - of the *Lost Patrol* disappearing within the Devil's Triangle.

As to the authenticity of ***Ghost,*** he will tell you: "If Mystery Island had been found in 1943 instead of 1946, U-boat activities in the South Atlantic *might* have been eliminated or greatly curtailed.

Mr. Pearce is a graduate of the University of Florida College of Journalism and Communications.